Ⓗ™

NEW YORK TIMES AND

SUSAN MALLERY

ONLY MINE

A Fool's Gold Romance

"Susan Mallery is

D0092266

Collect all three charming tales
in the *Fool's Gold* series from
New York Times and *USA TODAY* bestselling author

SUSAN MALLERY

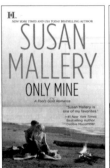

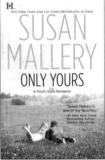

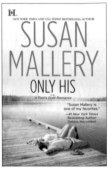

Available now!   September 2011.   October 2011.

And don't miss these two classic tales
in the *Fool's Gold* series:

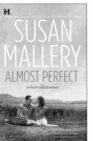

Available in print and ebook today!

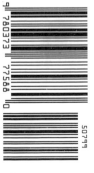

ISBN-13:978-0-373-77588-0

www.Harlequin.com

PHSSM0811V3IFC4C

SUSAN MALLERY

ONLY MINE

HQN™

Recycling programs
for this product may
not exist in your area.

ISBN-13: 978-0-373-77588-0

ONLY MINE

To Marilyn, my sister of the heart.
You are sweet and generous and funny, just like Dakota. This one's for you.

ONLY MINE

CHAPTER ONE

"WHAT'S IT GOING TO take to get you to cooperate? Money? Threats? Either works for me."

Dakota Hendrix looked up from her laptop to find a very tall, stern-looking man standing over her. "Excuse me?"

"You heard me. What's it going to take?"

She'd been warned there would be plenty of crazies hanging around, but she hadn't actually believed it. Apparently she'd been wrong.

"You have a lot of attitude for someone wearing a plaid flannel shirt," she said, standing so she was at least something close to eye-level with the guy. If he hadn't been so obviously annoyed, she would have thought he was pretty decent-looking, with dark hair and piercing blue eyes.

He glanced down at himself, then back at her. "What does my shirt have to do with anything?"

"It's plaid."

"So?"

"It's hard to be intimidated by a man wearing plaid. I'm just saying. And flannel is a friendly fabric. A little down-home for most people. Now if you were in all black, with a leather jacket, I'd be a lot more nervous."

His expression tightened, as did a muscle in his jaw. His gaze sharpened, and she had a feeling that if he were just a little less civilized, he would throw something.

"Having a bad day?" she asked cheerfully.

"Something like that." He spoke between clenched teeth.

"Want to talk about it?"

"I believe that's how I started this conversation."

"No. You started by threatening me." She smiled. "At the risk of sending your annoyance level from an eight to a ten, sometimes being nice is more effective. At least it is with me." She held out her hand. "Hi. I'm Dakota Hendrix."

The man looked as if he would rather rip off her head than be polite, but after a couple of deep breaths, he shook hands with her and muttered, "Finn Andersson."

"Nice to meet you, Mr. Andersson."

"Finn."

"Finn," she repeated, being more perky than usual, simply because she thought it would bug him. "How can I help you?"

"I want to get my brothers off the show."

"Hence the threats."

He frowned. "Hence? Who says that?"

"It's a perfectly good word."

"Not where I come from."

She glanced down at the worn work boots he wore,

then back to his shirt. "I'm almost afraid to ask where that is."

"South Salmon, Alaska."

"You're a long way from home."

"Worse, I'm in California."

"Hey, you're in my hometown. I'll thank you to be polite."

He rubbed the bridge of his nose. "Fine. Whatever. You win. Can you help me with my brothers or not?"

"It depends. What's the problem?"

She motioned to the seat across from her small desk. Finn hesitated for a second, then folded his long body into a scated position. She took her chair and waited.

"They're here," he said at last, as if that explained everything.

"Here instead of back in South Salmon?"

"Here instead of finishing their last semester of college. They're twins. They go to UA. University of Alaska," he added.

"But if they're on the show, then they're over eighteen," she said gently, feeling his pain, but knowing there was very little she could do about it.

"Meaning I don't have any legal authority?" he asked, sounding both resigned and bitter. "Tell me about it." He leaned toward her, his gaze intense. "I need your help. Like I said, they're one semester from graduating, and they walked away from that to come here."

Dakota had grown up in the town of Fool's Gold and had chosen to return after she'd finished her schooling, so she didn't understand why anyone wouldn't want to live in town. But she would guess Finn was a lot more worried about his brothers' future than their location.

He stood. "Why am I even talking to you? You're one of those Hollywood types. You're probably happy they've given up everything to be on your stupid show."

She rose as well, then shook her head. "First of all, it's not my stupid show. I'm with the town, not the production company. Second, if you'll give me a moment to think instead of instantly getting angry, maybe I can come up with something that will help. If you're like this with your brothers, I'm not surprised they want to get a couple thousand miles away from you."

Given the little she knew about Finn from their thirty-second relationship, she half expected him to snarl at her, then disappear. Instead he surprised her by grinning.

The curve of his lips, the flash of teeth, wasn't anything unique, but it hit her in the stomach all the same. She felt as if all the air had rushed out of her lungs and she couldn't breathe. Seconds later, she managed to recover and told herself it was a momentary blip on her otherwise emotionally smooth radar. Nothing more than an anomaly. Like a sunspot.

"That's what *they* said," he admitted, returning to his seat with a sigh. "That they'd hoped being at college would be far enough away, but it wasn't." The grin faded. "Damn, this is hard."

She sat down and rested her hands on the table

between them. "What do your parents say about all this?"

"I'm their parents."

"Oh." She swallowed, not sure what tragedy had brought that about. She would guess Finn was all of thirty, maybe thirty-two. "How long ago…?"

"Eight years."

"You've been raising your brothers since they were what? Twelve?"

"They were thirteen, but yes."

"Congratulations. You've done a good job."

The smile faded as he scowled at her. "How would you know that?"

"They made it into college, were successful enough to get to their final semester and now they're emotionally tough enough to stand up to you."

The scowl turned into a sneer. "Let me guess. You're one of those people who calls rain 'liquid sunshine.' If I'd done my job with my brothers, they would still be in college, instead of here, trying to get on some idiotic reality show."

There was that, Dakota thought. From Finn's perspective, nothing about this was good.

He shook his head. "I can't figure out where I went wrong. All I wanted was to get them through college. Three more months. They only needed to stay in school three more months. But could they do that? No. They even sent me an email, telling me where they were—like I'd be happy for them."

She reached for the files on her desk. "What are their names?"

"Sasha and Stephen." His expression cleared. "Is there something you can do to help?"

"I don't know. As I said, I'm here representing the town. The producers came to us with the reality show idea. Believe me, Fool's Gold wasn't looking for this kind of publicity. We wanted to say no, but were concerned they would go ahead and do it anyway. This way, we're involved and hope to have some kind of control over the outcome."

She glanced at him and smiled. "Or at least the illusion of control."

"Trust me. It's not all it's cracked up to be."

"I'm getting that. All the potential contestants were vetted thoroughly, background checks on everyone. We insisted on that."

"Trying to avoid the truly insane?"

"Yes, and criminals. Reality television puts a lot of pressure on people."

"How did the TV people hear about Fool's Gold if the town wasn't courting them?" he asked.

"It was just plain bad luck. A year ago a grad student writing her thesis on human geography discovered we had a chronic man shortage in town. The hows and whys became a chapter in her project. In an effort to bring attention to her work, she shopped her thesis around various media outlets, where the part about Fool's Gold was picked up."

He frowned. "I think I remember hearing about that. Didn't you get busloads of guys coming in from all over?"

"Unfortunately. Most of the reports made us sound like a town of desperate spinsters, which isn't true at all. A few weeks later, Hollywood came calling in the form of the reality show."

She flipped through the stack of applications of those who had made it to final selection. When she saw Sasha Andersson's picture, she winced. "Identical twins?" she asked.

"Yes, why?"

She pulled out Sasha's application and passed it to Finn. "He's adorable." The head shot showed a happy, smiling, younger version of Finn. "If he has a personality more exciting than that of a shoe, he's going to get on the show. What's not to like? Plus, if there are two of them..." She set down the folder. "Let me put it another way. If you were the producer, would you want them on the show?"

Finn dropped the paper. The woman—Dakota—had a point. His brothers were charming, funny and young enough to believe they were immortal. Irresistible to someone looking to pull in ratings.

"I'm not going to let them ruin their lives," he said flatly.

"The show is ten weeks of filming. College will still be there." Her voice was gentle and hinted at compassion. Her dark gaze was steady. She was pretty enough—had he been looking for that kind of thing. All he cared about right now was getting his brothers back to college.

"You think they'll want to go back after all this?" he demanded.

"I don't know. Have you asked them?"

"No." To date he'd only lectured and issued orders— both of which his brothers had ignored.

"Did they say why they wanted to be on this show?"

"Not specifically," he admitted. But he had a theory or two about their thinking. They wanted to be out of Alaska and away from him. Plus, Sasha had been dreaming of fame for a long time.

"Have they done this sort of thing before? Run off against your wishes, given up on school?"

"No. That's what I don't get. They're so close to being finished. Why couldn't they suck it up for one more semester?" It was the responsible thing to do.

Until now, Sasha and Stephen hadn't given him much grief. There'd been the usual driving too fast, a few parties with friends and plenty of girls. He'd sweated bullets waiting to hear one of his brothers had gotten a girl pregnant. But so far that hadn't happened. Maybe his thousands of lectures about using birth control had gotten through. So them wanting to leave college for a reality show had stunned him. He'd always figured they would at least finish school.

"They sound like great kids," Dakota said. "Maybe you should trust them."

"Maybe I should tie them up and throw them in the back of a plane headed for Alaska."

"You wouldn't like jail."

"They'd have to catch me first." He stood again. "Thanks for your time."

"I'm sorry I can't help."

"Me, too."

She rose and circled the table so she was standing in front of him. "To repeat a cliché, if you love something, set it free."

He stared into her dark eyes. They were an interesting contrast to her wavy blond hair. "If it comes back, it was meant to?" He managed a smile. "No, thanks. I fall into the 'if it doesn't, hunt it down and shoot it' category."

"Should I warn your brothers?"

"They already know."

"Sometimes you have to let people mess up."

"This is too important," he told her. "It's their future."

"The key word being *theirs,* not yours. Whatever happens here isn't unrecoverable."

"You don't know that."

She looked as if she wanted to argue more. She wasn't a yeller, and he appreciated that. Her points were well thought out. But there was no way she could change his mind on this. Come hell or high water, he was getting his brothers out of Fool's Gold and back to college, where they belonged.

"Thanks for your time," he told her.

"You're welcome. I hope the three of you can come to terms." One corner of her mouth twitched. "Please remember we have a very efficient police force in town. Chief Barns doesn't take kindly to people breaking the law."

"I appreciate the warning."

Finn walked out of the small trailer. Filming or shooting or whatever they called it was due to start in two days. Which gave him less than forty-eight hours to come up with a plan to either convince his brothers to return to Alaska on their own or physically force them to do what he wanted.

"I OWE YOU," Marsha Tilson said over lunch.

Dakota picked up a French fry. "Yes, you do. I'm a highly trained professional."

"Something Geoff doesn't appreciate?" Marsha, the town's sixty-something mayor, asked, her blue eyes sparkling with amusement.

"He does not. I have a Ph.D.," Dakota muttered. "I should make him call me doctor."

"From what I know of Geoff, I'm not sure that would help."

Dakota bit into her fry. She hated to admit it, but Mayor Marsha had a point. Geoff was the producer of the reality show that had invaded the town—*True Love or Fool's Gold*. After randomly sorting twenty people into couples, the pairs would be sent on romantic dates, which would be filmed, edited and then shown on television with a one-week delay. America would vote off the couple least likely to make it.

At the end, the last couple standing would receive $250,000 to share and a free wedding, if they were really in love.

From what Dakota could tell, Geoff didn't care about anything except getting good ratings. The fact that the town didn't want the show around hadn't bothered him at all. In the end, the mayor had agreed to cooperate on the condition that there be someone on his staff who was looking out for the interests of the good citizens of Fool's Gold.

All that made sense to Dakota, though she still didn't know why *she'd* gotten the job. She wasn't a public relations specialist or even a city employee. She was a psychologist who specialized in childhood development. Unfortunately, her boss had offered her services, even agreeing to pay her salary while she worked with the production company. Dakota still wasn't speaking to him.

She would have turned down the assignment, except Mayor Marsha had pleaded. Dakota had grown up here. When the Mayor needed a favor, the good citizens agreed. Until the production company had shown up, Dakota would have sworn she would happily do anything for her town. And, as she'd told Finn a couple of hours before, it was only for ten weeks. She could survive nearly anything that long.

"Have the contestants been picked?" Marsha asked.

"Yes, but they're keeping it a secret until the big announcement."

"Anyone we need to worry about?"

"I don't think so. I've looked over the files and everyone seems fairly normal." She thought about Finn. "We do have a family member who isn't happy." She explained about the twenty-one-year-old twins. "If they're half as good-looking in person as they are in their pictures, they're going to be on the show."

"Do you think their brother will make trouble?"

"No. If the boys were still underage, I would worry that he would try to ground them. As it is, he can only worry and threaten."

Marsha nodded sympathetically. Dakota knew the mayor's only daughter had been something of a wild child, then had gotten pregnant and run away. It couldn't be easy, raising a child. Or in Finn's case, two brothers. Not that she knew about being a mother.

"We can help," Marsha said. "Look out for the boys. Let me know if, or maybe when, they're chosen for the show. We don't have to like that Geoff brought us this mess, but we can make sure to keep it contained."

"I'm sure the twins' brother will appreciate that," she murmured, suspecting Finn might be grateful but wouldn't have much expectation for the town helping.

"You're doing a good thing," Marsha told her. "Keeping an eye on the show."

"You didn't give me much of a choice."

The mayor smiled. "That's the secret to my success. I box people into a corner and force them to agree."

"You're very good at it." Dakota sipped her diet soda. "The worst part is I actually like reality TV. Or I did until I met Geoff. I wish he'd do something illegal so Chief Barns would arrest him."

"We can always hope." Marsha sighed. "You've given up a lot, Dakota. I do want to thank you for taking on the show and protecting the town."

Dakota shifted in her seat. "I haven't done all that. I'm on set and making sure they don't plan anything truly insane."

"I feel better knowing you're around."

She was good, Dakota thought, eyeing the older woman. Years of experience. Marsha was the longest-serving mayor in the state. Over thirty years. She thought of all the money the town had saved on letterhead. It never had to change.

While this was far from Dakota's dream job, working for Geoff had the potential to be interesting. She knew nothing about making a television show, and she told herself she would enjoy the opportunity to learn about the business. At least it was a distraction. Something she wanted these days—anything to avoid feeling so... broken.

She reminded herself not to go there. Not everything could be fixed, and the sooner she accepted that, the better. She could still make a good life for herself. Acceptance would be the first step in moving on. She was a trained professional, after all. A psychologist who understood how the human mind worked.

But knowing and believing were two different things. Right now it seemed as if she would never feel whole.

"THIS IS GOING TO BE GREAT," Sasha Andersson said as he leaned against the battered headboard. He glanced down at the copy of *Variety* he'd bought from the old guy at the bookstore. Someday, he would be making thousands, or even millions, and he would subscribe and have it delivered to his phone, as the real stars did. Until then, he bought a copy every few days, to keep costs down.

Stephen, his twin brother, lay across the other bed in the small motel room they shared. A worn *Car and Driver* sat open on the floor. Stephen dangled his head and shoulders off the mattress as he flipped through an issue he'd probably read fifty times.

"Did you hear me?" Sasha asked impatiently.

Stephen looked up, his dark hair falling over his eyes. "What?"

"The show. It's going to be great."

Stephen shrugged. "If we get picked."

Sasha tossed the paper to the foot of the bed and grinned. "Hey. It's us. How could they resist?"

"I heard there were over five hundred applicants."

"They narrowed that number down to sixty and we're going to make the final cut, too. Come on. We're twins. TV audiences love that. We should make it seem like we don't get along. Fight and stuff. Then we'll get more camera time."

Stephen shifted on the bed, then rolled onto his back. "I don't want more camera time."

A fact that was both irritating and true, Sasha thought grimly. Stephen wasn't interested in the business.

"Then why are you here?"

Stephen drew in a deep breath. "It beats being back home."

Something they agreed on. Home was a tiny town of eighty people. South Salmon, Alaska. In the summer, they were flooded with tourists wanting to see the "real" Alaska. For nearly five months, every waking moment was spent working impossible hours, struggling to keep up with the crowds, to get the job done and get paid before moving on to the next job. In winter, there was darkness, snow and crushing boredom.

The other residents of South Salmon claimed to love everything about their lives. Despite being direct descendants of Russian, Swedish and Irish immigrants who had settled in Alaska nearly a hundred years before, Sasha and Stephen wanted to be anywhere but there. Something their older brother, Finn, had never understood.

"This is my chance," Sasha said firmly. "My shot. I'm going to do whatever it takes to get noticed."

Without even closing his eyes, he could see himself being interviewed on *Entertainment Tonight,* talking about the blockbuster movie he was starring in. In his mind, he'd walked a million red carpets, celebrated at

Hollywood parties, had women show up naked in his hotel room, begging him to sleep with them. Which he graciously agreed to do, he thought with a grin. Because that's the kind of guy he was.

For the past eight years, he'd wanted to be on TV and in movies. But the industry never made it to South Salmon, and Finn had always dismissed his dreams as something he would outgrow.

Finally old enough to be able to do what he wanted without his brother's permission, Sasha had been waiting for the right opportunity. A casting notice for *True Love or Fool's Gold* had been it. The only surprise had been when Stephen had wanted to come with him on the interview.

"When I get to Hollywood," he began, playing a familiar game, "I'm going to buy a house in the hills. Or at the beach."

"Malibu," Stephen said, rolling onto his back. "Girls in bikinis."

"Right. Malibu. And I'll meet with producers and go to parties and make millions." He glanced at his brother. "What are you going to do?"

Stephen was quiet for a long time. "I don't know," he said at last. "Not go to Hollywood."

"You'd like it."

Stephen shook his head. "No. I want something different. I want…"

He didn't complete the sentence, but then he didn't have to. Sasha already knew. He and his twin might not share the same dreams, but they still knew every-thing about each other. Stephen wanted to find a place to belong, whatever the hell that meant.

"It's Finn's fault you're not excited about this," Sasha grumbled.

Stephen looked at him and grinned. "You mean be-cause he's so hell-bent on us finishing college and having a good life? What a jerk."

Sasha chuckled. "Yeah. Where does he get off de-manding we're successful?" His humor faded. "Except it's not about us. It's about him. He just wants to say he's done a good job."

Sasha knew it was more than that, but he wasn't will-ing to admit it. Not out loud, anyway.

"Don't worry about him," Stephen said, reaching for the magazine. "He's a couple thousand miles away."

"Right," Sasha said. "Why let him ruin our good time? We're going to be on TV."

"Finn will never watch the show."

True enough. Finn didn't do anything for fun. Not anymore. He used to be wild—before…

Before their parents had died. That's how all the An-dersson boys measured time. Events were either before or after the death of their parents. But their brother had changed after the accident. Today Finn wouldn't know a good time if it bit him on the ass.

"Just because Finn knows where we are doesn't mean he's going to come after us," Sasha said. "He knows when he's beat."

Someone knocked on the door.

Since Sasha was closer, he stood and leaned over far enough to reach the knob. The door eased open. Finn stood there, looking as mad as he had the time the twins had trapped a skunk and left it in his bedroom.

"Hello, boys," he said, stepping inside. "Let's talk."

CHAPTER TWO

FINN TOLD HIMSELF that yelling wasn't going to accomplish anything. His brothers were technically adults, although it wouldn't be hard to make a case that, over eighteen or not, they were idiots.

He stepped into the tiny motel room, crammed with two full-size beds, a dresser, battered television and the door to an equally small bathroom.

"Nice," he said, glancing around. "I like what you've done with the place."

Sasha rolled his eyes as he sank back on his bed. "What are you doing here?"

"Coming after you."

The twins exchanged a look of surprise.

Finn shook his head. "Did you really think an email telling me you'd left college to come here was enough? That I would simply say, 'No problem. Have fun. Who cares if you abandon college in your last semester?'"

"We said we were fine," Sasha reminded him.

"Yes, you did and I do appreciate it."

As there weren't all that many motels in Fool's Gold, locating the twins had been relatively easy. Finn knew that money would be tight, which had eliminated all the nice places. The motel manager had recognized them immediately and hadn't minded giving Finn their room number.

Stephen watched him warily but didn't speak. He'd always been the quieter of the twins. Despite the fact that they looked nearly exactly alike, they had different personalities. Sasha was outgoing, impulsive and easily distracted. Stephen was more silent and usually considered his actions. Finn could understand Sasha taking off for California, but Stephen?

Stay calm, he reminded himself. Having a conversation would get him further than shouting. But when he opened his mouth, he found himself yelling from the very first word.

"What the hell were you thinking?" he demanded, slamming the door shut behind him and planting both hands on his hips. "You had one semester left of college. Just one. You could have finished your classes and graduated. Then you would each have had a degree. Something no one could take away from you. But did you think of that? Of course not. Instead you took off, quitting before you were finished. And for what? Some chance to be in a ridiculous show?"

The twins looked at each other. Sasha sat up and sucked in a breath. "The show isn't ridiculous. Not to us."

"Because you're both professionals? You know what you're doing?" He glared at them both. "I want to lock you in this damn room until you figure out how stupid you're being."

Stephen nodded slowly. "That would be why we didn't tell you until after we were here, Finn. We didn't want to hurt you or scare you, but you're holding on too tight."

Words Finn didn't want to hear. "Why couldn't you finish college? That's all I wanted. Just to get you through college."

"Would it really end there?" Sasha asked him, coming to his feet. "You said that before. That all we had to do was finish high school and you'd get off our butts. But you didn't. There you were, pushing for college, staying on us about our grades, our classes."

Finn felt his temper rising. "How is that wrong? Is it bad that I want you to have a good life?"

"You want us to have your life," Sasha said, glaring at him. "We appreciate all you've done. We care about you, but we can't do what you want anymore."

"You're twenty-one. You're kids."

"We're not," Stephen said, sitting up. "You keep saying that."

"Maybe my attitude has something to do with your actions."

"Or maybe it's just you," Stephen told him. "You've never trusted us. Never given us a chance to prove what we could do on our own."

Finn wanted to put his fist through a wall. "Maybe because I knew you'd pull something like this. What were you thinking?"

"We need to make our own decisions," Stephen said stubbornly.

"Not when they're this bad."

Finn could feel control of the conversation slipping from him. The sensation got worse when the twins exchanged a look. One that said they were communicating silently, in a way he'd never understood.

"You can't make us go back," Stephen said quietly. "We're staying. We're going to get on the show."

"And then what?" Finn asked, dropping his hands to his sides.

"I'm going to Hollywood to be on television and in the movies," Sasha told him.

Hardly news, Finn thought. Sasha had been starstruck for years.

"What about you?" Finn asked Stephen. "Want to become a spokesmodel?"

"No."

"Then come home."

"We're not going back," Stephen told him, sounding strangely determined and mature. "Let it go, Finn. You've done all you needed to. We're ready to be on our own."

They weren't. That's what killed Finn. They were too young, too determined to screw up. If he wasn't nearby, how could he keep them safe? He would do anything to protect them. Briefly he wondered if he could physically wrestle them into submission. But then what? He couldn't keep them tied up for the entire trip back. The thought of kidnapping wasn't pleasant, and he had a vague notion that he would be flirting with felony charges the second he crossed state lines.

Besides, getting them back to Alaska wouldn't accomplish anything if they weren't willing to stay and finish school.

"Can't you do this in June?" he asked. "After you graduate?"

The twins shook their heads.

"We don't want to hurt you," Stephen told him. "We really do appreciate all you've done. It's time to let go. We're going to be fine."

Like hell they were. They were kids playing at being adults. They thought they knew it all. They thought the world was fair and life was easy. All he wanted was to protect them from themselves. Why did that have to be so hard?

There had to be another way, he thought as he stalked out of the small motel room and slammed the door behind him. Someone he could reason with. Or, at the very least, threaten.

"GEOFF SPIELBERG, no relation," the long-haired, scruffy-looking man said as Finn approached. "You're from the city, right? About the extra power. Lights are like ex-wives. They'll suck you dry if you let them. We need the power."

Finn studied the skinny guy in front of him. Geoff "with a G" was barely thirty, wore a T-shirt that should have been tossed two years ago and jeans with enough rips to make a stripper nervous. Not exactly Finn's mental image of a television executive.

They stood in the middle of the town square, surrounded by cords and cables. Lights had been set up on stands and strung up on trees. Small trailers lined the street. Two trucks carried enough Porta-Potties for a state fair, and tables and chairs were set up by a tent with a buffet line.

"You're producing the show?" he asked.

"Yes. What does that have to do with my power? Can I get it today? I need it today."

"I'm not from the city."

Geoff groaned. "Then go away and stop bothering me."

Even as he spoke, the producer was heading toward a trailer parked on the street, his attention on the smartphone in his hand.

Finn kept pace with him. "I want to talk about my brothers. They're trying to get on the show."

"We've made our casting decisions. Everything will be announced tomorrow. I'm sure your brothers are great and if they don't make it on this show, they'll find another." He sounded bored, as if he'd said those same words a thousand times.

"I don't want them on the show," Finn said.

Geoff looked up from his phone. "What? Everybody wants to be on TV."

"Not me. And not them."

"Then why did they audition?"

"They want to be on the show," he clarified. "I don't want them to be."

Geoff's expression shifted to disinterest again. "Are they over eighteen?"

"Yes."

"Then it's not my problem. Sorry." He reached for the handle of the trailer door.

Finn got there first and blocked his way.

"I don't want them on the show," he repeated.

Geoff sighed audibly. "What are their names?"

Finn told him.

Geoff flipped through files on his phone, then shook his head. "You're kidding, right? The twins? They're going to make it. The only way they'd be better for our ratings is if they were girls with big boobs. Viewers are gonna love them."

Not a surprise, Finn thought. Disappointing, but not a surprise. "Tell me what I can do to change your mind. I'll pay you."

Geoff laughed. "Not enough. Look, I'm sorry you're not happy, but you'll get over it. Besides, they could be famous. Wouldn't that be fun?"

"They should be back in school."

Geoff's attention had been captured by his phone again. "Uh-huh," he murmured as he scrolled through an email. "Right. You can make an appointment with my secretary."

"Or I could convince you right here. You like walking, Geoff? Want to keep being able to do that?"

Geoff barely glanced at him. "I'm sure you could take me. But my lawyers are a whole lot tougher than your muscles. You won't like jail."

"You won't like a hospital bed."

Geoff looked at him then. "Are you serious?"

"Do I look serious? We're talking about my brothers. I'm not going to let them screw up their lives now because of your show."

Finn didn't enjoy making threats, but nothing was more important than making sure Sasha and Stephen finished their degrees. He would do what he had to. If that meant physically crushing Geoff, then he would do it.

Geoff shoved his phone in his pocket. "Look, I appreciate your position, but you have to see mine. They're already on the show. I have nearly forty people working for me here, and I have a contract with every one of them. I'm responsible to them and to my boss. This is a lot of money."

"I don't care about the money."

"You wouldn't, mountain man," Geoff grumbled. "They're adults. They can do what they want. You can't stop them from doing this. Say I kick them off the show. Then what? They head to L.A.? At least while they're here, you know where they are and what they're doing, right?"

Finn didn't like the logic, but he appreciated it. "Maybe."

Geoff nodded several times. "You see what I'm saying. Better they're here, where you can keep an eye on them."

"I don't live here."

"Where do you live?"

"Alaska."

Geoff's nose wrinkled, as if he'd just smelled dog excrement. "You fish or something?"

"I fly planes."

The scruffy producer brightened immediately. "Planes that hold people? Real planes?"

"As opposed to those that are remote controlled? Yes."

"Sweet. I need a pilot. We're already planning a trip to Vegas and we're flying commercial to keep costs down. But there are other places, maybe Tahoe and Frisco. If I rented a plane, you could fly it, right?"

"Maybe."

"It would give you a reason to stick around and watch your kids."

"Brothers."

"Whatever. You'll be part of the production staff." Geoff placed his hand on his chest. "I have family. I know what it's like to care about someone."

Finn doubted Geoff cared about anything or anyone but Geoff. "I would be there while you were filming?"

"As long as you didn't get in the way or cause trouble.

Sure. We've got some chick from the city hanging around already." He shrugged. "Denny, Darlene. Something."

"Dakota," Finn said dryly.

"Right. Her. Stick with her. She's gotta make sure we don't hurt her precious town." Geoff rolled his eyes. "I swear, my next gig is going to be filming in the wilderness. Bears don't have demands, you know? That's a whole lot easier than this. So what do you say?"

What Finn wanted to say was no. He didn't want to hang around while they filmed their reality show. He wanted his brothers back in college, and he wanted to return to South Salmon and get on with his life.

Standing between him and that was the fact that his brothers weren't going to go home until this was over. His choices were to agree or walk away. If he walked away, how could he make sure Geoff and everyone else didn't screw them?

"I'll stay," he said. "Fly you where you need to go."

"Good. Talk to that Dakota chick. She'll take care of you."

Finn wondered how she would feel about him hanging around.

"Maybe the twins will be voted off early," Geoff said, opening the trailer door and stepping inside.

"My luck's not that good."

DAKOTA WALKED to her mother's house. The morning was still cool, with a bright blue sky and the mountains to the east. Spring had come right on time, so all the trees were thick with leaves, and daffodils, crocuses and tulips lined nearly every walkway. Although it was before ten, there were plenty of people out on the sidewalks, residents as well as tourists. Fool's Gold was the kind of place where it was easier to walk to where you were going. The sidewalks were wide, and pedestrians always had the right of way.

She turned onto the street where she'd grown up. Her parents had bought the place shortly after they'd married. All six of their children had grown up here. Dakota had shared a room with her two sisters, the three of them preferring to live in the one bedroom through high school, even after their older brothers had moved out.

The windows had been replaced a couple of years ago, the roof a few years before that. The paint color was cream instead of green, the trees taller, but little else had changed. Even with all six kids out on their own, Denise still kept the house.

She walked around to the backyard. Her mother had said she would be spending much of the week working on the garden.

Sure enough, when she opened the gate, she found Denise Hendrix kneeling on a thick, yellow pad, digging vigorously. There were tattered remains of unworthy plants scattered on the grass by the flower beds. Her mother wore jeans, a Tinkerbell hoodie over a pink T-shirt and a big straw hat.

"Hi, Mom."

Denise looked up and smiled. "Hi, honey. Was I expecting you?"

"No. I just stopped by."

"Good." Her mom stood and stretched. "I don't get it. I cleaned up the garden last fall. Why do I have to clean it again in the spring? What exactly are my plants doing all winter? How can everything get so messy, so quickly?"

Dakota crossed to her mother and hugged her, then kissed her cheek. "You're talking to the wrong person. I don't do the garden thing."

"None of you do. I obviously failed as a parent." She sighed theatrically.

Denise had been a young bride to Ralph Hendrix. Theirs had been a case of love at first sight, followed by a very quick wedding. She'd had three boys in five years, followed by triplet girls. Dakota remembered a crowded house with plenty of laughter. They'd always been close, drawn more so by the death of their father nearly eleven years before.

Ralph's unexpected passing had crushed Denise but not destroyed her. She'd pulled herself together—most likely for the sake of her children—and gone on with her life. She was pretty, vibrant and could pass for a woman in her early forties.

Now she led the way through the backdoor, into the kitchen. It had been remodeled a few years ago, but no matter how it looked, the bright open space was always the center of the home. Denise was nothing if not traditional.

"Maybe you should get a gardener," Dakota said as she collected two glasses from the cupboard.

While her mother pulled out a pitcher of iced tea, Dakota filled the glasses with ice cubes, then checked the cookie jar. The smell of fresh chocolate chip cookies drifted to her. She tucked the ceramic ladybug container under one arm and made her way to the kitchen table.

"I would never trust a gardener," Denise said, sitting across from her daughter. "I should plow the whole thing under and pour cement. That would be easy."

"You've never been into easy. You love your flowers."

"Most days." She poured iced tea. "How's the show going?"

"They announce the contestants tomorrow."

Humor brightened her mother's dark eyes. "Will we see you on the list?"

"Hardly. I wouldn't have anything to do with them if Mayor Marsha hadn't guilted me into agreeing."

"We all have a civic responsibility."

"I know. That's why I'm doing the right thing. Couldn't you have raised us not to care about others? That would have been better for me."

"It's ten weeks, Dakota. You'll live."

"Maybe, but I won't like it."

Her mother's mouth twitched. "Ah, that maturity that always makes me so proud."

The teasing was good, Dakota thought. Things were about to get a lot more serious.

She'd put off this conversation for several months now, but knew it was time to come clean. It wasn't that she wanted to keep things a secret, it's that she knew the truth would hurt her mother. And Denise had already been through enough.

Dakota took a cookie and put it on a napkin in front of her but didn't taste it. "Mom, I have to tell you something."

Nothing about Denise's expression changed, yet Dakota felt her stiffen. "What?"

"I'm not sick or dying or going to be arrested."

Dakota drew in a breath. She studied the placement of the chocolate chips, the rough edges of the cookie, because it was easier than looking at the one person who loved her best.

"You know at Christmas I talked about wanting to adopt?"

Her mother sighed. "Yes, and while I think it's wonderful, it's a little premature. How do you know you won't find a wonderful man and get married and want to have kids the old-fashioned way?"

Material they'd been over a dozen times before, Dakota thought, knowing she only had herself to blame. Regardless of her mother's opinion, she'd gone ahead with the paperwork and had already been vetted by the agency she'd chosen.

"You know my period has always been difficult for

me," she began. While her sisters sailed through "that time of the month," Dakota had suffered from a lot of pain.

"Yes. We went to the doctor a few times about it."

Their family doctor had always said everything was fine. He'd been wrong.

"Last fall things seemed to get worse. I went to my gynecologist and she did some testing." Dakota finally raised her gaze and looked at her mother. "I have a form of polycystic ovarian syndrome and pelvic endometriosis."

"What? I know what endometriosis is, but the other?" Her mother sounded worried.

Dakota smiled. "Don't panic. It's not all that scary or contagious. PCOS is a hormone imbalance. I'm handling it by keeping my weight down and exercising. I take a few hormones. On its own it can make getting pregnant really difficult."

Denise frowned. "All right," she said slowly. "And the pelvic endometriosis? That means what? Cysts or growths?"

"Something like that. Dr. Galloway was surprised I had both, but it can happen. She cleaned things up so I don't have the pain anymore."

Her mother leaned toward her. "What are you saying? Did you have an operation? Were you in the hospital?"

"No. It was a simple outpatient thing. I was fine."

"Why didn't you tell me?"

"Because that was the least of it."

Dakota swallowed. She'd been so careful not to let anyone know. She hadn't wanted to have to listen to sympathy, to hear people say it would be fine when she'd known it wouldn't be. She'd been in a place where words would only make things worse.

But weeks, then months, had passed and the old cliché about time healing all wounds was nearly true. She wasn't healed, but she could finally say the truth aloud. She should know—she'd been practicing in her small rented house for days now.

She forced herself to look into her mother's concerned, dark eyes. "The PCOS is under control. I'm going to live a long, healthy life. Either condition makes it more difficult to get pregnant. Having both of them means it's pretty unlikely I can get pregnant the old-fashioned way, as you said. Dr. Galloway says it's about a one-in-one-hundred shot."

Denise's mouth trembled and tears pooled in her eyes. "No," she whispered. "Oh, honey, no."

Dakota had half expected recriminations. A cry of "Why didn't you tell me?" Instead her mother stood, then pulled her to her feet and held on as if she would never let go.

The warmth of the familiar embrace touched Dakota's cold, dark places. Those buried so deep, she hadn't even known they were there.

"I'm sorry," her mother told her, kissing her cheek. "You said you found out last fall?"

Dakota nodded.

"Your sisters mentioned something had upset you. We thought it was a man, but it was this, wasn't it?

Dakota nodded again. She'd gone into work after finding out what was wrong and had started sobbing in front of her boss. While she'd never told him the cause, her grief hadn't exactly been subtle.

"I shouldn't be surprised you kept it to yourself," her mother told her. "You were always the one to think things through before talking to anyone."

They sat back at the table.

"I wish I could fix this," Denise admitted. "I wish I'd done more when you first had these problems as a teenager. I feel so guilty."

"Don't," Dakota told her. "It's just one of those things."

Denise drew in a breath. Dakota could see the determination returning to her mother's eyes.

"Regardless," Denise said firmly, "you're healthy and strong and you'll get through this. As you said, there are things that can be done. When you get married, you and your husband can decide what you want to do." She paused. "This is why you're adopting. You want to be sure you have children."

"Yes. When I found all this out, I felt broken inside."

"You're not broken."

"I know that in my head, but in my heart I'm not so sure. What if I never get married?"

"You will."

"Mom, I'm twenty-eight years old. I've never been in love. Isn't that weird?"

"You've been busy. You had your doctorate before you were twenty-five. That took tremendous effort."

"I know, but…" She'd always *wanted* a man in her life. She just couldn't seem to find him. At this point, she wasn't even searching for Mr. Right. A reasonably decent guy who didn't run screaming into the night at the sight of her would be pretty darned fabulous.

"I don't want to wait anymore. I'm perfectly capable of being a single mom. It's not like I'll be alone—not in this town, or with my family."

"No, you wouldn't be alone, but having children will make it difficult to find the right man."

"If I meet someone who can't accept all of me, including an adopted child, then he's not the guy for me."

Denise smiled. "I raised such wonderful children."

Dakota laughed. "Because it's all about you."

"Sometimes." She leaned forward. "All right, adoption it is. Have you started looking? Can I help?"

Emotions swelled inside of Dakota—the most powerful was gratitude. No matter what, she could always depend on her mom.

"I couldn't go through it without you. Adopting as a single parent isn't easy. I researched international adoptions and applied with an agency that works exclusively in Kazakhstan."

"I don't even know where that is."

"Kazakhstan is the ninth largest country in the world

and the largest country that is completely landlocked." Dakota shrugged. "I did research."

"I can tell."

"Russia is to the north, China to the southeast. The agency was very open and encouraging about the adoption. I filled out the paperwork and prepared to wait."

Her mother's mouth dropped open. "You're getting a child."

Dakota winced. "No. In late January, after I'd finished the paperwork and had the home and background checks, they called and said they had a little boy for me. But the next day they called back and said there's been a mistake. He was going to another family. A couple."

She drew in a breath to keep from crying. At some point the body should just run out of tears, but she had enough personal experience to know that didn't happen.

"I'm not clear if it was an honest mistake or if they prefer couples and that's why I didn't get him. I'm still on the waiting list and the director of the agency swears it's going to happen."

Her mother leaned back in her chair. "I can't believe you've been through all this on your own."

"I couldn't talk about it," Dakota said quickly. "Not with anyone. At first I felt too frail to discuss it at all. Then I was afraid I'd jinx the adoption. It wasn't you, Mom."

"How could it be?" Denise asked. "I'm practically perfect. But still."

For the second time, Dakota laughed. It felt good to find humor in life again. She'd had a few months where nothing had been happy or right.

Dakota touched her arm. "I'm dealing. Most days it's okay. Sometimes it's hard to get out of bed. Maybe if I'd been in a relationship, I wouldn't have felt so unlovable."

"You're not unlovable. You're beautiful and smart and fun to be with. Any man would be lucky to have you."

"That's what I tell myself. Apparently the entire gender is blind and stupid."

"They are. You'll find someone."

"I'm not so sure. I can't blame my lack of love life on the man shortage here. Not entirely. I didn't date when I was away at college, either." She shrugged. "I haven't told anyone, Mom. I'll talk to Nevada and Montana in a few days. If you wouldn't mind, I thought you could tell my brothers after that." Denise would explain what had happened in simple terms, and it would be a whole lot less embarrassing than coming from her.

Her mother nodded. Once her sisters knew, they would want to rally, but there wasn't anything to do. Her body was different. Most of the time she was okay with that.

"You're still on the list to get a baby from Kazakhstan?" her mother asked.

"Yes. Eventually I should get a call. I'm staying positive."

"That's important. I know you don't love working on the reality show, but it's a nice distraction."

"It's beyond crazy. What were they thinking? Mayor Marsha is terrified something bad is going to happen. You know how she loves the town."

"We all do," Denise said absently. She frowned slightly. "Just because you haven't fallen in love yet doesn't mean you're not going to. Loving someone and being loved is a gift. Relax and it will happen."

Dakota hoped she was right. She leaned toward her mother. "You got really lucky with dad. Maybe it's a genetic thing, like being a good singer."

Her mother grinned. "Meaning I should start dating again? Oh, please. I'm too old."

"Hardly."

"It's an interesting idea, but not for today." She rose and walked toward the refrigerator. "Now, what can I fix you to eat? A BLT? I think I have some frozen quiche, too."

Dakota thought about pointing out that this wasn't a problem that could be fixed by food. Not that her mother would listen. Denise was nothing, if not traditional.

"A BLT would be nice," she said, knowing it wasn't the sandwich that would make her feel better, but the love that went into it.

DAKOTA WAS MEETING her sisters at Jo's Bar. She arrived a little early—mostly because her house had gotten too quiet, with only her thoughts to keep her company.

She crossed to the bar, prepared to order a lemondrop martini, only to realize that Finn Andersson was standing in the center of the room, looking more than a little confused.

Poor guy, she thought as she walked toward him. Jo's Bar wasn't the usual kind of hangout where a man went at the end of a difficult day.

Until very recently, most of the businesses in Fool's Gold were owned by and catered to women. Including everyone's favorite bar.

Jo was a pretty woman in her thirties. She'd moved to town a few years ago, bought the bar and converted it into the kind of place where women felt comfortable. The lighting was flattering, the bar stools had backs and hooks for hanging purses, and the big-screen TVs were tuned to *Project Runway* and pretty much anything on HGTV. Music always played. Tonight it was '80s rock.

The men had their place—it was a small room in back with a pool table. But without preparation, Jo's Bar could be shocking to the average male.

"It's okay," Dakota said, coming up behind Finn and leading him to the bar. "You'll get used to it."

He shook his head as if trying to clear his vision. "Are those walls pink?"

"Mauve," she told him. "A very flattering color."

"It's a bar." He looked around. "I thought it was a bar."

"We do things a little differently here in Fool's Gold," she told him. "This is a bar that mainly caters to women.

Although men are always welcome. Come on. Have a seat. I'll buy you a drink."

"Is it going to have an umbrella in it?"

She laughed. "Jo doesn't believe in putting umbrellas in drinks."

"I guess that's something."

He followed her to the bar and took a seat. The padded stool seemed a bit small for his large frame, but he didn't complain.

"This is the craziest place I've ever been," he admitted, glancing at her.

"We're unique. You heard about the man shortage, right?"

"The very piece of information that brought my brothers to town."

"A lot of jobs traditionally held by men are held by women here. Nearly all the firefighters, most of the police, the police chief and, of course, the mayor."

"Interesting."

Jo walked over. "What'll you have?"

The words were right, Dakota thought, telling herself not to blush, but Jo's look of speculation promised many questions to come.

"I'm meeting my sisters," Dakota said quickly. "I rescued Finn. It's his first time in."

"We generally serve your kind in the back," Jo told him. "But because you're with Dakota, you can stay here."

Finn frowned. "You're kidding, right?"

Jo grinned. "Not the brightest bulb. Too bad." She turned to Dakota. "Your usual?"

"Please."

Jo strolled away.

Finn glanced at Dakota. "She's not going to serve me?"

"She's bringing you a beer."

"What if I don't want a beer?"

"Do you?"

"Sure, but…" He shook his head again.

Dakota held in a laugh. "You'll get used to it, don't worry. Jo's a sweetie. She just likes messing with people."

"You mean men. She likes messing with men."

"Everyone needs a hobby. So how are things? Have you convinced your brothers to leave?"

His expression tightened. "No. They're determined. Solidarity in numbers and all that."

"I'm sorry things aren't working out, but I'm not surprised. You're right about the solidarity thing. I'm a triplet and my sisters and I always protected each other." She thought about the conversation she was going to have with them later. "We still do."

"Identical triplets?"

"Uh-huh. It was fun when we were younger. Now it's less thrilling to be mistaken for someone else. We try to look as different as possible." She tilted her head. "Now that I think about it, looking different has gotten easier as we've gotten older and started developing our own style." She glanced down at the blue sweater she'd pulled over jeans. "Assuming we have something close to style."

Jo appeared with her lemondrop and a beer. She set down the drinks, winked at Finn, then walked away.

"I'm going to ignore her," Finn muttered.

"Probably for the best." Dakota took a sip of her drink. "What happens now? If your brothers are staying, are you going back to Alaska?"

"No. I talked to Geoff." He took a drink of his beer. "I threatened him, he threatened me back."

"And you're taking a house together on the shore?"

"Not exactly. He said Sasha and Stephen were both going to be on the show, so I volunteered to work as his pilot. Flying contestants around, that sort of thing. I'm staying."

Dakota told herself that having a tall, handsome, caring man in town was a meaningless bit of info. That any pleasure she took in sitting next to him, having a drink, was just her natural joy in spending time with a fellow human. She wasn't impressed by the strong line of his jaw, the crinkles by his eyes when he smiled or the way he filled out his plaid shirt.

"You're a pilot?"

He nodded absently. "I have a cargo company back in South Salmon." He picked up his beer. "I'd rather knock both of them senseless and drag them back home," he said. "But I'm doing my best to show restraint."

"Think of this as a growing experience," she said.

"I'd rather not."

She smiled. "Poor you. Do you have a place to stay for a few weeks?" The words replayed in her mind. "I, ah, mean that if you want something other than a hotel room, I can recommend a couple of furnished rentals, or..." She swallowed and held on to her drink.

Finn turned to her, the stool shifting until he faced her. His dark eyes started on her face, dropped a little lower, before returning to lock with her gaze.

There was something intense about all that attention. Something that made her previous rocklike stomach give a little wiggle. Nothing overt. Just the slightest quivery shift.

"I have a place," he said, his voice low and a little gravelly. "Thanks."

"You're welcome. I, ah, do think your brothers could be on the show for a while."

"That's what I'm afraid of." He leaned toward her. "I have a life back in Alaska. The plane cargo business comes with a partner. Bill is going to explode when I tell him I have to stay." He ran one hand through his dark hair. "It's early spring. In about six weeks, we'll start our busy season. I need to be back by then. They should have come to their senses by then, right?"

She wanted to give him hope, but knew it would be silly to lie. "I don't know. It depends on how much they're enjoying themselves. They could get voted off early."

"And then head for L.A." He grimaced. "That's what

Geoff said. At least here, I can keep my eye on them. Kids. Giant pain in the ass. You have any?"

"No." She sipped her drink, searching for a shift in topic. "It's just the three of you?"

"Yeah. Our parents were killed in a plane crash."

"I'm sorry."

"It was a long time ago. For years it was just us, you know? My brothers were great when they were young. There were a few scrapes, but they tried to be responsible. What the hell happened?"

She stared into his dark eyes. "Don't take it personally. You've done a great job with them."

"Obviously not."

She touched his arm, feeling heat through the soft cotton of his shirt. *Note to self,* she thought. It had been a very long time since she'd had a man in her bed. She would have to do something to fix that.

He was staring at her. It took her a second to remember she'd been making a point.

"Um, this is just a blip in their lives. You see it as huge, but I don't think it will be. They're testing boundaries, testing themselves, but you'll be here if they need help." She carefully removed her hand, then waited for the sense of heat and strength to fade.

It didn't.

"They won't ask for help," he grumbled, obviously not the least bit affected by her. Which was very annoying.

"Maybe they will. Besides, you should take pride in

the fact that they're comfortable enough with themselves and their lives to risk disappointing you. They're not worried about losing your love and support."

The glower from that morning returned. "You're way too happy a person. You know that, right?"

She laughed. "I'm actually pretty normal on the happy scale. I think you're jaded."

"You got that right." He drained his beer, then tossed a couple of bills on the bar. "Thanks for listening."

"You're welcome."

He stood. "I guess I'll see you at the show or on the set."

"I'll be there."

Their eyes locked. For a second, she thought he might lean in and kiss her. Her mouth was more than ready to take him for a test drive. But he didn't. Instead he gave her a slight smile and headed out.

She stared after him, her gaze dropping to his very nice butt and lingering. They knew how to grow 'em in South Salmon, she thought, raising her glass toward the north. At least she thought it was north.

She told herself that finding Finn attractive was a good thing. As far as she could tell, she hadn't had a single sexual thought since last fall, when her gynecologist had told her about her inability to have children. If she was stirring, so to speak, then it must mean she was healing. Healing was good.

Having Finn kiss her would have been better, but at this point, she would take whatever she could get.

CHAPTER THREE

"WHO'S THE GUY?" MONTANA asked as she walked up to Dakota. "He's cute."

"His brothers will probably be on the show and he's not happy. He wants them to finish college."

Montana raised her eyebrows. "Good looking *and* responsible. Is there a wife?"

"Not that I know of."

Montana grinned. "Better and better."

Jo waved at her and pointed to a table that had opened up in the corner. Unlike regular bars, Jo's was more crowded midweek when it was easier for women to get away. Come weekends, the place went more "date night," and that wasn't as appealing to the regulars.

Dakota grabbed her drink and followed her sister to the empty table. Montana had been letting her hair grow out. It came more than halfway down her back, a cascade of different shades of blond. Last year it had been brown—the blond looked better.

All three sisters had their mother's coloring with blond hair and dark brown eyes. Denise said it was the result of her surfing childhood—a humorous claim considering she'd been born and raised in Fool's Gold and the town was over two hundred miles from the nearest ocean.

Dakota settled across from Montana. "How's it going?" she asked.

"Good. Max is keeping me busy. Some guy from the government came by earlier in the week. I'm not sure which agency he works with, mostly because he didn't tell us. He'd heard about the work Max does and wanted to test some of our dogs for their ability to differentiate scent."

Last fall Montana had left her position at the library and gone to work for a man who trained therapy dogs. She'd attended several seminars, had learned to train the dogs and seemed to be loving everything about her new job.

Dakota sipped her lemondrop as a Madonna song played in the background. "Why?"

Montana leaned toward her and lowered her voice. "I think they would be trained to sniff out explosives. The guy wasn't very clear. He knew Max from before, which makes me curious about his past. Not that I'm asking. I know Max likes me and all but I swear sometimes when he looks at me, he's wondering if I even have half a brain."

Dakota laughed. "You're being too hard on yourself."

"I don't think so."

Nevada walked up to the table. Although she was the same height and weight as her sisters, she managed to look completely different. Maybe it was the short hair or the jeans and long-sleeved shirts she favored. While Montana had always been on the girly end of the spectrum, Nevada preferred the tomboy look.

"Hi," she said as she sat down across from Dakota. "How's it going?"

"You should have been here earlier," Montana said with a grin. "Dakota was with a guy."

Nevada had raised her arm to wave at Jo. She froze in place and turned her brown eyes toward her sister. "Seriously? Anyone interesting?"

"I'm not sure if he's interesting, but he's yummy," Montana said.

Dakota knew there was no point in fighting the inevitable. Even so, she tried. "It's not what you think."

Nevada dropped her arm and grinned. "You don't know what I'm thinking."

"I can guess." Dakota sighed. "His name is Finn and his brothers are here to appear on the reality show." She briefly outlined the problem—at least the one from Finn's point of view.

"You should offer to comfort him in his hour of need," Montana told her. "A hug that lingers. A soft kiss with a whisper of need. Soul-stirring touches that..." She looked at her sisters. "What?"

Nevada glanced at Dakota. "I think she's slipped over the edge."

"I think she needs a man," Dakota told her, then looked at Montana. "Soul-stirring touches? Seriously?"

Montana dropped her head to her hands. "I need to spend some quality time with a naked man. It's been too long." She straightened, then smiled. "Or I could get drunk."

"Whatever works," Nevada muttered, accepting the tall vodka tonic Jo handed her. "Montana's slipping over the edge."

"It happens to the best of us," Jo said cheerfully, passing Montana a rum and Diet Coke.

As Jo left, the front door opened and Charity and Liz walked in. Charity was the city planner, married to cyclist Josh Golden, while Liz had married the triplet's brother, Ethan. Both women saw the sisters and headed over.

"How are things?" Charity asked as they approached.

"Good," Dakota said, eyeing her friend. "You look amazing. Fiona is what—three months old? You'd never know you just had a baby."

"Thanks. I've been walking a lot. Fiona is sleeping longer, so that helps."

Liz shook her head. "I remember those baby nights. Thank goodness mine are older."

"Wait until they start wanting to drive," Nevada told her.

"I refuse to think about that."

"Want to join us?" Montana asked.

Liz hesitated. "Charity's been reading my work-in-progress and wants to discuss a couple of things. Next time?"

"Sure," Dakota told them.

Liz wrote a successful detective series that had, until recently, featured victims who looked surprisingly like their brother Ethan. Now that he and Liz were together, Dakota had a feeling the next dead body would be completely different.

The two women walked to another table.

"How's work?" Nevada asked Montana.

"Good. I'm training a couple of new puppies. I talked to Max about the reading program I've been researching. I have an appointment with a couple of school board members to talk about a trial program."

Montana had discovered several studies that explained that kids who were bad readers improved more quickly when they read to dogs instead of people. Something about dogs being all support and no judgment, Dakota thought. When her sister had approached her about the studies, Dakota had done a little research and found even more supportive literature.

"I love the idea of going into schools and helping kids," Montana said wistfully. "Max says we're going to have to expect to do it for free in the beginning. Once we show results, the schools will hire us." She wrinkled her nose. "Honestly, most of what we do is for free. I can't figure out where he gets his money. Someone is paying my salary and to take care of the dogs. Even if he owns the land and the kennel is paid for, there's still upkeep."

"He hasn't said where the support comes from?" Nevada asked.

Montana shook her head.

"You could ask him," Dakota told her.

Montana rolled her eyes and picked up her drink. "That's not going to happen."

Montana wasn't big on confrontation, Dakota thought. She turned to Nevada. "How are things with you?"

"Good. The same." Her sister shrugged. "I'm in a rut."

"How can you say that?" Montana asked. "You have a great job, you've always known what you want to do."

"I know. I'm not saying I want to stop being an engineer and take up pole dancing, but sometimes…" She sighed. "I don't know. I think my life needs to be shaken up a little."

Dakota smiled. "We could always set Mom up on a date. That would be a distraction."

Both her sisters stared at her.

"Mom date?" Montana asked, her eyes wide. "Has she said anything?"

"Not seriously, but she's vibrant and attractive. Why wouldn't she date?"

"It would be weird," Montana said.

"Or uncomfortable." Nevada picked up her drink. "She would probably find a guy in fifteen seconds. I can't remember the last time I was on a date."

"That's what I thought, too," Dakota admitted. "But don't you think one of us should be successful at the dating thing?"

"You don't see the humiliation of that person being our mother?" Nevada asked.

Dakota grinned. "There is that."

Montana shook her head. "No. She can't. What about Dad?"

Dakota studied her. "It's been over ten years since he died. Doesn't she deserve a life?"

"Don't get all logical and therapist-y on me. I'm very comfortable not being the mature one."

"Then you shouldn't worry. We were just joking about it." As a way to release tension, Dakota thought sadly. As a distraction from the truth about her inability to have children.

"She didn't sign up for the show, did she?" Nevada asked. "Not that I wouldn't support her if she did."

"No, she didn't."

"Thank God." Nevada leaned back in her chair. "Speaking of the show, when do they announce the contestants?"

"Tomorrow. They've already made their casting decisions, but they're not telling anyone in advance. I think they're broadcasting live or something. I'm trying to stay out of it as much as I can."

"Will Finn be there?" Montana asked.

"Nearly every day."

Montana raised her eyebrows. "That will keep things interesting."

"I'm sure I don't know what you mean," Dakota said lightly. "He's a nice man, nothing more."

Nevada grinned. "You expect us to believe that?"

"Yes, and if you don't, I expect you to pretend."

AURELIA DID HER BEST to tune out the rant as she carefully put dishes into the dishwasher. The tirade was a familiar one. That Aurelia was a terrible daughter, selfish and cruel, who cared about no one but herself. That her mother had cared for her for years so it wasn't wrong to expect a little support and comfort in her old age.

"I'll be gone soon," her mother declared. "I'm sure you're counting the days until I'm dead."

Aurelia turned slowly to face the woman who had raised her on a secretary's salary. "Mama, you know that's not true."

"So I'm a liar?" her mother demanded. "Is that what you tell people?" Her mother's face crumpled. "I've only ever loved you. You're the most important person in my life. My only child. And this is the thanks I get?"

As always, Aurelia couldn't quite follow the train of the argument. She was clear on the fact that she'd messed up—she always messed up. No matter what she did, she was a constant disappointment. Much like her father, who had abandoned both his wife and daughter.

Aurelia didn't know if her mother had been a professional victim before he'd left, but she'd certainly taken on star status in the "poor me" department after.

"Look at you," her mother continued, pointing to Aurelia's long, straight hair. "You're a mess. You think this is how to find a man? They don't even see you. This is

Fool's Gold. There aren't that many men. You have to try harder to get one here."

Harsh words that were true, Aurelia thought. She moved through the world in a bubble. Doing her job, going out to lunch with her work friends, invisible to every man, including the president of the company. She'd worked for his firm for nearly two years, and he still had trouble remembering her name.

"I want grandchildren," her mother declared. "I ask for so little, but do you give them to me?"

"I'm trying, Mama."

"Not hard enough. You're with businessmen all day long. Smile at them. Flirt a little. Do you even know how? Dress better. You could lose a little weight, too. I didn't put you through college so you could be alone your whole life."

Aurelia closed the dishwasher and then wiped down the counter. Technically her mother hadn't paid for college at all. Aurelia had received a couple of small scholarships, a few grants and had worked to pay the rest. However, she had lived at home for free, so that was support. Her mother was right—she *should* be more grateful.

"You'll be thirty soon," her mother went on. "Thirty. So old. When I was that age, you were five and your father had been gone four years. Did I have time to be young? No. I had responsibilities. I had to work two jobs. Did I complain? Never. You lacked for nothing."

"You were good to me, Mama," she said dutifully. "You still are."

"Of course I am. I'm your mother. You need to take care of me."

Which was what had happened a few years ago. Aurelia had graduated, gotten her first job and moved out. A year or so later, her mother had mentioned money was a little short and asked her to help her out. A few dollars here and there had become the reality of nearly supporting her mother.

While her accounting job paid well, paying rent on two places, not to mention utilities and groceries, didn't leave very much left over.

Other parents seemed proud of their children's successes. Not her mother. She complained that Aurelia took horrible care of her. In this household, being a child meant a never-ending debt that only grew with time.

Aurelia stared out the kitchen window at the backyard beyond. Instead of a neat garden, she saw a giant balance sheet covered in red. Near-physical proof that she was trapped forever.

It wasn't supposed to have been like this, she thought sadly. She'd always had dreams of finding someone special, of falling in love. She just wanted to belong without having to feel there was always a payment to be made.

An impossible fantasy, she reminded herself. She wasn't especially pretty or interesting. She was an accountant who actually loved her work. She didn't go to clubs or bars, and should a man ever speak to her, she wouldn't have a clue what to say back.

"If you get picked for that show," her mother warned, "don't embarrass me by saying or doing something stupid. Be on your best behavior."

"I'll try."

"Try!" Her mother, a small woman with penetrating dark eyes, threw her arms in the air. "It's always *try* with you. Never *do*. You try and then fail."

Not exactly a pep talk designed to make her feel better, Aurelia thought, walking through the kitchen to the small living room. She hadn't wanted to audition for the reality show being filmed in town, but her mother had bullied her until she'd agreed. Now she could only hope she wasn't chosen.

She'd even tried to get out of it by saying that she had to work, but when she'd mentioned the application to her boss, it had been one of the few times he'd seemed interested in her. He'd told her she could take off time during the day whenever she needed as long as she got her work done later.

"I need to get home," she said. "I'll see you in a couple of days."

"Your own apartment," her mother said with a scowl. "So selfish. You should move back here. Think of the money you'd save. But no. It all has to go for your pleasure, while I have nothing."

Aurelia thought about pointing to the check she'd left on the table by the door. The one that would cover the rent and utilities for the month. Her mother was still working, earning what she'd always earned. So where was her money going? Perhaps for things like the new car in the garage and the stylish clothes she favored.

Aurelia shook her head. There was no point in going there. After all, once she gave her mother the money, it wasn't her business how it was spent. A gift was to be given freely.

Although the checks never felt like a gift. They were much more a guilt payment.

She grabbed her purse, told her mother goodbye and stepped out onto the small porch. Her own apartment was only a few blocks away and she'd walked.

"I'll see you soon," she called over her shoulder.

"You should move back," her mother yelled.

Aurelia kept walking. She might not be able to stand up to her mother, but she was determined that she would never live with her again. She didn't care if she had to work five jobs or sell her own blood. Moving back would be the end of anything close to a life.

As she walked along the tree-lined streets, she wondered where she'd gone wrong. When had she decided it was okay for her mother to treat her so badly, and how was she supposed to figure out how to stand up for herself without allowing a lifetime of guilt to get in her way?

FINN HAD NEVER BEEN on a movie set, so he couldn't speak to what happened there, but from what he could tell, television was all about the lighting.

So far the crew had spent nearly an hour adjusting

lights and big reflectors in a newly built soundstage on the edge of town. Rows of chairs had been set up for the audience that was due to arrive, and there had been at least three sound checks on microphones and the canned music, but it was the lights that seemed to have everyone frantic.

He kept out of the way, watching from a far corner. Nothing about the situation interested him. He would rather be back in South Salmon, getting ready to ferry shipments north of the Arctic Circle. Unfortunately, his regular life wasn't much of an option. Not until he could drag his brothers with him.

A few people walked toward the stage. He thought he recognized the tall man wearing a suit and what looked like an inch of makeup. The host, Finn thought, wondering what was the least bit appealing about being on TV. Sure, the pay was good, but at the end of the day, what had anyone really accomplished?

The host guy and Geoff had a long conversation with plenty of arm waving. A few minutes later, all the would-be contestants were led on stage. The curtain had a logo of the cable company on it—the stylized letters meaningless to Finn. He rarely watched network television, much less cable.

He saw a few people well over forty, a lot of good-looking kids in their twenties, a few ordinary types who were seriously out of place and the twins.

It was all he could do not to stomp onto the stage, grab one under each arm and head for the airport. Only a couple of things stopped him. First, the fact that it was unlikely he could actually wrestle either of his brothers into submission. They were as tall as him, and while he had more muscle and experience in a fight, he cared about them too much to really hurt them. Second, he had a feeling someone with the production company would call the police and the situation would go downhill from there.

"You're looking fierce about something," Dakota said, coming up and standing next to him. "Plotting to kidnap them?"

Finn was impressed by her mind-reading skills. "Want to be an accomplice?"

"I make it a rule to avoid situations that end with me going to jail. I know that makes me less fun at a party, but I can live with that."

He glanced at her and saw her brown eyes were bright with laughter.

"You're not taking my pain seriously enough," he told her.

"Your pain is in your head. You know your brothers are capable of making their own decisions."

"If we exclude their present situation."

"I don't agree with that." She turned to the stage. "Everyone deserves to follow his or her dream."

"They'd do better to finish college and settle down," he grumbled.

"Did you?"

He studied his brothers. "Sure. I'm the poster boy for responsible."

"Because you had to be. What were you like before your parents died and you were left with two thirteen-year-olds? Something tells me you were a lot wilder than they've ever been."

She was right, damn it. He shifted. "I can't remember."

"Do you expect me to believe that?"

"I might have been slightly less responsible."

"Slightly?"

He'd been crazy, he thought, refusing to admit it to her. He'd loved parties and women and defying every law of physics in his airplane. He'd gone beyond testing boundaries—he'd been reckless.

"That was different," he said. "We didn't know what could happen."

"Meaning they do and should act accordingly? They're twenty-one. Give them a break."

"If they go back to college, I'll give them a break."

"Silly, silly man." Her gaze was both amused and slightly pitying.

Under normal circumstances, that probably would have annoyed him, but he found he liked spending time with Dakota. Even when she disagreed with him, he liked hearing what she had to say.

He was aware of her standing close to him in the dark shadows of the back of the soundstage. They would see everything, and no one knew they were there. For a second, he wondered what he would have thought of her under other circumstances. If he weren't here because of his brothers. If he didn't have to worry about their welfare. If he was just a guy intrigued by an attractive woman with a killer smile.

But these circumstances didn't allow for distraction. He'd promised himself that once he got his brothers through college, it would be *his* turn to follow *his* dream. After eight years of taking care of them, he'd earned it. He didn't want to spend the rest of his life flying cargo. But that thought was for later—after he'd gotten his brothers out of this mess and knew that they were safe.

On stage, Geoff shooed everyone out of view. The potential contestants were gathered together.

Dakota glanced at her watch. "Show time," she murmured.

From what he'd been able to figure out, there would be a combination of live scenes and taped segments of the various potential contestants. Whatever it took to drag out the show, he thought grimly. He stared at his brothers, willing them to suddenly come to their senses. Neither of them noticed him.

The big lights went on, someone called "We're live in five, four, three…" Cameras were moved silently, then the host began.

He welcomed the viewers, explained the premise of the show and started introducing the potential cast. Dakota reached for Finn's hand and drew him through the darkness to the other side, where they had a better view of a wide-screen television.

She released his fingers and leaned toward him. "That's the feed going out," she murmured, her voice soft, her breath tickling his ear.

He inhaled a feminine scent—something floral and clean. Heat from her body seemed to slip across his arm, making him aware of her curves. For a second he considered pulling her deeper into the darkness and paying attention to her mouth instead of the screen.

Don't go there, he told himself. *Big mistake.* He had to remember what was important, and right now that was the twins.

On stage, the host began calling names. Finn found himself stiffening. The first couple was older. Late '50s early '60s. He ignored them. A blond guy got paired up with a dark-haired, busty Amazon. At least that was something, he thought. The girl looked like she could take Sasha and Stephen together.

"I promised you some fun contestants," the host said with a smile. "Here's where it gets interesting." He motioned for Sasha and Stephen to join him on stage.

"Twins," he said with a grin. "Can you believe it? Sasha and Stephen."

Finn watched his brothers carefully. They looked at ease on the stage. They smiled at the camera, chatted with the host. They looked like they belonged.

"Now which one of you is which?" the host asked.

Sasha, wearing jeans and a blue pullover, the same

damn color as his eyes, grinned. "I'm the better-looking one. So I must be Sasha."

Stephen gave his brother a shove. "I'm better-looking. We could take a vote."

The host laughed. "You boys are going to do just fine. Now let's find out if you made it on the show."

Finn felt his fingers curl into fists. Tension swept through his body. If only, he thought. But he knew what was going to happen. It had been inevitable from the day his brothers had left South Salmon.

The host looked at the card in his hand. He turned it over and showed it to the camera. Sasha's name was clearly visible. The audience, mostly bused in for the show, although a few locals had shown up, applauded. The host drew another card from his suit pocket. The girls waiting just behind him leaned toward the camera. A couple seemed ready to grab Sasha and run for the hills. A sentiment Finn could understand, although his reasons were different.

"Are you ready?" he asked Sasha.

Sasha grinned for the camera. "I can't wait to meet her."

"Then let's get the two of you together." The host turned the second card toward the camera. "Lani, come meet Sasha."

A petite, dark-haired, beautiful young woman stepped toward Sasha. Her eyes were large, her smile welcoming. She moved with an easy grace that had every man in the room watching her. Even Finn noticed her beauty.

Sasha's expression was comical as his eyes bugged out, and he leaned so far forward, he nearly lost his footing. He and Lani moved toward each other.

"Hi," she said softly. "Nice to meet you."

"Ah, nice to meet you, too."

They stared at each other. If Finn didn't know better, he would swear he was witnessing love at first sight. But he did know better. Or rather he knew his brother. Sasha would never let a girl stand between him and what he wanted.

"They look good together," Dakota said. "Or should I not point that out? Are you dealing okay?"

"I'll survive, if that's what you're asking."

"Not that you'll like it?"

He glanced at her. "What's to like?"

"You're not really a go-with-the-flow kind of guy, are you?"

"What gave me away?"

"Something tells me we're going to be seeing a lot more of those two," the host said cheerily.

Finn had yet to meet the man. He didn't know his name, but he knew he didn't like him. He couldn't imagine having to listen to him for ten or twelve weeks, or however the hell long the show lasted. Although disliking the host was the least of his problems right now.

Sasha and Lani linked hands and stepped to the side of the stage. The host put his arm around Stephen. "Guess you're next. Nervous?"

"More excited than nervous," Stephen said.

The host nodded to the girls waiting behind them. "Got a favorite?"

Stephen smiled. Unlike his brother, he didn't feel the need to charm the world. He'd always been serious. More studious. He had a sincerity the girls had always liked. If Sasha was the flash, then Stephen was the substance.

"Do I have to pick just one?" his brother asked.

The host chuckled. "You need to leave some for the rest of the contestants. How about if I pick one for you?"

Steven turned back to the camera. "Whichever one you pick is fine with me."

The host called for quiet. Finn wanted to point out that no one was talking but knew his comments wouldn't be appreciated. Once again the host removed a card from his suit pocket and held it up for the camera.

"Aurelia."

The camera panned across the girls, then paused as one of them stepped forward. Finn frowned. It wasn't that the girl was unattractive, or even badly dressed. She was just…different from the other girls. Less polished, less sophisticated. Plain.

She wore a navy dress that fell past her knees, low-heeled shoes and no makeup. Her long hair fell in her face, making it hard to see her eyes, not that she looked up as she approached. When she finally stepped next to Stephen and glanced at him, her expression was more one of horror than anticipation.

Finn studied her for a second, then frowned. "Wait a minute. How old is she?"

"Aurelia?" Dakota shrugged. "Twenty-nine or thirty. She was a year or two ahead of us in school."

He swore. "There's no way this is happening. I'm going to crush Geoff. I'm going to leave him bleeding and broken on the side of the road."

"What's wrong?"

He spun toward Dakota and glared at her. "Can't you see it? She's what? Nearly ten years older than Stephen. There is no way in hell I'm going to stand by while my brother is devoured by some cougar."

The corners of Dakota's mouth twitched. "Seriously? You think Aurelia is a cougar?"

"What else would she be? Look at her."

"I am," Dakota said. "*You* look at her. She's mousy. She was always like that in high school. I don't know her whole story but I'm pretty sure I remember she has an awful mother. Aurelia never got to do anything. She wasn't allowed to go to school dances or football games. It's kind of sad. You don't have to worry—she's not the type to trap him by getting pregnant or something."

"Cry me a river. I don't care about her past, I care about her being with my brother." He froze. "Pregnant?" He swore. "She can't get pregnant."

Dakota winced. "I shouldn't have said that. Stop worrying. She's no danger to Stephen. Come on, Finn, she's a nice girl. Isn't that what you want for your brother? A nice girl?"

"Sure I want a nice girl, but I want a nice girl who's his age."

Dakota grinned. "It may seem like a big age difference now, but when he's forty-two she'll only be fifty."

"You're not making me feel better. I don't think you're even trying."

Finn was done talking. Bad enough that his brothers had come to Fool's Gold to be on the stupid show. Maybe he could learn to live with that, but he was not going to stand here and let his brother be set up for a fall.

But before he could stomp down to the front of the stage and disrupt the live broadcast, Dakota stepped in front of him.

"Don't go up there," she said firmly, staring into his eyes. "You'll regret it, but more important, the boys will be humiliated on live television. They'll never forgive you. Right now you're an annoying older brother who wants to keep them safe. That's a livable condition. I'm serious, Finn."

He could see the truth in her eyes, and as much as he didn't want to believe her, he knew he had to. But the thought of leaving his brother alone with that woman...

"He doesn't have any money."

"Aurelia isn't after his money."

"How do you know that?"

"She has a great job. She's an accountant. From what I've heard, she does amazing work. There's a waiting list to be one of her clients." Dakota grabbed his arm again and stared into his eyes. "Finn, I know you're worried. Maybe you have reason to be. It would have been great if your brothers had stayed in college like you wanted them to. But they didn't. Please don't make this worse by going out there and acting like an idiot."

"I know you're trying to help," he said, realizing he sounded frustrated.

"Look at it this way. If she is as boring as I think she is, they'll get voted off early."

"If she's not, he'll be in trouble."

She dropped her hands to her sides. "You'll be here to make sure nothing bad happens."

"Assuming he'll listen."

He glanced toward the stage. Aurelia stood next to Stephen. If her body language was anything to go by, crossed arms, averted gaze, posture so stiff it was as if she were made of steel, she really wasn't happy about the situation. Maybe he would get lucky and they wouldn't last a date. He was due for some luck.

"You're quite the tough guy," Dakota told him. "Is that an Alaska thing?"

"Maybe." He took a deep breath and looked into her dark eyes. "Thank you for talking me off the ledge."

"I'm a paid professional, it's my job."

"You're good at it."

"Thank you."

He continued to stare into her eyes, mostly because

he liked it. She was easy to be around. And his body couldn't help but be aware of the smoothness of her skin, the shape of her mouth.

"I need to get going," she said. "Can I trust you to stay here on your own?"

"Sure."

"Have a little faith," she said, stepping back. "It's going to be okay."

She couldn't know that, he thought. But for today, he was going to believe her.

He waited until she had left before walking out of the sound studio. After pulling his cell phone out of his pocket, he dialed the number for his office in Alaska.

"South Salmon Cargo," a familiar voice said.

"Hey, Bill, it's me."

"Where the hell are you, Finn?"

"Still in California." Finn shifted the phone to his other ear. "Looks like I'm going to be stuck here for a while. They both got on the show."

A couple of thousand miles away, Bill sighed. "We're going to get busy soon. I can't do this by myself. If you can't get back here soon, we're going to have to freelance a couple of extra pilots."

"I know," Finn said heavily. "Go ahead and start looking. If you find somebody good, hire him. I'll be back as soon as I can."

"I need faster than soon," his partner told him.

"I'll do my best."

The business mattered, he thought as he ended the call. But his brothers would always be more important. He was stuck here until he finished the job he'd come to do.

CHAPTER FOUR

THE AIRPORT AT THE NORTH END of Fool's Gold was typical for its size. There were two runways and no tower. Pilots were responsible for staying out of each other's way. Finn was used to flying under those conditions. It was the same in South Salmon but with a lot worse weather.

He got out of his rented car and walked to the main office of Fool's Gold Aviation. He'd been told this was the best place to find out about renting a plane. He was also going to talk to the owner about picking up some extra work. There was no way he could stay in town for any length of time without doing something more productive than flying show contestants a couple of times a week.

He knocked on the open door and stepped into the two-room office. There were a couple of battered desks, a coffeepot on a rickety table by the window and a view of the main runway. An older woman sat at the larger of the desks.

When he entered, she looked up. "Can I help you?"

"I'm looking for Hamilton." He'd been given a single name and little else.

The woman, a pretty redhead in her fifties, sighed. "He's out with his planes. I swear, if he could sleep with them, he would." She pointed to the west. "That way."

Finn nodded his thanks and went around the building. He saw an older man bent low over the right tire of a Cessna Stationair.

Finn was familiar with the plane. It had a 310 fuel-injected horsepower engine and could cruise for nearly seven hours. The rear double doors made it easy to load cargo.

Hamilton looked up as Finn approached. "Thought I felt the tire go when I landed last night," he said, straightening. "Seems fine now."

He walked toward Finn and held out his hand. Hamilton had to be in his seventies, with wild white hair and a permanently lined face.

"Finn Andersson," Finn told him, shaking hands.

"You a pilot?"

"On a good day." Finn told him about his cargo business up in Alaska.

"That's wild flying," Hamilton said. "We don't get weather like that here. We're below twenty-five hundred feet, so we miss the worst of the snow and wind. There's some fog, but nothing like what you deal with. What brings you to Fool's Gold?"

"My brothers," Finn admitted and told Hamilton about the twins and their involvement with the show.

"They're going to use me to fly people around. I guess to save money."

"I don't care who rents my planes as long as they know what they're doing. Sounds like you do."

Finn knew the old man would need more than his word, but confirming credentials would be easy. "I'm stuck here for a few more weeks and wondered if you needed a pilot. I can fly cargo or people."

Hamilton grinned. "I do have some extra business. I hate to turn it away, but I've only got one set of hands and can only take on one flight at a time." He sighed. "There's plenty to be done. Rich people like to fly back and forth to town. Makes 'em feel special. The restaurant at the lodge is all fancylike and I fly in their fish. I have contracts with a few delivery companies, that kind of thing. Just tell me when you want to work and I can keep you busy."

"I'd appreciate that," Finn told him, relieved to know he wouldn't have to spend his day sitting around and watching his brothers.

"Let's go back to my office and see what's on the schedule. I guess I'll need to make it official and check on your license. We can go for a flight when we're done with the paperwork, if you have time."

"I have time," Finn told him.

"Good."

Back in the building, they went into Hamilton's office. It was smaller than the front room, but tidy. There were pictures of old planes covering the walls.

"How long have you been here?" Finn asked.

"Since I was a kid. Learned to fly before I could drive,

that's for sure. Never wanted to do anything else. My wife keeps bugging me to move to Florida, but I don't know. Maybe soon." He glanced at Finn. "The business is for sale, if you're interested."

"I have a business," Finn told him. "Although you could do a lot here." Not just charter and deliveries, he thought. Air tours could be lucrative. And there was that idea of his about teaching flying.

Dreams for another day, he reminded himself. When he knew for sure his brothers were grown-up enough that nothing bad would ever happen to them.

"If you change your mind, let me know," Hamilton told him.

"You'll be the first."

IN HER REGULAR LIFE, Dakota spent her days working up curricula for math and science programs. In theory, a year or two from now, students from around the country would be able to come to Fool's Gold and spend a month immersed in a math or science program. Dakota and Raoul worked hard to solicit donations from corporate and private benefactors. It was work that excited her. It was work that made a difference. But was she doing that important work now? No. Instead, she'd spent the past hour on the phone with various hotels in San Diego, negotiating room rates so reality show contestants could have a dream date.

The door to her makeshift office opened and Finn stepped inside. She hadn't seen him in a couple of days, not since the contestants had been announced. She half expected to read an article in the local paper saying that two twenty-something twins had gone missing. But so far, Finn seemed to be holding it all together.

"Am I interrupting?" he asked.

"Yes, and I'm desperately grateful." She tossed the papers she'd been holding. "Do you know I have a doctorate? I can make people call me doctor. I don't, but I could. Do you know what I'm doing with that degree right now?"

He took the seat across from her desk. "Not loving your job?"

"Not today," she said with a sigh. "I tell myself I'm doing the right thing. I tell myself I'm helping the town."

"Let me guess. It's not working."

"I'm getting very close to wanting to bang my head against the wall. That's never a good sign. As a health care professional, I'm very aware of that."

She leaned back in her chair and studied him. Finn looked good. Hardly a surprise. When had the man looked bad? He was solid. Dependable. His concern about his brothers proved that. She supposed her next line of thought should be that he was nice. Instead she found herself acknowledging that he was every woman's definition of a hot, sexy guy.

"Can I help?" he asked.

"I wish." She sighed. "Let's talk about something else. Nearly any topic would be more cheerful." She pointed to the papers on her desk. "I see Geoff kept his word. You're the pilot of choice for several of the dates. What you're doing for your brothers—" she smiled "—let's just say, parents across America will be so proud."

"That's one way of looking at it," he said. "I'd rather not have to be here at all." He looked at her. "Present company excluded."

"Thanks. Are you still going to come between Stephen and Aurelia?"

Finn shrugged. "Once I figure out how. They haven't been on a date yet, and both my brothers are avoiding me."

"Are you surprised?"

"No. If I were them, I'd be avoiding me, too." He shook his head. "Why couldn't they rebel in Alaska?"

"Missing home?" she asked.

He swung his gaze back to her and shrugged. "Some. This is very different."

"The landscape or the people?"

"Both," he admitted. "Compared to where I come from, Fool's Gold is the big city. Back in South Salmon, there's still snow piled ten-feet deep. But the days are getting longer and warmer. Bill—that's my business partner—and I should be gearing up for the busy season. Instead Bill's doing it himself." Finn sank lower in the seat. "We're going to have to hire a couple of temporary pilots."

"That can't be good," she said.

"It's a pain in the ass."

"You blame your brothers."

He raised one dark eyebrow. "Any reason I shouldn't?"

"Technically, you don't have to be here."

"Yes, I do." He glanced out the window. "If I wasn't worried about my brothers and work, being here wouldn't be so bad."

She smiled. "Are you saying you like Fool's Gold?"

"The people are friendly enough." He straightened. "I went out to the airport and talked to a guy there about renting planes for the show. I'm going to work with him while I'm here."

"Flying cargo?"

He nodded.

"I didn't know we flew cargo in and out of Fool's Gold."

"You'd be surprised what comes in by air. Even here. He also has charters. Taking people to remote places."

"Do you do that in South Salmon?"

"Some, although Bill and I focus mostly on cargo. I've thought about expanding, or even starting a new company. Bill wants to avoid dealing with passengers. It may be hard to believe, but I'm more of a people person." He grinned.

She reacted with a burst of heat to her belly and the knowledge that he'd made her toes curl. Thankfully, the latter was something he couldn't see.

"You're willing to take on the tourists?" she asked, trying to speak without having to clear her throat.

"They can be fun. I've also thought about opening a flying school. There's freedom up there, but you can't be stupid about it. My dad used to say the only time he knew I wasn't taking crazy chances was when I was flying." He chuckled. "Of course, he was wrong about that. Still, it teaches responsibility."

"Sounds like a calling."

"In some ways it is." He gazed at her. "You've been nice to me. I know you don't have to be, and I appreciate your counsel."

Nice? Great. She wanted him to think she was sexy and irresistible. Someone he couldn't wait to get in his bed. Wouldn't you just know it—the first man to get her attention in nearly a year thought she was nice.

"I do what I can," she said lightly. "If there are any particular goods or services you need in town, just let me know."

His dark gaze settled on her face. His mouth curved into one of those smiles designed to make a woman do just about anything. "I've been looking for a place to have dinner," he said. "Somewhere quiet. Somewhere a man can have a conversation with a beautiful woman."

If she'd been standing, she would have been in danger of tumbling over in shock. Was Finn asking her out to dinner? Or was he talking about someone else? It was pretty presumptuous of her to assume she was the beautiful woman in question. If he had said reasonably attractive, that she could have bought into.

"Well, I…" She paused, not sure what to say.

Finn shook his head. "I'm obviously out of practice. I was trying to ask you out to dinner, Dakota."

"Oh." Now was her turn to smile. "I'd like that." Then before she could stop herself, she added, "What if I cook? I mean, you could come to my place. I don't do gourmet or anything, but I know a couple of good recipes."

"Sounds perfect," he told her. "Just tell me when and I'll be there."

"How about tomorrow?"

"Works for me."

They settled on a time and she gave him her address. When he left, Dakota found herself smiling just a little more broadly as she picked up the phone to call another hotel in San Diego.

AURELIA STOOD in front of Geoff's desk and did her best to look confident, rather than horrified. Despite his jeans and worn T-shirt, a Hollywood producer intimidated her. Not a huge surprise, she thought. Most people intimidated her. The only place Aurelia felt confident was at work. In her office, with her computer and her numbers, she ruled her world. Everywhere else, it was all she could do not to apologize for simply breathing.

"There's been a mistake," she said, forcing herself to stare at him rather than at the ground. "I really appreciate being picked for the show. I didn't expect to be. It's just…"

How to say it? How to explain the truth without confessing her deepest, darkest secrets?

"I'm not a cougar," she said, speaking very quickly. "I'm actually allergic to cats. I'm not a man magnet." She could feel herself blushing. The man magnet statement was ridiculous. Geoff could tell what she was and wasn't simply by looking at her.

The producer glanced up from the laptop on his desk and frowned, as if he hadn't known she was in the room. "Who are you?"

"Aurelia. I'm paired with Stephen. He's one of the twins. They're twenty-one." She twisted her fingers together, not sure how she was going to make him understand. "Maybe there was a mistake. Or we could make a change. What if I was with someone older? Maybe a widower with a disadvantaged kid. I could do that."

Geoff returned his attention back to his laptop. "Not gonna happen. We need ratings. There are no ratings with a widower and some kid. Cougars are hot right now. It'll be fun."

She could tell he'd already lost interest in the conversation. Normally, she would simply accept whatever the circumstance was and go with it. But this time she couldn't. This time she had to fight.

She squared her shoulders and stared at the man who held her destiny in his indifferent hands. "No," she said firmly. "I'm not a cougar. Look at me." When he didn't glance up from his computer screen, she repeated the instruction. "Look at me!"

Reluctantly, Geoff raised his gaze from his screen. "I don't have time for this," he began.

"You're going to make time," Aurelia told him. "I'm only on this show because my mother insisted. She makes my life a living hell, and you don't get to do that to me, too. Sure I want to meet someone. Sure I want to get married and have children. I want a normal life. But I'm never going to have that with her around, dragging me down. I thought maybe, just maybe, if I did this, I could catch a break."

She felt her eyes starting to burn with tears and did her best to blink them back. "And look what happened. You put me with a *child!*"

When she'd finished, she expected Geoff to tell her to get out and return his attention to his computer. Instead he leaned back in his chair, folded his hands behind his head and studied her.

She felt his slow gaze start at her mousy brown hair and move down to her knees, which was about all that was visible, what with her standing in front of his desk.

She'd come straight from work, so she was dressed in one of her conservative navy suits. They were a uniform of sorts. She had five, along with two black suits and one in pale gray for when it was really hot in the summer.

On the same rack in her closet were an assortment of blouses. On the carpet below were a row of sensible, low-heeled pumps. Hers was not a wardrobe any cougar would be caught dead in.

Geoff dropped his hands to the desk. "You're right—you're not a cougar. But sex sells and a woman on the prowl is interesting to viewers."

"Not when that woman is me. I've never prowled."

His mouth turned up slightly. "You never know. People might feel sorry for you."

She held in a wince. How nice. The pity vote.

"I can't do this."

Geoff shook his head. "I hate to be a pain in your ass, Aurelia, but here's the thing. You're with Stephen or you're out."

While the words weren't a surprise, she had been hoping for a miracle. Apparently the universe was fresh out. Or busy with someone else.

"I have to do this," she said earnestly. Contestants were paid twenty thousand dollars. It wasn't a huge amount, but it was enough. When added to the small amount she'd managed to save, she would finally be able to buy a condo. She would own her own home.

The dream was better with a husband and child, but right now she was willing to take what she could get.

"Then do it," he told her. "If you need to be on the show to get your mother to back off, you have to take the chance. Go through with it. What's the worst that could happen?"

The humiliating possibilities were endless, but that wasn't the point. Geoff was right. If she believed the show was her way out, then she had to be willing to do the show.

"For what it's worth," Geoff said, "Stephen isn't a bad guy."

"Can I get that in writing?"

He laughed. "No way. Now get out of here."

Aurelia felt a little better as she stepped out of Geoff's office. She *could* do this, she told herself. She could be strong. She might even be able to fake being a...

Her proud, brisk exit walk came to a halt when she slammed into someone tall and broad.

"Oh, sorry," she said, then found herself looking up and up until she fell into the dark blue gaze of Stephen Andersson.

She'd only seen him one other time—during the initial filming, taping, whatever they call it, of the show. During those brief minutes, she'd barely glanced at him. All she'd been able to think about was her humiliation. The reality that he was absolutely the last man she could ever imagine dating. Okay, Gerard Butler would have been worse, but only marginally.

"You really think it's going to be that bad?" he asked. "Being with me?"

The question was horrible enough, but worse was the realization that he had heard at least part of her conversation with Geoff. She felt herself flush.

"It's not you," she said quickly. "It's me. I'm sure you're a great guy."

"Don't say nice," he warned her. "That only makes it worse."

"Okay, then," she said slowly. "I'm sure you're not nice. Is that better?"

He surprised her by smiling. A casual but friendly smile. One that made her forget how to breathe.

"Not by much." He took her elbow and led her into an empty meeting room. "So what's the deal? Why don't you want to be on the show with me?"

It was hard to think with his fingers curled around her elbow like that. In her world, men didn't touch her. They barely knew she was alive.

He was standing too close. How was she supposed to think with him taking up all the air in the room? While this would be a good time to self-edit, the truth bubbled up before she could stop it.

"Look at you," she said. "You're this gorgeous guy. You could have anyone. You should be hitting on coeds. You're not anyone who would be interested in someone like me. Even ignoring the age difference, I'm not your type. Do you know what I do in my regular life? I'm an accountant. Look up boring in the dictionary and you'll find some version of me."

Knowing that if she didn't get some small measure of self-control soon, she was going to make an even deeper hole to fall into, Aurelia pulled her arm free and stepped back.

Instead of looking horrified, Stephen appeared amused. Humor brightened his eyes, and one corner of his mouth twitched slightly.

"That's quite a list," he told her. "Where should I start?"

"No," she said with a sigh. "I understand this is my fault. I should never have signed up to do the show. I didn't really want to, it's just…" She twisted her hands together. "At the risk of being a cliché, my mother made me do it. She's always on me about stuff. And the money. I thought…maybe, if there was someone else, it would be easier to stand up to her." She groaned. "That makes me sound so pathetic."

"Hey, I get it. I know what it's like when someone in your family thinks they can run your life. Not wanting to do what they say doesn't mean you don't love them."

Aurelia wasn't sure what she felt for her mother. Love, of course, but sometimes the love felt more dutiful than sincere. Which made her a horrible person, she knew.

"My brother flew here from Alaska to yell at me about leaving college," Stephen said. "That's how much he doesn't want me to do this."

"What's wrong with you doing the show?" She did the math in her head, then looked at him. "You're really close to graduating, aren't you?"

Stephen, all six plus feet of hunky guy, shifted uncomfortably. "I was in my last semester."

"Before graduating?" she asked, her voice a slight shriek. "You left school for this?"

"Now you sound like my brother."

"Maybe he has a point."

"I couldn't do it anymore. I had to get away."

She shook her head. "You get how idiotic that is, right?"

The smile returned. "Maybe, but I'm still not going back."

"I feel the need to take your brother's side in this."

"But you're not going to, are you?" Stephen shoved his hands into his front pockets. "Because if I leave, you don't do the show."

Something she hadn't thought about. "Why are you here? I mean really, why are you here? I can't believe school was that difficult."

"It wasn't hard, if that's what you mean." He sighed. "Our folks died about eight years ago. There was Sasha and Finn and me, and no one else. We were close before, but losing them changed everything. It was hard."

Aurelia had a feeling the word *hard* didn't begin to describe what they'd gone through. "At least it brought you together," she said, thinking that the loss of her father hadn't brought her and her mother together.

"Finn won't let go. He's holding on too tight. Sasha found the audition in the paper. He's the one who wants to be on TV. I just want to be anywhere but South Salmon." He stared into her eyes. "It seems to me, we could help each other. I get your mom off your back and you protect me from Finn."

"I'm not sure you need protecting."

"Everyone needs protecting now and then."

There was something about the way he said the words. A vulnerability that only made him more appealing.

Maybe Stephen wasn't as scary as she had first thought. But scary or not, she was taking a big risk. So much could go wrong.

"I won't let anything bad happen to you," he said quietly.

His words stunned her. It was as if he could read her mind. No one had ever done that before, probably because no one had ever taken the time to get to know her.

"You can't know that," she said, wanting to believe him, but afraid to try.

"Sure, I can. Why don't we try being here for each other?"

A tempting offer, she thought.

She stared into his eyes, searching for the truth. As she looked, she realized the answer wasn't to be found in Stephen. It was in herself. Either she gathered the courage to take the next logical step, or she was trapped forever.

"Let's do it," she said and promised herself there would be no regrets.

DAKOTA STARED at the raw chicken in the pan, not sure if she should put it in now or wait until Finn arrived. What had she been thinking, inviting him over to dinner? In truth, he'd sort of invited himself, but still. Their evening was clearly a date, which should have been good but wasn't because now she was rattled. Worse, her thighs had been quivering all day.

Before she could decide about the chicken, the door-bell rang. She hurried toward the door, only to run back into the kitchen, pull open the oven and set the pan inside. Dinner would be ready in forty minutes. They would have to figure out a way to fill the time until then.

She sucked in a breath, squared her shoulders and opened the front door.

"Hi," she said.

It was good she spoke quickly, before she could really see him. Once she took in the long, lean body, the hand-some face, the cotton shirt that wasn't plaid, she found herself feeling the tiniest bit disoriented.

"Hi, yourself," Finn said with a smile, as he handed her a bottle of red wine. "I hope this is okay." He pointed at the wine. "I stopped at a store in town to pick it up. The guy made several recommendations. I'm not much of a wine guy. I wouldn't mind learning about it. You probably know something about wine, what with all the wineries around here."

As his words swirled around her, she realized he was talking too quickly. Was it possible Finn was nervous, too? The thought made her feel a whole lot more com-fortable about the evening.

"I know nothing about wine," she said, holding up the bottle. "Except that I usually like it. Come on in."

He followed her into the kitchen. She only had to search two drawers before finding the corkscrew. Finn took the bottle from her and made quick work of the cork. She set glasses on the counter and he poured. After they toasted each other, she led the way back into her living room.

The house was small—two bedrooms—and a rental. Intelligent thinking and her slightly feminist sensibilities had told her to buy a house. After all, she was a professional who could take care of herself. But she was enough of a traditionalist to want to buy her first house with the man she loved. Hence, the rental.

Finn sat on the overstuffed chair her brother Ethan had talked her into buying. At the time, she'd thought it was too big for the room. Now, seeing Finn in it, she knew her brother had been right.

"This is nice," Finn said, glancing around the room. "Thank you."

They stared at each other, then looked away. Dakota felt disaster looming. She knew she wasn't much of a dater, and, based on what Finn had told her, he didn't date much, either. This could be bad.

"I hope you're okay not eating meat," she said quickly. "I'm a vegetarian."

He looked slightly trapped, but nodded bravely and said, "Vegetarian is fine."

"Oh, great. So you like tofu. A lot of guys refuse to eat it."

He swallowed visibly. "Tofu?"

"Uh-huh. It's one of my favorite casseroles. Tofu, a special sauce mostly based on green vegetables. Soy ice cream for dessert."

"Sounds delicious."

She could see the panic in his eyes and couldn't help laughing softly. "I'm kidding. I made chicken."

His gaze narrowed. "Seriously? That's your idea of fun? Torturing me?"

"Everyone needs a hobby."

He leaned back in his chair and studied her. "You're not predictable, are you?"

"I try not to be. Besides, you're easy."

"It was the sauce made with green vegetables that pushed me over the edge."

"Not the soy ice cream?"

"I figured I'd leave early."

"Coward."

They smiled at each other. She felt the bad tension bleed away and a nice, new boy-girl tension take its place.

"You grew up with brothers, didn't you?" he asked.

"How can you tell?"

"You're not worried about my ego."

"Interesting observation," she said, then sipped her wine. "I hadn't thought about that, but you're right. I have three older brothers."

He raised his eyebrows. "Six kids?"

"Yes. I think my mom really wanted a girl. Instead she got three for the price of one."

"That had to have been a shock."

"I'm sure it was. Apparently having triplets is really hard on the woman's body. She was in the hospital after we were born. For a while, the doctors were concerned she wasn't going to make it. My dad had to have been freaked out, and my brothers were really young and missing their mom. Complicating everything was the fact that it was Christmas. To distract them, he told them they could name us, but that all three of them had to agree on the names."

She paused and wrinkled her nose. "Which is why we're Dakota, Nevada and Montana."

"Very patriotic."

She laughed. "When I used to get frustrated at their choice, my mom would point out that it could have been a lot worse. Apparently Oceania was in the running."

"Sounds like a fun family."

"It is." She shifted on the sofa. "What was it like for you? Before you lost your family?"

"Good. Fun. We were close." He shrugged. "My brothers are a lot younger than me, which influenced the relationship."

"You must have been devastated when your parents died."

He nodded. "I was. I didn't know how I was going to do it. Raise the boys and not screw up."

"Be proud of what you've accomplished. I don't think I could have done it. We lost my dad ten years ago. My sisters and I were just out of high school, ready to start college. My brothers were either in college or done. There was nothing for me to do but get through the mourning. And it was hard every day. I can't imagine having to deal with the emotional loss and raise two younger brothers."

Finn looked uncomfortable with the praise. "I did what had to be done. Some days I think I did okay. Others, like when I'm in my hotel room here in Fool's Gold, I think I screwed up completely."

"You didn't. What they're doing now has nothing to do with you."

He looked at her. "I want to believe you."

"Then you should."

"You're bossy. Has anyone ever told you that?"

"Are you kidding? With three brothers? I have a crown. I'm the queen of bossy."

Finn laughed. The warm sound filled the room and made her smile. They continued talking until, in the kitchen, the timer dinged.

"Come on," she said, rising to her feet. "Our tofu surprise awaits."

FINN ENJOYED HIS DINNER. Not just the chicken and mashed potatoes, which were the best he'd had in months. Maybe years. But also the conversation. Dakota told funny stories about growing up in Fool's Gold. He knew what small towns were like, but South Salmon made Fool's Gold look like New York City. Where he lived, people tended to keep to themselves. Sure, you could count on a neighbor to help, but everyone minded their own business. From what Dakota said, Fool's Gold was the town that meddled.

"If you'd come here under other circumstances," she said, "I'm sure you would've liked it a lot more."

"I like Fool's Gold just fine," he told her.

"This is always going to be the place your brothers ran off to."

"Look at it this way," he said. "When Sasha moves to L.A., I'll hate it there, instead."

"That's not very comforting."

They smiled at each other across the table. He liked how the light played on her hair, bringing out the various shades of blond. When she laughed, her eyes crinkled in a way that made him want to laugh, too. Dakota was easy to talk to. He'd forgotten how nice it could be to enjoy a woman's company for an evening.

"How come your boss is so understanding?" he asked. "You said you had another job. What's he doing while you're working with the show?"

Dakota wrinkled her nose. "Not missing me," she grumbled. "Raoul is busy playing house with his new wife. Do you follow football?"

"Some. Why?"

"My boss is Raoul Moreno."

"The Dallas Cowboys quarterback?"

"That's him. When he retired, he wanted to settle down and found his way here. There was an old abandoned camp up in the mountains. He bought it and refurbished it. He hired me to coordinate the various programs. He had this whole idea to use it year-round. In the winter we were going to offer math and science programs. Intensive learning for middle-school-age kids. Get them all interested in the possibilities."

Sounded like a good idea, he thought. "What happened?"

"One of the local elementary schools burned down. It was a freak thing with the furnace. Raoul offered the camp to the school district. That was last September. Until the new school is built and the kids move back, the camp is full. Our big plans are on hold. Which is one of the main reasons he didn't mind me helping out with the reality show."

She leaned toward him. "The other reason is, he recently got married. Pia, his wife, is pregnant with twins. She's due in a couple of months, and that's keeping him busy."

"What are you going to do between the end of the show and when the school is done using the camp?" he asked.

"Raoul wants me to keep working for him. There's plenty to do. We have to apply for grants, find corporate sponsors, come up with a curriculum."

"All of which you'd rather be doing," he said.

She smiled. "Absolutely."

"Is leaving an option? Do you ever think about living anywhere else?"

"I've lived other places. Got my undergraduate degree at UCLA, my masters and Ph.D. at Berkeley. But Fool's Gold is home. It's where I belong. Do you think about leaving South Salmon?"

At one time he had. When he'd been Sasha and Stephen's age he'd dreamed of seeing the world. But then his parents had died and he'd had two brothers to raise. There hadn't been time for dreams.

"I have a business there," he said. "Leaving is impractical."

"And you're a practical guy?"

"I've learned to be," he admitted.

"You said you were wild before." Her gaze locked with his. "Would I have liked you?"

"I would've liked you."

He felt the awareness crackling between them. Everything about Dakota appealed to him. Sure, she was pretty, but it was more than that. He liked listening to her. He liked her opinions and how she looked at the world. Maybe part of him liked that she was as firmly connected to Fool's Gold as he was to South Salmon. They couldn't make a mistake because it couldn't go anywhere.

Wanting stirred. It had been a long time since he'd had the time or energy to be interested in a woman. Given how concerned he was about his brothers, it was extraordinary he was interested now. Which begged the question—what did he do next?

"I have dessert," Dakota said, coming to her feet. "And it's not soy-based. Interested?"

He stood as well, then came around the table. He supposed he should ask. After all, this wasn't just about him. Dakota was a rational, thoughtful woman. She would appreciate getting all the details out of the way first, assuming she was interested at all. But instead of asking, he moved closer. He cupped her face in his hands, leaned in and kissed her.

CHAPTER FIVE

DAKOTA HAD EXPECTED SOMETHING along the lines of, "What flavor of ice cream do you have?" She hadn't expected Finn to kiss her.

His hands were warm on her face, which was nice enough. But what really got her attention was the feel of his mouth on hers. His lips were soft enough to tempt her and firm enough to allow her to relax. He kissed her gently, but deliberately enough to let her know that he really meant it. He kissed like he was hungry and she was an unexpected buffet.

His lips teased hers, moving lightly, as if searching for the best place to land. It'd been a long time since a man had kissed her. A long time since she'd wanted one to. Last fall, before she discovered she was broken inside, she would have said she wanted to be in a relationship. After, everything had changed. Now she wasn't sure. But with Finn, it didn't matter. He wasn't staying and anything between them wasn't permanent.

A very freeing concept.

He dropped his hands to her waist and drew her against him. She wrapped her arms around him and leaned in to the embrace. Her head tilted, he moved closer. He tasted of the wine they'd had with dinner. He smelled clean and masculine. As she moved her hands from his shoulders to his arms, she felt the strength of him.

The kiss continued. Skin on skin, warm. Appealing. Then something changed. Maybe it was the way he shifted his hands to her back and spanned the length of her spine. Maybe it was her thighs brushing his. Maybe it was the placement of the moon in the sky. Or maybe it was finally time for something good to happen to her.

Regardless of the reason, one second she was enjoying a perfectly respectable kiss from a very charming man. The next, fire swept through her body. It was as unexpected as it was intense. Heat was everywhere. Heat and hunger and the kind of wanting that stole a woman's will and left her prepared to beg.

Instead of holding on to him, she found herself clinging. The need to get closer grew until it overwhelmed her. She parted her lips, hoping to deepen the kiss. Thankfully, he read her mind. His tongue swept inside, brushing against hers.

It was heaven. Every stroke made her insides clench, her legs shake. She kissed him back, enjoying the growing sense of arousal. She wanted to be swept away, to be reminded of exactly what her body could do.

She'd been numb for so long, she realized. Disconnected from everything but the pain. She'd blocked off nearly all emotions, going through the motions so well, she'd even fooled herself.

He kissed her more deeply. She closed her lips around his tongue and sucked gently. He tensed in her embrace, as if holding back.

He was going to stop. But he couldn't. She needed this. He had to...

Only he didn't have to do anything. This wasn't her, she told herself firmly. She didn't attack guys in her kitchen—or anywhere else. The polite course of action seemed to be to step back.

Oh, but she wanted him. Her breasts ached. Her nipples were so sensitive, the feel of her bra was nearly agony. Between her legs, she was swollen and hungry. She wanted his big hands to touch her everywhere. She wanted to see him naked and hard in her bed. She wanted to be filled over and over until she found her release and with it, maybe a little healing.

It took every ounce of self-control, but somehow she managed to drop her hands to her sides and put some room between them. She was aware of her frantic breathing and hoped she didn't look too desperate. Sexual confidence was attractive. Desperation tended to send a man running.

Finn's eyes were dark with passion, which was nice. She was tempted to glance down to see if there was physical proof of his feelings, but she couldn't figure out how to do it without being obvious. Still, there was every chance he'd been offering a polite kiss and she'd gone after him like a sex-starved monkey.

"I, ah, don't know what to say," she admitted, not quite meeting his gaze.

"I shouldn't have done that," Finn mumbled. "You weren't… That's not why you…" He cleared his throat.

She frowned, not sure if he was apologizing or trying to escape. Hope shoved embarrassment out of the way.

"I'm glad that you did that," she said, telling herself that being brave built character.

"You are?"

She forced herself to look at him and found him staring at her. Oh, yeah. That was some serious passion.

"Very glad."

One eyebrow raised. "Me, too."

Heat stained her cheeks, but she plunged ahead anyway. "We could do it again."

"We could. There's only one problem."

He was married? He used to be a woman? He was gay?

"I'm not sure I'll want to stop," he admitted.

The relief was nearly as good as the kiss had been. Dakota stepped toward him and didn't stop until her body was plastered against his. Which answered the question about his feelings on the subject.

"That works for me," she whispered.

She'd planned to say more, to suggest they move to her bedroom, but she didn't get the chance.

Once again, Finn kissed her. And while it wasn't as unexpected as the first time, she still found herself swept away.

She surrendered to his strong embrace, wanting to feel his arms around her. She parted her mouth, and he plunged inside, teasing her into passionate frenzy. Even as his mouth claimed hers, his hands were everywhere. He stroked her back, then dropped lower, to her rear. He cupped the curves, squeezing until she instinctively arched forward.

Her belly rubbed against his erection. He was hard and thick, and the image that contact painted made her whimper. Without thinking, she reached behind her and grabbed his hands, then brought them around to her breasts.

The second he touched her, she began to melt. His hands cupped her curves, caressing the skin as he learned every inch of her. His thumbs and forefingers found her nipples and teased them. Then he grabbed the hem of her sweater and tugged it over her head.

He'd barely had time to toss it away when she was pulling at the hooks on her bra. The bra went flying. Her only thought was to hope the stove was off so if it landed there, nothing bad would happen.

While she was doing that, Finn pulled off his shirt and kicked off his shoes. Then he bent down and drew her right nipple into his mouth. He licked the hard, sensitive tip before sucking deeply. She felt the connection all the way down her belly. Wanting tugged her center.

The combination of the movement, the heat, the moisture and the friction nearly drove her to her knees. She held on to him to keep standing. He switched to her other breast and used his fingers to caress the first. She ran her fingers through his hair, then brought his face to hers so she could kiss him again.

As their tongues tangled, he unfastened the button on her jeans. She stepped out of her flats. Seconds later, her jeans and bikini briefs hit the floor. Finn followed, dropping to his knees, parting her thighs and kissing her intimately.

There was no warning, she thought frantically. No way to prepare herself for the gentle assault of his lips and tongue. She was defenseless as he explored all of her before returning again and again to her swollen center.

With each erotic lick, she felt herself getting closer. Her legs trembled until it was nearly impossible to stay upright. She dug her fingers into his shoulders, but it wasn't enough. She could feel herself starting to sink.

He caught her as she fell, pulling her into his embrace and against his chest. His skin burned hot against hers. As he stood, her feet left the floor, then he was carrying her through the small house.

She thought about giving directions, but as there were only two bedrooms on a single floor, she knew he could figure it out. Sure enough, he went directly into her bedroom, where he placed her on the quilt. Before he joined her, he sent his jeans and boxers skidding to the other side of the room.

He slid down next to her and put his hands on her body. He began at her forehead, lightly tracing her skin. He touched her cheekbones, her ears, her jaw. He traced her shoulders, her collarbone, before settling his hands on her breasts.

From there, he journeyed down her waist, over her hips, to the vee between her legs. She'd thought he might linger, finish what he started. But instead he continued down her thighs to her knees, her calves to her ankles.

He made the return trip more slowly. When he reached the soft skin of her inner thighs, he shifted between her legs, parted her and bent down to kiss her.

His tongue went immediately to where she was most sensitive. The steady stroking, a back and forth rhythm designed to drive her to madness, made her moan. Her body was not her own. He controlled every reaction, every sensation. Over and over again. Up and down.

Her muscles tensed. She felt herself straining toward the finish.

Not yet, she thought frantically. It was too good. She had to make it last. But it was impossible. The sureness of his touch, the feel of him against her. She felt herself nearing the end, nearing the inevitable.

Then he shifted slightly and inserted a finger deep inside of her. He pushed in once, twice, and she was lost. Her body dove into the pleasure. It swept through her, over her and around her. It was everywhere, and she never wanted it to end.

But gradually, the shuddering slowed. She felt herself resurfacing, returning to the real world. Lethargy battled with contentment. She hadn't felt this good in a really long time.

Just as the last of her climax faded away, Finn straightened, then put his hands on her hips. He entered her with one smooth, determined thrust. He was as big as she had imagined and filled her completely.

When he was all the way inside, she opened her eyes and smiled at him. "Nice," she whispered.

He managed a grin. "You like?"

"I do."

She wrapped her legs around his hips and drew him closer. When he withdrew and thrust in again, she urged him to go deeper. She wanted to take all of him. She wanted to get lost in what they were doing. This was life. This is what people who were alive did.

Every time he filled her, she found herself moving a little closer to who she had been before. Her body accepted him, widening and stretching to accommodate him. She felt him get closer. She felt herself getting more aroused.

Next time, she promised herself. Next time she would come again. But for now it was enough to feel him tensing. To feel him straining. To hold him as he lost himself in her.

SASHA AND LANI both sat cross-legged on the only bed in her motel room. The space he shared with his brother was bigger, but not by much. Once they'd been picked for the show, the production company paid for their food and lodging. Not that Geoff saw the need to pay for anything extravagant. So they were all stuck where they started.

When the show was over, they each got twenty grand. More than enough to finance his move to L.A.

Lani spread out several sheets of paper onto the bedspread. A few were new, but some of the pages looked old, with stains, tears and creases from being folded and unfolded again and again.

"I want to be a household name by the time I'm twenty-two," Lani said, her dark brown eyes bright with conviction. "Movies would be great, but TV feels like more of a sure thing. I flew to L.A. last year for pilot casting season." She paused and looked at him.

Sasha nodded. He knew enough about how the media worked to be familiar with pilot season.

Every year the networks and cable stations produced pilots for potential television series. Then the executives at the various stations decided which shows got a chance to be seen and which were dumped before they'd even begun. Casting was a big part of making a pilot, and unknowns were welcome to try.

Getting onto a pilot was huge, but once cast, there were no guarantees. Even if the show got picked up—a one in a million shot—your part could get recast with someone else. It was an actor's version of the lottery.

"How did you do?" he asked.

She sighed. "I got on two pilots. Neither went anywhere."

She raised her arms above her head and stretched. As she moved, her T-shirt pulled across her boobs.

Sasha watched, mostly out of habit. Lani was beautiful.

Her features were exotic, and he would bet she would photograph great.

"What about modeling?" he asked.

"I'm too short," she told him. "Five-five. It's not going to happen. I've done some swimsuit stuff back home. Catalogues, that kind of thing. Of course I've had tons of offers to do nude shots, but there's no way. I wouldn't want those pictures to come back and haunt me when I'm up for an Oscar."

He wanted to get out of Alaska and be famous and very rich. Being a star was a way to make that happen. But Lani wanted it all. A serious acting career, awards and scores of paparazzi following her every move.

"We need to nail down our plan," she said, shuffling the papers. Her long, dark, wavy hair tumbled over her shoulders.

He supposed he should want to have sex with her or something. If she took off her clothes and offered, he wouldn't say no. But he wasn't really interested in her that way. Lani was the first person he'd met who wanted the same thing he did, only more. He understood that if they worked together, they would have a better chance of getting it all.

"You know, if we win, we'll each get a hundred and twenty-five thousand dollars," he said, leaning back against the pillows. "Plus the twenty. I want to rent a house in Malibu."

"Don't be an idiot," she told him. "That's before taxes. We'll be lucky to walk away with seventy thousand.

And that has to last. I'm getting an apartment in the San Fernando Valley. Somewhere near the studios in Burbank, and an easy drive over the hills. That way I can be in Century City or Hollywood pretty fast. I know if I don't get picked up right away, I'll need to get a job." She looked at him. "Do you have your dream list of agents?"

Agents? "Ah, not really."

"I do. Once this show starts to air, I'm going to be making calls, asking their assistants to watch me. There's no way I'll get to the agent I want, but assistants love to take calls. They're looking for the next big thing. They want to find him or her and take that potential client to their boss."

Sasha stared at her. He and Lani might be about the same age, but he suddenly felt like a kid at the grown-ups' table. How did she know all this?

His questions must have shown because she grinned. "Don't look so surprised. I've been working the program since I was thirteen."

"I guess that should make me feel better."

She shook her head. "You'll catch on. It's not that hard. Everything is about capturing attention. Getting your fifteen minutes of fame and making it an hour. I've been thinking that we need a story line."

"What do you mean?"

"Regular dating isn't interesting. Who wants to watch that? What, we'll be sitting there talking?" She shook her head. "We need something better. We need a better reason for viewers to want us to win."

He leaned toward her. "Okay. Like what? Something from a movie?"

"I thought one of the classic love stories," she admitted. "But I'm not sure that's the way to go. Too many people will be familiar with the plot. Plus, it's not enough. It's not like we can have people kidnap us, although that would be fabulous."

She pulled out one of the pieces of paper and waved it at him. "I watched soaps. Some of the story lines are really great. When you think about it, people watch soaps because something is always happening. That and they care about the characters. So we have to get people to care about us and we have to give them something interesting to watch." She looked at him. "Sex sells."

"I can do sex," he said with a grin.

Lani rolled her eyes. "I already told you, no porn. But that doesn't mean we can't do romantic and passionate. People love that. I'm thinking we could have one of those great relationships where we're always falling in love and fighting and then breaking up and then getting back together. The camera loves drama. The camera loves action. If we give the director something interesting to film, we'll get the most TV time. And that's what we want."

"I can do action," Sasha said, still a little stunned by Lani's determination and willingness to do anything to get what she wanted. The most he'd done was walk away from college and his brother. At the time, that had seemed huge. Now he wasn't so sure.

"We'll be the couple everyone is talking about," she said eagerly.

"Absolutely. So what's the plan?"

Lani grinned. "I'm not sure." The grin widened. "Are you afraid of fire?"

THERE WAS A LOT MORE to filming a television show than Dakota had realized. With ten couples, nearly as many locations and what seemed to her to be a very small crew, chaos reigned. Each couple was going to get a local date, and a few of them would get travel dates. It seemed to her that getting a travel date the first week made it a lot easier to stay on the show.

She'd always been a huge fan of shows like *Project Runway* and *Top Chef.* But she'd had no idea of all the work that went into forty-five minutes of air time. Today two couples were getting to know each other while they walked around Fool's Gold. A very nice first date in reality, but from what she could see on the monitors, it didn't make for exciting television.

She checked her clipboard to see how long the "date" was supposed to last. As she glanced back at the couple, she saw a tall, yummy-looking man walking toward her.

She hadn't seen Finn for nearly two days. Not since he'd been at her place and they'd engaged in acts that had the potential to send her to a higher plane. A quality she could really grow to like in a man.

As she wondered if she would be embarrassed or feel awkward around him, her body began a quivering dance of anticipation. As if her whole being had been invaded by sex-starved DNA.

"Morning," he said as he approached.

"Hi."

She stared into his blue eyes and found herself smiling. No bad feelings for her, she thought, relieved. The quivering got even better when he smiled back.

"How's it going?" she asked.

"Better," he told her. "I've been dealing with a few work-related crises back home, I flew some cargo to Eugene, Oregon, then spent most of yesterday trying to talk the twins into going back to Alaska."

"How did that go?"

"When we were done, I pounded my head against a wall just to make myself feel better."

"Ouch. Did you really expect your brothers to get on a plane and go back with you?"

He shrugged. "A guy can dream, right?" He shook his head. "No, I really didn't expect them to come with me. I knew it wasn't going to work, but I was compelled to try. Call me an idiot."

"Actually, I think you're someone who really cares about his family. You're misguided, but that happens to all of us."

He chuckled. "Thanks, I think."

"I was being nice," she told him.

"In a very subtle way."

She laughed. It was good to know she hadn't imagined that being around Finn was fun. The morning after could be an awkward time, even several days later, but she felt just as comfortable with him as she had before they'd made love.

"About the other night," he began.

Talk about being on the same wavelength, she thought. "I had a great time."

"Me, too. It was a surprise, not that I'm complaining." He looked at her. "Are you complaining?"

"I've never felt better."

The slow, sexy smile returned. "Good." The smile faded. "What with it being unexpected and all," he said, "I didn't use anything. Is that a problem?"

It took her a second to realize what he was talking about. Protection, as in birth control.

"There's no problem," she told him.

"You're on the Pill?"

The easiest thing would be to say yes. It's what people expected the answer to be. But for some reason, she didn't want to lie to Finn.

"I don't need to be," she told him. "I can't have kids. It's a medical thing. Technically, if all the planets aligned, on the day of an eclipse, with the aliens landing, it could happen. The phrase 'one in a million' was tossed around."

She gave Finn credit. He didn't back away or even look ridiculously relieved. Instead, sympathy crossed his face and he said, "I'm sorry."

"Me, too. I always wanted kids. A regular family. I am at heart someone who planned to be a mother."

There it was, she thought, the sadness. When she first found out what was wrong with her, she thought she might drown in it. The sadness had overwhelmed her, sucking the life from her. Despite all her training, all the classes and papers and lectures, she'd never truly understood depression. She'd never understood how a person could lose all hope.

Now she knew. There had been days when she had barely been able to move. Taking her own life or hurting herself wasn't part of her personality. But pulling herself out of a constant state of apathy had been one of the hardest things she'd ever had to do.

"There's more than one way to get what you want," he told her. "But then you already know that."

"I do. I tell myself that all the time. On my good days, I believe me." She studied him. "You, on the other hand, aren't looking for a family at all."

"A good guess or your professional assessment?"

"Both. Am I wrong?"

"No. Been there, done that."

His words made sense, she thought. Finn had been forced to take on unexpected responsibility at a time in his life when he had planned to play. Why would he want to start over, with a new family?

A good reminder, she told herself. She liked Finn. They'd had fun together. But they wanted very different things, and if she continued to spend time with him, she needed to remember that. The last thing she needed right now was a broken heart.

"Have I freaked you out?" she asked.

"No. Were you trying to?"

She laughed. "No. Not really. I just don't want things to be awkward between us."

"They're not."

"Good." She moved a little closer, then looked up at him. "Because the other night was really fun."

One eyebrow raised. "I thought so, too. Want to do it again sometime?"

Sex with a man who definitely wasn't staying? All the fun with none of that commitment? She'd never been that kind of girl. Maybe it was time for that to change.

She smiled. "I think I would."

CHAPTER SIX

DAKOTA COULDN'T REMEMBER the last time she'd been this cold. Although the calendar claimed it was mid-spring, a cold front had blown through, dropping the temperature nearly twenty degrees and depositing over a foot of snow in the mountains.

She pulled her coat tighter and wished she'd thought to wear gloves. Unfortunately, she'd already packed away most of her winter clothes and had had to make do with layering. The thick blanket of clouds weren't helping, she thought, staring at the pale gray sky.

She heard someone call her name and turned. Montana waved as she hurried down the street, looking warm and comfy in a thick down jacket. A colorful knitted cap covered her head, and she had on matching mittens.

"You look cold," her sister said as she approached. "Why aren't you in something warmer?"

"I packed it all away."

Montana grinned. "Sometimes it pays to procrastinate."

"Apparently."

"It's supposed to warm up in a few days."

"Lucky me."

Montana moved close and linked arms. "We'll share body heat." She pointed to the lake. "What's going on?"

"We're filming a date."

"Outside? They're making contestants be outside on water when it's three degrees above freezing?"

"Somebody didn't look at the weather report. Worse, it's one of the older couples. They're supposed to be having a romantic picnic lunch. Last I heard, the sound guy is complaining he can't understand anything. Between the wind howling and their teeth chattering, there's not much conversation."

Montana studied the small boat in the middle of the black, choppy water. "TV isn't anything like I thought. It's not very interesting. Or romantic."

"Taping segments takes a long time. I won't miss this when they're gone."

"I can see why." Montana frowned. "There's no music. Do they add that later?"

"Probably." Dakota shivered. "The next few dates are out of town. Stephen and Aurelia are going to Las Vegas, then Sasha and Lani were supposed to go to San Diego, but Geoff freaked about the price of rooms, so they might be staying here."

Temperatures in both places were supposed to be well into the seventies. She was hoping for San Diego for sure.

"Those are the twin boys, right?" Montana asked. "They're gorgeous."

"A little young for you," Dakota said dryly.

"Oh, I know. I wouldn't be interested. I'm just saying, they're very nice to look at."

Dakota laughed. "Looking is allowed. Just don't let Finn catch you. He's still determined to get his brothers back home."

"How's the plan going?"

"Not very well, but not for lack of trying on his part."

Finn was determined. He was a lot of other things she really liked, but she wasn't going to share those with Montana. The last thing she needed was her sisters speculating about her personal life. While the attention would be well-meant, it would still be more than she could handle.

"So he's sticking around?" Montana asked.

"I suspect to the bitter end."

"Poor guy." Montana glanced to her left, then nudged Dakota. "Is that him?"

Dakota turned and saw Finn walking toward them. He wore a leather jacket. His head and hands were bare, but he didn't look the least bit cold. Probably because, compared to a brisk South Salmon spring, these temperatures were practically balmy.

"That's him," she said. "Don't embarrass me."

Montana freed her arm. "When have I ever done that?"

"We don't have enough time for me to start the list."

Montana started to say something, but mercifully stopped before Finn got close enough to hear.

"Whose fool idea was this?" he asked. "It's too cold for them to be out on the lake. Does anyone plan ahead?"

Dakota did her best not to smile. "Finn, this is my sister Montana. Montana, this is Finn. His two brothers are on the show."

Finn glanced at them both. "Sorry. I was distracted." He held out his hand to Montana. "Nice to meet you."

"Nice to meet you, too," Montana said. "It doesn't sound like you're having a good time."

"Is it that obvious?" He shook his head. "Never mind. I don't think I want you to answer that." He glanced between them, paused, then looked more thoroughly. "You really are identical, aren't you?"

Dakota laughed. "Because we'd lie about it?"

"Good point," Finn said. "My brothers are identical twins," he told Montana. "They've always said they have a relationship I can't understand. Are they telling the truth?"

"Sorry," Montana told him. "But they are. It's a weird thing to be identical to someone else. You kind of always know what they're thinking. I can't imagine life any other way, but I've been told it's not like that for other people."

"I figured you'd say that," he admitted. "Dakota said the same thing."

"But you didn't want to believe me?" Dakota asked, not sure if she should be annoyed or not.

Finn looked at her. "I believed you. I just wanted you to be wrong."

"At least he's honest," Montana said. "The last honest man."

"Don't say that," Finn told her. "I couldn't stand the pressure." He looked at Dakota. "I hear we're going to Las Vegas tomorrow."

"Have you ever been?" she asked. Las Vegas didn't strike her as a Finn kind of town.

"No. It's not my thing. I'm sure Stephen will love it, though." He sighed. "Damn show."

"You'll get it figured out," she told him.

"Want to tell me when so I have something to look forward to?"

"I wish I knew."

He turned to Montana. "It was nice to meet you."

"Nice to meet you, too."

Finn waved, then turned and walked away.

Dakota watched him go. She enjoyed the way he moved, his easy confidence. While she felt badly that he was worried about his brothers, there was a part of her that was looking forward to being with him in Las Vegas. She'd been there a couple of times with girlfriends, and it had been fun. She could only imagine what that town would be like with a man like Finn.

"Interesting," Montana said. "Very, very interesting. How was the sex?"

Dakota nearly choked. "Excuse me? What kind of question is that?"

"An obvious one. Don't try to pretend nothing happened. I know you. You and Finn have had sex. I'm not asking for a lot of details, I just want to know how he was. Hardly an unreasonable request. It's not like I'm getting any. Living vicariously through one's sisters is a time-honored tradition."

"I, ah…" Dakota swallowed. She knew better than to try to fake her way out of telling the truth. With someone else she might have a prayer, but not with one of her sisters.

"Fine. Yes, I was with Finn. It was great." She smiled. "It was better than great."

"Are you going to do it again?" Montana asked.

"The possibility is on the table. I'd like to."

Montana studied her. "Is it serious?"

"No. Even if I was tempted, it can't be. Finn isn't staying. He practically lives on another planet and my life is here. Besides, neither of us is looking for anything significant or long-lasting. So we'll be fine."

"I hope you're right," her sister told her. "Because sometimes when things are going really well, we find the one thing we're pretending we're not looking for."

"WHAT DO YOU MEAN the shipment came in early? All three hundred and eighty boxes? Are you telling me there are three hundred and eighty boxes sitting in our warehouse?" Finn asked.

"Not boxes," his partner Bill said. "Crates. Goddamn crates. What is he building? An ark?"

This wasn't happening, Finn told himself. It couldn't be happening. Not now. Not while he was stuck here.

The air charter company survived on contracts. That's where the main money came from. The one-time deliveries were great, but the annual contracts paid the bills.

One of their largest customers had decided to build a boat. By hand. He'd ordered it from God knows where and had arranged to have the pieces delivered to South Salmon. Now they had to be airlifted to his property three hundred miles north of town.

When Finn had first heard about the project, he'd figured they were talking a half dozen boxes at most. Apparently, he'd been wrong.

"The weight's listed on the side of each crate," Bill said. "We're talking three to four crates per trip, at best. You want to do the math?"

Finn swore. One hundred trips? "It's not possible," he said, more to himself than to Bill. "We have other customers."

"He's willing to pay," Bill said. "Finn, we can't lose this guy. He keeps us going all winter."

His partner was right. The majority of their work came between April and October. But a hundred trips?

"I've already put the word out," Bill told him. "We've got the planes. I've shifted around the schedule. What we need is pilots. You have to come back."

Finn stared at the Southwest Airlines plane at the

gate. The flight was already boarding. Stephen and the cougar were going to Las Vegas, and he had to be there to make sure everything was going to be okay. He didn't trust that woman, or Geoff or anyone associated with the show. Excluding Dakota. Like him, she was doing what she had to.

"I can't," he said. "Sasha and Stephen need me."

"That's bullshit. They're twenty-one. They'll be fine on their own. This is where you belong, Finn. Get your ass back here."

He'd been responsible for his brothers for the past eight years. There was no way he could walk away now.

"Who have you called? Did you try Spencer? He's a good pilot and is usually available this time of year."

There was a long silence before Bill spoke again. "So that's your answer? Hire someone else?"

Finn turned his back on the other passengers and lowered his voice. "How many times have you needed me to cover for you? Before you got married, how many times did you have a hot date down in Anchorage or want to go trolling for lonely tourists in Juneau? I've always said yes to whatever you asked me to do. Now I'm asking you to give me a break. I'll be back when I can. Until then you have to handle it."

"All right," Bill said, sounding pissed. "But you'd better get back here pretty quick. Or there's going to be a problem."

"I will," Finn said, wondering if he was telling the truth.

He closed his phone and shoved it in his pocket, then joined the line of passengers waiting to board. Guilt battled with annoyance. To make matters worse, he was flying commercial. He hated flying commercial. He hated flying when he wasn't in charge. But the tickets to Vegas had been cheaper than renting a plane, and Geoff was trying to save money.

Finn stalked onto the plane and shoved his small duffel into the first overhead compartment.

"Sir, you might want to take that with you," the flight attendant said. "That way it will be closer to where you're sitting."

"Fine," Finn growled between gritted teeth.

He grabbed the duffel and continued down the aisle. When he spotted Dakota with an empty seat next to her, he stopped. Of course there was no room for his carry-on here. Cursing under his breath, he stepped over her, dropped into the middle seat, and shoved his duffel into the space where his feet should go.

"Tell me this isn't a five-hour flight," he grumbled.

"Aren't you perky this morning." Dakota turned to him. "What has you all grumpy?"

He leaned back in his seat and closed his eyes. "Is grumpy the technical term? Are you asking me as a psychologist?"

"Do you want me to?"

"Maybe we could just skip the talk therapy and go

directly to electric shock treatment." A few thousand volts of electricity coursing through his body would put everything else in perspective, he thought.

Dakota touched his arm with her hand. "Seriously? It's that bad? You're not blowing things just a little out of proportion?"

"Let's see. I just talked to my business partner. We have an unexpected delivery of nearly four hundred crates that have to be flown several hundred miles. We can get maybe four crates on each plane. I should be there helping. Instead I'm stuck on a plane I'm not piloting, going to Las Vegas. Why, you ask? Because my brothers decided to leave college in their last semester. Even as we speak, Sasha is planning to destroy his life by moving to Hollywood. And Stephen is about to be devoured by a cougar." He turned to her. "You tell me. Am I blowing things out of proportion?"

Her mouth twitched a little.

He narrowed his gaze. "This isn't funny."

"It's a little funny. If you weren't you, you would think it was funny."

He leaned back in his seat. "Go away."

"I'm sorry," she told him. "I'll take this more seriously, I promise. I really can't help with your business problem. Although the good news is, you have a lot of new business. Is your partner going to hire another pilot?"

"He has to. He'll probably charge me for it. I'd do it to him."

"You could go home. You don't really have to be here."

"I do. Someone has to look out for them." He hesitated, then glanced around to make sure no one was listening.

"Years ago, when our parents died, it was a mess. There was a plane crash and the media got involved. Reporters crawled all over town, we were the hot story of the week, at least up in Alaska. Some even sent money to help us out."

Dakota stared at him. "I have a feeling you hated that."

"I did. I knew it was a temporary thing, but that's not what Sasha got from it. He wants to be famous because he believes being cared for by the world at large will keep him safe. Sure, he's twenty-one, but that thirteen-year-old kid who lost his folks has never gone away."

He leaned back in his seat. "Stephen is going along with this. I'm guessing it's to make sure Sasha is okay. I know they're technically adults. But they lived in a small town until they went to college. They don't know about this world. They're too trusting and don't know enough to protect themselves. I have to be there for them."

"I'm sorry," she said, putting her hand on his. "I didn't know."

He shrugged. "I have to let them go. I'm good with that. But not like this. Not when they're dealing with men like Geoff."

"Agreed. But you do realize that at some point you

have to let go. At some point you have to trust them to make their own decisions."

"Maybe you're right. But not today." He looked around. "Have you seen her?"

"Who?"

"The cougar out to destroy my brother. The one you said was going to get pregnant to trap him." He wanted to think she would miss the flight, but his luck wasn't that good.

Dakota's eyes widened. At the same time, Finn heard something very much like a whimper coming from in front of them.

Dakota cleared her throat. "Ah, yes. Aurelia is on the plane. In fact, she's sitting in the row in front of us. Had you been paying attention, you would have noticed." She jabbed him in the side. "And I never said she was going to get pregnant. Oh, look." She pointed. "There's your brother. He's going to sit next to her." Dakota turned to him. "Perhaps he can explain why you're such an idiot."

Finn almost regretted what he said. Almost. He was sure that under normal circumstances Aurelia was a perfectly decent human being. But he couldn't trust a woman who had gone on a reality show to find a man. Who did that? She was too old for Stephen. He was going to do everything in his power to keep them apart.

He glanced out the window. "When does the flight leave?"

"I swear, if you plan to spend the entire hour flight

asking, 'Are we there yet?' I'm going to drop something heavy on your groin."

Despite everything going on and his growing level of frustration, Finn laughed. "Okay, you win. I'll behave."

"Can I get that in writing?" she asked.

"Sure."

She settled back in her seat and took his hand in hers. "You are so lying."

"Maybe not."

"I'll believe it when I see it. So tell me, what would you be doing if you were back in Alaska? Flying?"

"Probably."

"You're on a plane now. That's practically the same thing."

He laced his fingers with hers. "It's not the same thing. When you're the pilot, you're in charge."

"We could ask the flight attendant if you can have a pair of those little wings they give kids. You could pin them on your shirt. That might make you feel better."

"You think you're pretty funny, don't you?"

"I *am* pretty funny."

"I'll give you pretty, but that's as far as I'm going."

She smiled. "I can live with that."

AURELIA HAD NEVER BEEN to Las Vegas before. She'd seen it on TV and in the movies, but she found that real life was much, much better. The short plane ride had passed painfully slowly, as she'd desperately wished to disappear into her seat. Finn's cruel assumptions about her and why she was on the show had made her feel horrible. She'd spent most of the trip berating herself for not standing up to her mother more. Because if she had something close to a spine, she wouldn't be in this situation.

Now they'd arrived at the huge airport in Las Vegas, she was determined to shake off her bad feelings and simply enjoy the experience. She might never come back, and she had a feeling she would want these memories later.

Stephen stood next to her as they waited for their luggage. Geoff had said to pack for an evening on the town. That was tomorrow. This afternoon's agenda was supposed to be a lot of quick shots of them in the casino and around town.

As the luggage carousel started, she caught sight of Finn and Dakota walking toward the taxi stand. As they weren't going to be on television, they'd been able to pack light and only needed carry-on bags. Aurelia had been forced to borrow a couple of fancy dresses from women at the office, with the idea that at least one of them should be okay for their dressy evening.

As she watched, Finn put his hand on the small of Dakota's back. It was a simple, polite gesture, but one that made Aurelia long for a man in her life. Someone who would be there for her, just like she wanted to be there for him. Someone who would care.

"Point out your bag and I'll grab it," Stephen told her.

She nodded.

He was sweet, she thought wistfully. But too young. That's what she wanted to tell Finn—that she'd already come to terms with the fact that she and his brother could only be friends. But she was afraid if she told Stephen, he would act different and Geoff would notice. Aurelia didn't want to be voted off the show too soon. The longer she stayed, the more she didn't have to deal with her mother. Oddly enough, the more she was around Stephen, the stronger she felt.

She saw her bag, and Stephen lifted it off the carousel. He had his. Karen, one of the production assistants, ushered them toward a limo. The camera guy was already waiting for them.

"Don't look so scared," Stephen said, leaning toward her and speaking softly. "They're going to think you don't want to be with me."

"That's not true," she said, doing her best not to remember Finn's outrageous claim she would trap his brother by getting pregnant.

"Because I'm exactly who you've been waiting for all your life?" he asked, his voice teasing.

She smiled. "I've always had a desperate longing for someone who could tell me the difference between Hilary Duff and Lindsay Lohan."

He winked. "I knew it."

They were still looking at each other as they got into the limo.

She'd never been good at talking to men, let alone flirting, but Stephen made it easy. Maybe because she knew she was safe with him. He was…nice. Probably not a word to excite him, but for her, it was plenty.

They left the airport and drove toward the Strip. She could see all the hotels rising toward the sky, their various heights and shapes standing out against the sand-colored mountains. As they got closer, she made out the different structures. The big, black pyramid at the Luxor, the Eiffel Tower in front of the Paris Hotel and the vast expanse that was Caesars Palace.

"Do you know where we're staying?" she asked.

"There."

Stephen pointed to the right. As they rounded the curve in the road, Aurelia saw the tall towers of the Venetian Hotel. The limo pulled into the covered entry and their door was opened.

She was vaguely aware that the cameras were filming everything, but she couldn't seem to pay attention to them. Not when there was so much to see.

They stepped into a massive lobby with a painted ceiling. Every inch was beautiful—from the huge sprays of flowers to the gilded posts. Even the carpets were gorgeous.

There were people everywhere. She could hear a dozen different languages flowing around her, and the air was lightly scented with a slightly citrus fragrance.

"You're already checked in," Geoff told her, and handed over her keys. "Your rooms are next door to each other. If you decide to do anything interesting, call one of us. We want to be there."

Aurelia felt her eyes bug out. Call him? What? If any of the contestants decided to have sex, he wanted it on film?

"I can't really see that happening," she murmured.

Geoff sighed. "Tell me about it. Still, if you get drunk enough, we all might get lucky."

With that, he walked off.

Aurelia stood in the center of the lobby. The crowd moved around her, as if she wasn't there. Hardly a surprise. She'd spent most of her life being invisible.

"Ready to go to the rooms?" Stephen asked, joining her. "Geoff said we're already checked in."

She held up her key.

He glanced at the number. "We're next to each other. That's great. We can send coded messages through the wall."

She stared into his blue eyes and told herself it was enough that Stephen was nice. Going through this with a guy who was a jerk would have been unbearable.

"Do you know any codes?" she asked.

"No, but we could learn one. Or make one up. You're good with numbers, right?"

She smiled. "I'll work on it."

They made their way to the room elevators. Thankfully, the camera guy took a different elevator, leaving them alone for a few minutes.

Once they reached their floor, they made their way to their rooms. They were actually across from each other, rather than next door, but still close enough. A different camera guy was already waiting for them.

"Who do you want to go in with?" she asked.

He shrugged. "Your room. Stephen, go with her."

Like they were sharing a room? She blushed at the thought, then shoved her key into the lock and opened the door.

Aurelia hadn't traveled much and rarely stayed in a hotel. Still, she knew what a regular room looked like, and this wasn't it.

To her right was a beautiful bathroom done in marble and glass. There was a stall shower and a big tub, double sinks, a vanity and plenty of mirrors. It was like a movie set or something out of a fairy tale. Past the bathroom was the bedroom. Except it was more than a bedroom. There was a king-size bed with beautiful linens and big nightstands. Beyond that, three steps led to a sunken living room. Floor-to-ceiling windows offered her a view of the pirate boat floating in front of Treasure Island.

She turned in a slow circle, taking in the room again, then looked at Stephen. "I don't understand," she said. "This can't be my room. It's so beautiful." She laughed. "Tell me we never have to leave."

"If we win big downstairs, we can stay as long as you like," he told her.

Aurelia smiled. "I'd like that."

They agreed to meet in half an hour and go down to the casino. Aurelia used her time to put her brown hair into hot rollers and pray that it came out okay. She changed into white jeans and a turquoise-colored silk blouse she'd bought on sale nearly a year ago.

She normally didn't spend much money on her casual wardrobe. All of her clothing budget was spent on work clothes, and everything she didn't spend on her own living expenses either went to her mother or her small savings account. But the shirt had been so beautiful, she'd been unable to resist it.

After spreading out her newly purchased cosmetics on the marble counter, she carefully applied moisturizer, then concealer. The powder foundation went on as easily as the girl at the makeup counter had promised. She kept her eye shadow simple by brushing on a light taupe color. After mascara, she applied blush, then lip gloss. The last step was pulling out the hot rollers and finger combing her hair. She bent at the waist and doused herself in hairspray. As she stood, she flipped her head back and surveyed the look.

In a bathroom full of mirrors, there was no escaping reality. But this time it wasn't so bad. Aurelia looked at herself from several angles. She would never be stunning, but for once in her life she was pretty. At least she felt pretty, and that might be enough.

She'd barely slipped into her shoes when Stephen

knocked on her door. She picked up her purse and went to meet him.

"Hi," she said, hoping she didn't sound as breathless as she felt.

"Hi, yourself," he began, then stopped and stared at her. "Wow, you look great."

"Thanks."

She was aware of the man and the camera just beyond Stephen's shoulder. For a moment she wished it could just be the two of them. That even a small part of their time together could be real. But it wasn't. She had to keep reminding herself of that.

"What do you want to do first?" Stephen asked. "Slots, blackjack, or do you prefer roulette?"

"I've never gambled," she admitted. "What do you suggest?"

As they spoke they walked toward the elevators. Stephen pushed the button for them to go down. The doors opened immediately. As they stepped onto the elevator, she felt him put his hand on the small of her back.

It was nothing, she told herself. Men did that sort of thing all the time. She'd just noticed Finn doing it to Dakota. But she couldn't help being aware of how he touched her. The silk of her shirt seemed to intensify the heat from his hand. As the elevator started down, she felt a little light-headed and told herself it was from the vertical movement and nothing else.

They walked out of the elevator and into the craziness. It was fun and bright and loud. Aurelia didn't know where to look first.

"Are you hungry?" Stephen asked, pointing to the Grand Lux Café.

"Maybe later," she said. Right now she was too excited to eat. There was too much to see.

An older couple walked past them. "Don't you love seeing a family traveling together, George?" the woman asked. "She brought her baby brother to Las Vegas. Isn't that nice?"

Aurelia stepped away from Stephen. She didn't know if he'd heard the comment or not. The camera guy had his lens trained on the old people, so she knew that moment was going to make the show.

She started walking, not sure where she was going. Humiliation heated her cheeks and stole the pleasure she felt at being here. She thought about running after the couple and telling them what was going on, but what was the point?

Stephen kept pace with her. "You okay?" he asked.

His obvious confusion told her he hadn't heard their words, at least not yet. Reminding herself they were just friends didn't make her feel any better.

She stopped in the center of the casino and faced him. He was so nice, she thought. A good guy. But there was no way...

"Excuse me. What are you doing?"

Aurelia and Stephen turned toward the well-muscled man in the dark suit. The name badge said that he was with security. His expression told them he was very serious about his job.

He pointed to the camera guy. "You can't film here."

"We're doing a reality show," Stephen said. "Didn't the production company clear this with you?"

"No." The man from security moved toward the camera. "Turn that off now or I will turn it off for you."

"I'll get Geoff," the camera guy said as he turned and practically ran away.

"Is he coming back or do I have to chase him down?"

Aurelia wasn't sure if the security man was talking to them or not. Apparently, it didn't matter. He pulled a walkie-talkie out of his jacket pocket and spoke into it. She had a feeling that this wasn't going to end well.

"We'll go," she said taking Stephen's hand in hers.

Stephen glanced at the security guy's annoyed face and nodded. "I don't think either of us would like jail."

They turned.

For a second, Aurelia wondered if they would be allowed to simply walk away. But nothing happened as they dashed up an escalator. As the stairs carried them to another floor, she was able to draw in a deep breath.

"You okay? I thought you were going to faint," Stephen told her.

"I was terrified," she admitted. "I can't believe Geoff brought us all here without making arrangements with the hotel. It's not a surprise they don't want us filming. They don't know what we're going do with it. It could be a scam. Or a trick to cheat or something."

She had more to say but suddenly couldn't speak. Stephen was riding on the step behind her. Without warning, he rested one hand on her hip as he leaned toward her.

Aurelia did her best to act casual. Shrieking in surprise wasn't very appropriate. Besides, she'd taken his hand in hers to pull him away from the security guy—although that had been different. She couldn't explain why, but knew it was.

When they reached the top of the escalator, they stepped off. She planned to continue her analysis of what it all meant, only she couldn't. Not when it seemed as if they'd entered another world.

Above them, the ceiling was painted sky blue with clouds that almost appeared to float by. They were in the hotel, but she felt like they really could be outside. There were stores and restaurants and...

"Look," she breathed, pointing to the narrow boats floating on a man-made canal. "Gondolas."

"Want to ride?" he asked, then urged her forward. "Come on. It'll be fun."

There wasn't much of a line, so in a matter of minutes, she was carefully stepping into the gondola. It wobbled on the water, but she managed to sit down without falling. Stephen sat next to her.

There wasn't a lot of room, so he was close. Close enough for her to feel the softness of his long-sleeved shirt against her hand and the pressure of his thigh against hers.

"Ever done anything like this before?" he asked as he looked around.

"No."

Never. Not even in her dreams.

They took the leisurely boat ride through a winding course. People walking by stopped to wave. Music echoed off the ceiling and reverberated all around them. She caught sight of stores whose names she'd only seen in magazines. Everything about the moment was perfect.

Then Stephen put his arm around her and it all got better.

When they rounded a corner, a man was waiting with a camera. He told them to smile, then snapped their picture. Once the ride was over, they went to check on the digital image displayed on a computer screen.

"You're beautiful," Stephen told her.

Aurelia knew he was being kind, but she was pleased with how the photo had turned out. They were both looking at the camera, with genuine smiles. She noticed they were leaning into each other and looked very much like a couple. If one ignored the age difference.

"We'll take two," he said, then paid for them.

"I should buy them."

"Why?"

Because she made more than him. Because he was still in college and this wasn't a date. But she didn't want to say any of that, so instead she simply said, "Thank you," when he handed her the thin bag containing the pictures in a paper frame.

"Hungry?" Stephen asked, pointing to one of the outdoor restaurants.

"Yes."

"Good. Me, too."

It was midafternoon, and there wasn't much of a crowd. They were seated immediately at a small corner table next to a plant. Despite being in the open, the space felt private. Intimate.

The server gave them menus. Even though she was hungry, Aurelia couldn't imagine eating. She chose a salad and iced tea. Stephen ordered a pizza and soda.

"You know why I decided to do the show," she said. "Why did you?"

He picked up his fork and turned it over in his hands. "A lot of reasons. I wanted to get out of South Salmon and this was a good way."

"A good way? You left college in your last semester. How is that smart?"

Stephan rolled his eyes but Aurelia persisted.

"Getting an education can't hurt. What are you going to do when the show is over?"

Stephen put down the fork and leaned toward her. "I don't want to fly."

"I don't understand. You want to drive back to Alaska?"

He laughed. "No. I mean I don't want to be a pilot,

like my brother. I don't want to go into the family business."

"Oh." She knew all about family expectations. Despite the fact that she was nearly thirty, she had never once been able to please her mother. "Is that what Finn wants? He expects you to go into the family business?"

"It's implied."

"Have you told him how you feel?"

"No. He doesn't care about that."

Aurelia shook her head. "You're talking about a man who flew a thousand miles to make sure you and your brother were okay. I think he cares a lot about you."

"That's different. He wants me home so he can control me. If I were to tell him that I wanted to be an engineer, he'd fly me up to ten thousand feet and kick me out of the airplane."

"Now you're talking like a kid."

"Hey!" He straightened. "Where do you get off saying that?"

"Look at your actions. You're not willing to sit down and talk to Finn. Instead, you ran off. How is that mature?"

"You're supposed to be on my side."

"I'm a disinterested third party." Disinterested probably wasn't the right word. Embarrassingly enough, she found herself more than a little interested in Stephen. Why couldn't he have been thirty instead of twenty? Life was nothing if not karmically cruel.

"Besides," she continued. "If you're one semester away from graduation, he already knows your major."

"The major isn't important as long as I come back home." He shook his head. "When our folks died, things were bad. Finn took care of us. Now he can't let that go. He thinks we're still the little kids who needed him."

"You should talk to him," she said. "Why wouldn't he be happy that you wanted to be an engineer? It's a good, solid job."

"I've known him all my life, Aurelia. You're going to have to trust me on this. Finn would never approve."

She wanted to argue but didn't. After all, there were plenty of people who would tell her to simply stand up to her mother. From the outside it seemed so easy. But from the inside, everything was different. She couldn't seem to survive the waves of guilt every time she tried. It was as if her mother had been given an instruction manual on how to manipulate her and had memorized every page.

Stephen had been one of the few people to accept her limitations. "I do trust you," she said.

In the square, someone called their names. She and Stephen turned toward the sound of several people running. One of the production assistants hurried up to them.

"There you are," Karen said, sounding breathless. "We've been looking everywhere. Geoff is furious. We're all packing up and going home. You have to come right now."

Aurelia looked at Stephen, who shrugged. "I guess we'll get something to eat at the airport," he said.

"Hurry," the production assistant said. "We have to get to the airport. Geoff is furious that there wasn't a date."

Aurelia and Stephen walked out of the restaurant. As they followed the production assistant to the elevators, he leaned close.

"Geoff was wrong," he whispered in her ear. "There was a date and I had a great time."

Deep inside of her, she felt her heart give a little tug. "Me, too," she whispered back.

He smiled at her and took her hand in his.

CHAPTER SEVEN

DAKOTA OPENED HER FRONT DOOR to find Finn standing
on her porch. It was a little after seven in the evening.
She and Finn had managed to catch the four-thirty flight
out of Las Vegas, which meant she hadn't even been
home an hour.

"I know, I know," he said, shuffling his feet. "You
have stuff to do. I shouldn't bother you."

"Yet here you are," she said with a smile. "It's okay.
I didn't have any hot plans."

She wasn't sorry to see him. As for hot plans, he
certainly qualified.

He stepped inside and handed her a bottle of wine. "I
come bearing gifts, if that counts."

"It does."

"I'm spending so much time at the wine store, the guy
there wants to know if he and I are planning to run off
together."

She laughed. "You know he was kidding, right?"

"I hoped he was. People don't joke like that in South
Salmon."

"Then people in South Salmon need to work on their
sense of humor." She led the way into the kitchen and

set the wine on the counter. "Is wine enough or do you want something to eat, as well?"

"You don't have to feed me," he told her.

"That wasn't the question." She walked to the refrigerator and pulled it open. There were salad fixings, some yogurt and a few raw almonds in a bowl. Not exactly man food.

She turned to him. "I'm going to have to take back my offer of food. I don't have anything you'd like. Want to order a pizza?"

He'd already opened the drawer where she kept the corkscrew. "Pizza sounds good. I'll even let you put something healthy on your half."

"You'll let me? How magnanimous."

He shrugged. "I'm just that kind of guy."

"Lucky me."

She ordered pizza, then they took their wine into the living room and sat down. She ignored the fact that she liked having Finn in her house. That was a road without a happy ending. Instead, she focused on why he'd shown up.

"There wasn't a date," she said. "So Stephen and Aurelia are in danger of being voted off. It doesn't make you happy?"

"Yes, as long as he goes back to college."

"You can't follow him around for the rest of his life. At some point you have to let him be an adult."

"When he acts like an adult, I'll treat him like one. Until then, he's just a kid."

Dakota leaned back in her chair and studied him over her glass. He still wasn't getting it. How his brothers acted had everything to do with how they had been raised and nothing to do with his presence in town. Whether he stayed or left, the twins' actions would be the same. But how to get him to believe that?

"Except for them going back to college without you dragging them, is there a win in this?" she asked.

"I don't know," he admitted. "I guess there has to be. What if they never go back to college? I need to know they're okay and that no one is taking advantage of them." He picked up his glass. "Something I don't want to think about. Let's change the subject. Are you sorry we left Las Vegas early?"

"I won't cry myself to sleep tonight, if that's what you're asking. But it would have been fun to stay. There's plenty to do. I heard there was great shopping at the hotel."

"You like shopping?"

She laughed. "I am a girl. It's practically genetic. You, on the other hand, buy the same shirt over and over again. And your socks come in a package of ten or twelve."

"It's easier that way," he said. "And what do you have against my shirts?" He glanced down at the light blue cotton shirt he wore. "I'm not wearing plaid. You should appreciate that."

"Oh, I do. I don't have anything against your shirt. I think you look nice."

"You're just saying that." He sighed dramatically. "Now you've hurt my feelings. I don't think I can talk about this anymore. It's just so hard when a man tries to look special and no one notices."

She put down her wine glass so she wouldn't spill it. Even as she tried not to laugh, she found herself chuckling. The teasing side of Finn was very appealing.

"Do you want me to say you're pretty?" she asked.

"If you mean it," he said primly. "Otherwise you're just messing with my feelings."

She stood and walked around the coffee table. After taking his wine and setting it down, she tugged him to his feet. She held both his hands in hers and stared into his eyes.

"I really, really like your shirt."

"I bet you say that to all the guys."

"No. Only to you."

She expected him to keep up with the game. Instead he drew her close and lowered his mouth to hers.

There was nothing playful about the kiss. He claimed her with an intensity that took her breath away. There was hunger in his touch, a need that echoed her own sudden, powerful passion. She wrapped her arms around him and gave herself over to the pleasure of feeling his body against hers.

He was strong and solid and powerful, she thought hazily. Everything she needed from a man. When he tightened his hold, she parted her lips and welcomed him inside.

Want filled her. Her breasts swelled in anticipation of his touch. Her belly throbbed in an ancient rhythm that made her want to squirm to get closer. When he started backing her toward the sofa, she went willingly.

Her legs had barely bumped against the cushions when she heard something in the background. An insistent knocking.

"The pizza guy," she mumbled against Finn's mouth.

"Let him get his own girl."

She laughed. "I have to pay him."

Finn straightened. "I'll get it."

He released her and walked toward the front door.

When his back was turned, she hurried out of the living room and down the short hall to her bedroom. Seconds later, she was barefoot, and the small lamp by her bed was on. Finn appeared in the doorway.

"Is this your way of telling me you're not all that hungry?" he asked.

She tilted her head. "I am. Just not for pizza."

His slow, sexy smile made her toes curl.

"You're my kind of girl," he told her as he crossed to her.

"I'll bet you say that to all the women."

"Only you," he whispered, right before he kissed her.

"CHARLIE IS BLOND to the bone," Montana said. "He's the sweetest guy, but I worry he's not bright enough to get into the program."

"When will you know for sure?" Dakota asked.

"Max will have a pretty good idea when Charlie is about six months old. Until then, I'll teach him the basics and we'll see how that goes." Montana rolled onto her side and rubbed Charlie's belly. "But you love everybody, don't you, big guy?"

The big guy in question was a three-month-old yellow Lab puppy. Charlie had feet the size of softballs. He was not going to be petite by anyone's definition.

"What happens to him if he doesn't make it into the program?" Nevada asked.

"He's given up for adoption. Max's dogs are bred to be family friendly, so there's always a waiting list. Charlie will find a good home. I'd just hate to see him go. He would have been the first dog I trained from birth. Well, six weeks. They can't do much when their eyes are still closed."

The three sisters lay stretched out on blankets in Montana's backyard. It was a warm Saturday afternoon. Unseasonable for this time of year and they were going to be back in the fifties tomorrow. Two other dogs played in the yard. An apricot-colored toy poodle named Cece and a labradoodle named Buddy sniffed in the grass and chased butterflies.

"I don't get the poodle," Nevada said. "Isn't she kind of small?"

"Cece is very well trained," Montana told her. "She works with really sick kids. Because she's so small, she can sit on their beds. A lot of times the kids aren't even strong enough to pet her. She sits close or curls up next to them. Having her there makes them feel better. Being a poodle, she doesn't shed like other dogs. She gets bathed before going to the hospital and carried in so she doesn't pick up germs on her feet. That means she can go into some of the special wards."

Dakota sat up. "Is that what you do with your day? Take dogs to visit sick children?"

"Sometimes. There are dogs that visit nursing homes. I take them there. And I spend part of the day training. The older dogs don't need much instruction, but the younger ones get regular reinforcement. The puppies take a lot of time. And I'm working on the reading program."

When Montana had said she was going to start working with therapy dogs, Dakota hadn't realized how much was involved. "You're very dedicated to your work."

Montana rolled onto her back, supporting herself on her elbows. "I think I've found what I'm supposed to be doing. You two have known for a long time, which is great for you but left me feeling inadequate. I'll never get rich doing this, but that's okay. I love the dogs, I love working with people. When you're lonely, having someone love you is really important. Even if that someone is just a dog."

Nevada sat up. "Now I feel like a slacker. All I do is design things."

"Houses," Montana said. "Everyone needs somewhere to live."

"I don't design houses. I work on remodels or I tweak existing designs."

Dakota looked at her sister. Nevada had always wanted to be an engineer. Was she regretting that decision now? "Don't you like working for Ethan?"

"I don't dislike it. It's just…" Nevada drew her knees to her chest and wrapped her arms around her legs. "Do you know I've never applied for a job? Sure, I had part-time jobs in high school and college, but I mean a real job. Once I chose engineering, everyone assumed I'd go to work for Ethan. I graduated and showed up at his office the next day. I didn't have to prove myself."

"Just because it was nepotistic, doesn't mean you aren't doing a good job," Dakota told her. "Ethan wouldn't keep you around if he didn't want you working there."

Nevada shook her head. "You really think Mom would let him fire me?"

Montana pulled Charlie onto her lap. "She has a point. Ethan can't fire her."

"Do you want him to?" Dakota asked.

"No. I work hard for him. I know he's happy with my work, but that's not the point. I went to work in the family business. I never thought about doing anything else. I just want to know if I'm in the right place. Doing the right thing."

"Is this a triplet curse?" Montana asked. "For so long I didn't know what I was doing. Now I'm finally happy and you're confused?"

"There's no curse," Dakota told her.

"I've been thinking about this for a while," Nevada admitted. "The thing is, I don't want to leave Fool's Gold. I like it here. It's my home. But it's not like there are a lot of other opportunities. I'm not comfortable working for another contracting firm. I don't want to be in competition with Ethan."

"So what's the solution?" Dakota asked.

Nevada straightened her legs and picked at a blade of grass. "Have either of you heard about Janack Construction?"

Dakota frowned. "The name is familiar. Wasn't there a guy in school named Tucker Janack? He was friends with Ethan and Josh. They went to a cycling camp together, way back when. I can't recall all the details."

"I remember," Montana said. "Tucker's father is super rich. Didn't he send a helicopter to pick up Tucker?"

"Yes and yes," Nevada said. "They're one of the largest construction companies in the country. Apparently, Tucker's father liked what he saw when he visited here all those years ago. He bought a couple hundred acres north of town."

"How could he do that?" Dakota asked. "Isn't that Indian land? They can't buy that."

"Tucker's father is one sixteenth Máa-zib. That's all you need to be. Apparently Tucker's mom is also part Máa-zib."

Dakota wondered how her sister knew so much about the Janack family. "Did you meet them sometime we don't know about?"

"The parents? No, I've never met them."

"What are they going to build there?" Montana asked. "Isn't two hundred acres a lot of land?"

"I've heard it's going to be an exclusive resort," Nevada said. "Big hotel, spa, casino and a couple of golf courses. There's some serious money going into the project. They're going to hire a lot of people."

"So you'd go work for them?" Dakota asked.

"I haven't decided. I might apply and see what happens. At least then I could say I've been on a job interview."

Dakota wondered if there was more going on than Nevada wanted to tell them. Was she not getting along with Ethan? Or was the situation exactly what she said—a need to prove herself?

"I haven't heard anyone talking about this project," Montana said. "I guess if they're on Indian land, they don't need City Council approval. But you'd think they'd at least talk to the mayor."

"Maybe they have and Marsha simply hasn't mentioned it to anyone," Dakota said. "There's plenty going on right now, what with the reality show and all the men still pouring into town."

"When are you going to decide what to do?" Montana asked.

"Not for a while," Nevada admitted. "They're still in the design stage. That could take months or even a year. Once I know they're actually moving forward with work, I'll think about what I want to do." She shifted on the blanket. "Please don't say anything to Ethan. It's not that I don't like working with him. I just need to know that I could work somewhere else, too."

"I'm not going to say anything," Montana said. "I've been flaky for years. I totally understand the need to figure out what you want to do."

"I won't say anything, either," Dakota promised. "If you need someone to listen, if you just want to bounce ideas off me, I'm always available."

"I know that," Nevada told her. "Thanks."

"Has it occurred to any of you that none of us have been on a date in months?" Montana asked. "Maybe there *is* something to this stupid man shortage."

"I'm dating," Dakota said.

"No. You're having sex with Finn. That's not dating."

"Did I know this?" Nevada asked. "When did you start sleeping with Finn?"

Dakota briefly explained her recent encounters with the twins' brother. "It's not serious," she said. "When he figures out that his brothers are more than capable of taking care of themselves, he'll go back to South Salmon. This isn't a long-term relationship. And technically, as Montana said, it's not really dating."

"Point taken," Nevada said with a grin. "So the question is, do you want a date or do you want to have sex?"

"Can't I have both?" Montana asked. "Do I have to pick?"

"Find the right guy and you can have both," Nevada told her.

"Is that what you want?" Dakota asked.

Nevada laughed. "I'll take the sex, at least for now. Love is too complicated."

"Sometimes sex is complicated, too," Montana reminded her.

Nevada shook her head. "I'm willing to take my chances." She looked at Dakota. "What about you? Is sex enough?"

There were things they didn't know, Dakota thought. How she couldn't have children and how knowing that had changed everything. She would tell them eventually, just not today. Not when they were having fun, enjoying such a beautiful day.

So she smiled at her sisters and said, "Is sex with Finn enough? Absolutely."

FINN WAITED with Sasha in the lobby of the Gold Rush Ski Lodge and Resort. The place was nice enough, he thought. If one was into attractive tourist hotels. He would rather be home.

Once Geoff found out what carting everyone to San Diego would cost, especially for the beachfront hotel he preferred, he'd decided to keep Sasha and Lani in town.

The pool area of the Lodge had been transformed into a tacky tropical paradise, with fake palm trees, twinkle lights and tiki torches. Unfortunately, the weather was anything but tropical. While it didn't phase Finn, everyone else was running around wearing thick coats and shivering.

"What if I gave you ten thousand dollars?" he asked his brother. "To go home and finish college. Would you do it?"

Sasha grinned at him. "The show is paying twenty, bro."

"Fine. Thirty. Go back to school and you'll have a check that day." His business was successful, and he didn't have a lot of expenses. The house where he and his brothers had grown up was paid for.

"What did Stephen say when you offered it to him?" Sasha asked.

"To shove it up my ass."

Sasha's grin broadened. "He read my mind."

"I figured," Finn said glumly. "But I had to ask. What's the plan for today?"

"It's all going down tonight. We were going to have a city tour, but since we're pretending we're not in Fool's Gold, I don't see that happening."

Finn glanced around at the fake greenery. "This is a crazy business."

"I like it."

He thought about pointing out that Sasha's love of fame was tied to their parents' death, but he and his brother had had that conversation a dozen times before. He suspected Sasha had to go through the process himself and learn the truth the hard way.

That was the part Finn objected to. Not the learning, but the inevitable pain that would follow. If only he could be sure that his brothers were ready to be on their own, that he'd done all he could to keep them safe. Then he could walk away. But how to know?

"You should chill," Sasha told him. "You're wound too tight. Relax."

"You've been spending too much time with Hawaii girl."

His brother laughed. "I like Hawaii girl. She's fun."

Finn was sure Sasha liked Lani well enough but suspected their relationship was far more a means to an end than anything romantic. Sasha's idea of a steady relationship was a date that lasted two hours. On the other hand, Stephen had always preferred long-term relationships. Despite being identical twins, the brothers were fairly different.

"You should do something fun," Sasha told him. "Think of this as a vacation."

"Except it's not. I'll 'chill' or 'relax' or whatever you want when you and Stephen get back to Alaska and finish college."

Sasha sighed. "Sorry. No can do. I wish you could let it go."

Before Finn could say anything, one of the production assistants called for Sasha to get ready for a lighting check. His brother waved at him and followed the girl toward the hotel.

Finn checked his watch. He had a group of tourists

to take on a flight in a couple of hours. They would be the second ones this week. The previous group had been a family, including a thirteen-year-old boy who'd been fascinated by the idea of flying a plane. Finn had talked to him about taking lessons.

"You're looking serious about something."

He glanced up and saw Dakota walking toward him. She carried a clipboard in her hands and stopped in front of him.

"For once, not the usual," he told her.

"Your brothers?"

"Work stuff."

"Everything okay back in South Salmon?"

"As far as I know."

She stood there, as if waiting for him to explain more.

"I was thinking about the tour I have later and the one I had a few days ago," he said slowly. "There was this kid. He was really into flying. Sometimes I think about opening a flight school, focusing on kids." He shrugged. "Who knows if it would work."

"Don't you have to be a certain age to get your pilot's license?"

"You can solo at sixteen, but training could start before that. Teaching a kid to fly gives him, or her, the ability to sense possibilities. You need math skills to do some of the calculations. There would have to be a way for them to raise money to pay for the lessons, or grants or something." He shook his head. "It's just something I play around with."

She tilted her head. "You should talk to Raoul. My boss. His whole thing is helping kids. His camp focused on bringing inner-city kids here to the mountains to get them out of their environment. He might have some ideas about how to get started."

"I will. Thanks." It beat worrying about the twins.

She gave him the contact information. "I'll let him know to expect your call."

He wondered if what he'd thought about doing was possible. There weren't a lot of inner-city kids in South Salmon. Of course, his cargo business was there.

But the thought of doing something a little different excited him. Cargo was paying the bills, but taking tours around was a lot more interesting. And doing something useful with kids appealed to him, as well. While he worried about his brothers, there was also a sense of satisfaction, of knowing he'd been the one to shape them into grown-ups. Of course, he had no idea yet if he'd done a decent job.

Dakota glanced around at the decorated pool area. "San Diego would have been a lot warmer. It's eighty there. I could have lain by the pool, ordered little drinks with umbrellas." She sighed.

"I thought you loved Fool's Gold," he teased.

"I do, but I love it more when it's warmer. It's spring. There should be plenty of heat." She shivered in her coat. "I had to dig out warmer clothes."

"It seems fine to me."

"You're from Alaska. Your opinion doesn't count."

He chuckled. "Come on. I'll buy you a cup of coffee."

"At Starbucks? A mocha latte would really help me feel better."

He took the hand that wasn't holding the clipboard. "You can even have whipped cream on it, if you want."

She leaned against him. "My hero."

CHAPTER EIGHT

A SHARP, INSISTENT RINGING called Dakota out of a dream that involved a panda, a raft and ice cream. She rolled over in the bed and picked up the phone.

"Hello?"

"Dakota? It's Karen."

Dakota glanced toward the clock, wondering why the production assistant was calling her. "It's one in the morning."

"I know." Karen's voice was muffled, as if she were trying to be quiet. "I'm out by the pool at the lodge. There's a Tahitian dancing team here. Or maybe it's not a team. I don't know what they're called."

Dakota flopped back on the bed and closed her eyes. "I appreciate the news flash, but I'm really tired. I can catch the dancers tomorrow." Which was technically later today, she thought.

"I don't want you to see them. Sasha is here and so is Lani. I think she knows some of the dancers. Geoff's filming the whole thing."

"Then I can see it on the show broadcast. I'm sure Sasha and Lani are great dancers. Thanks for telling me, Karen."

"Don't hang up. I called to talk to Finn."

That got Dakota's attention. She sat straight up and clutched the phone tighter. "Why would you think he was with me?"

"Oh, please. Do you know how small Fool's Gold is? Everybody knows you're sleeping with him. Which isn't the point. I need to talk with him. I'm afraid this is gonna get out of hand. Sasha is dancing with Fire Poi."

Dakota wanted to go back to the "everybody knows you're sleeping with him" remark, but the words "Fire Poi" got her attention.

"Fire, as in flames?"

"They're lighting them right now. Geoff thinks it will be great for the show. I'm scared Sasha will get hurt."

Dakota was already getting out of bed. "Finn's at his hotel. Do you have his cell number?"

"No."

Dakota gave it to her. "Tell him I'll meet him at the hotel."

"I will. Hurry," Karen said.

There might have been more, but Dakota didn't bother to listen. She shoved the phone back on the base and turned on the light. Seconds later, she'd pulled on jeans and shoved her feet into athletic shoes. After grabbing her car keys and her cell phone, she was out the door and heading for her car.

DAKOTA DROVE AS FAST as she could up the mountain and pulled into the parking lot. A car jerked to a stop next to her, and Finn got out of his rental. He was already swearing.

"I'm going to kill him," he growled, taking off toward the back of the hotel, where the pool was located.

Dakota raced after him. "They're filming. Just so you know."

Finn scowled as he grabbed her hand. "Meaning Sasha will resist any attempts to help him." He swore under his breath. "I want to blame Geoff for this, but my brother is the real idiot." He looked at her. "They don't call it Fire Poi because it only looks like fire, do they?"

"Karen said there were actual flames."

Finn picked up the pace. By the time they got to the pool, he was almost at a dead run. She had no way to keep up with him and arrived a few seconds later, barely able to breathe.

Note to self, she thought as she gasped for air. In the morning, she was really going to have to consider some kind of exercise program.

Any other thoughts on the exercise issue disappeared the second she stepped onto the patio area by the pool. About a half dozen Tahitian dancers stood by the water. Two of the guys were spinning balls of fire at dizzying speed. Sasha held a single ball of fire, connected to a chain. As she watched in horror, he raised his arm level with his shoulder and began to turn the fire.

What should have been darkness was illuminated by the lights from the two cameras. All that was missing was an insistent jungle drumbeat. That, and someone who knew what he was doing.

Urged on by the other dancers and Lani, Sasha spun the chain faster and faster. The fire created eerie circles of light. Dakota thought of Geoff lurking by the bushes. If Finn got a hold of him, there would be hell to pay. Normally she didn't condone any kind of violence, but Geoff made it clear that all he cared about was the show. The fact that Sasha could be seriously hurt was of no interest to him.

Finn stalked toward the dancers. Dakota followed, not sure if she was going to interfere or not. While she strongly believed Finn should let his brothers live their own lives, this was different.

"What the hell are you doing?" Finn asked as he approached. "Do you want to get killed? Put that down."

Sasha turned toward his brother. It seemed as if, just for a moment, he forgot he was holding a chain with a ball of fire on the end. He stopped turning the chain and the ball swung toward the ground. The arc of movement swept perilously close to Sasha's side.

She wasn't the only one who noticed. Even as Finn dove toward his brother, Lani screamed and one of the dancers yelled out a warning.

But it was too late. Sasha's T-shirt caught fire. He instantly dropped the chain and yelled. In the time it took Dakota to register the horror, Finn barreled into his brother, and they both tumbled into the pool.

"I'M GOING TO KILL HIM," Finn said as he paced the length of Dakota's living room. He'd showered and dried off, but hadn't cooled down.

"I don't care about the consequences. I'll plead guilty. I'll face the judge. Do you think there is any judge in this country who wouldn't understand why I have to kill my brother? And Geoff. What the hell. If I'm going to jail for murder, what difference does the second one make? Doesn't everyone like a two-for-one sale?"

Dakota sat on the sofa. For once she wasn't sure what to say. She believed Finn was hanging on too tight, but tonight Sasha had crossed the line. Legally, he was an adult. Apparently a stupid one. What kind of idiot started swinging around a ball of fire in the middle of the night? Sure it made good TV, but he wasn't going to have a career if he ended up with third-degree burns.

Although the paramedics had said he was going to be okay, they'd taken him to the hospital to be checked out. Dakota had been relieved when Finn hadn't climbed in the ambulance. She'd been concerned about having them alone in such a small space.

"I can't do this anymore," Finn said. "I'm going to tie them up and throw them on a plane. I know you think that will land me in jail but I'm good with that. If I get them back to Alaska and back in college, I will happily go to jail."

"If you're in jail, they'll just leave college. As for tying them up, they're about your size, Finn. You could probably take one of them but you can't take both."

He paused by the window and looked at her. "Want to bet? I'm mad enough to take on a Kodiak bear."

This probably wasn't the time to point out that the Kodiak bear would win.

"I can't believe Sasha did that," she admitted. "I can't believe he was that stupid."

"Despite the visual demonstration?"

"Even then. I'm so disappointed."

"Imagine how I feel." He crossed to the sofa and sat next to her. "I know you think I'm being controlling, but now do you see that Sasha will risk his life to get that damn fame he so desperately wants? I have to stop him. He's my family." He shook his head. "I'm never going to be done raising them, am I?"

She laid her head on his shoulder. "Yes, you are. But you're never going to stop worrying. There's a difference."

"And here I thought I'd be done by now." He wrapped his arm around her. "This is why I don't want more kids. It never ends. You can't get away from the responsibility. How do you know you've done a good job? How do you know they're going to be okay? It's too much. God, I want to go home."

Unexpected emotion swirled inside her. The sharp pain from the reminder that children might not be in her future. Disappointment that Finn didn't share her dream of family.

She and Finn didn't have a future. The fact that he didn't want children and had plans to return to South

Salmon wasn't news. She'd known from the first second she met him that he didn't want to be in Fool's Gold. As for the kid thing, she knew that, too.

But it was possible that sometime in the past week or so she'd allowed herself to forget that Finn wasn't a permanent part of her life. It was possible that he had managed to creep past her defenses, and now she cared about him. Which meant she had to get her feelings under control or she would be at risk of having her already fragile heart shattered.

"Sorry," he said with a sigh. "This isn't your problem."

"We're friends. I'm happy to listen. Besides, I'm something of a professional in this area. Feel free to pick my brain."

"I know what you think." He kissed her lightly. "You're not exactly reticent when it comes to sharing your opinion."

"I'm going to take that as a compliment."

"Good. That's how I meant it." He glanced at the clock on the wall. "It's late. We should get some sleep."

"You want to stay here?" she asked, before she could stop herself. What was she thinking? She just realized that she was at emotional risk with Finn, and now she was asking him to spend the night? It's not that she was afraid they were going to have sex. They were both tired and stressed. The real danger came from not having sex. From sleeping together. Sharing. Connecting.

"I'd like that," he said standing.

They walked into the bedroom and got undressed. She kept on her short-sleeved nightshirt, but took off her shoes and jeans. Finn dropped everything to the floor. They slid into her king-size bed and met in the middle. After she turned out the light, he lay on his back, she curled up next to him. He put his arm around her.

"Thank you," he murmured in the darkness. "You've been a rock."

"I'm happy to help." Which was the truth. Helping was easy. It was protecting herself that was going to be hard.

SASHA SAT ON A BED in the emergency room, waiting for the doctor to release him. He had minor burns on his right side and on the underside of his arm. Nothing that wouldn't heal in a few days.

They hurt like hell but had been worth it. On the ambulance ride over, Lani had told him that Geoff had already called a couple of reporters to tell them what had happened. His accident was going to give the show a lot of publicity, which was great for both of them.

The only downside in all the excitement was how pissed Finn was going to be at him. Like that was news, Sasha told himself. He'd survived it before, and he would survive it again. Finn was an old man who couldn't remember what it was like to be young and have dreams. Sasha had his whole life ahead of him.

The curtain to his small alcove parted, and Lani stepped in.

"How are you doing?" she asked, her voice low.

He motioned her close. "Are the guys out there?"

She nodded. "Both cameras. They're not supposed to film in the hospital without written permission, but you know Geoff. He's telling them to get what they can."

She settled on the side of the bed and grinned at him. "This is so cool. We're going to get tons of airtime. I was thinking, when we get back, we should stage a big fight. They can edit that in to make it look like you wanted to do the Fire Poi to prove something to me."

He tugged on her long, dark hair. "Have you been talking to Geoff?"

"Of course. Come on. We all want the same thing. Huge ratings. This is one way to get that. Geoff said he's already had a call from *Inside Edition*. They're talking exclusive interview. That would be beyond amazing."

Inside Edition?

For years now, the thing he'd wanted most in life was to get the hell out of South Salmon. As a kid, the dream had been about only that. He hadn't had another destination in mind—just a fervent need to be anywhere but there.

As he'd gotten older, he'd started to realize he needed a better goal. A place to reach toward, rather than away from. Which was how his idea of being a star had been born. Now he wanted to get on a TV series, or be in movies. He wanted to be someone, to be loved and cared for by millions. And if the price of that was a couple of burns, so be it.

"So we'll stage the fight and then there will be these scenes?" he asked.

"Uh-huh." She lowered her voice even more. "So I'm thinking I should probably cry and beg you to live."

He chuckled. "Sure thing. Then some loud kissing?"

She nodded and stood. "Let me go tell the guys."

Sasha watched her go. She was pretty enough, he thought. But there wasn't any chemistry between them. There were a lot of other women he would rather kiss and then sleep with. But whatever it took for him to get to the next level...

Lani returned. She stood by his bed, drew in a few deep breaths, then started to cry.

"Sasha," she said, her voice thick with emotion. "Sasha, you have to be okay. Please, please live. S-Sasha?" Her voice broke on his name.

Her talent impressed him. He stared at her for a second, then imagined how all this would feel if he really loved her and thought he was going to die.

"Don't go," he said, his voice low and husky, as if he was in extreme pain. "Lani, I need you."

"I'm right here. You know I'm here." She sniffed. "I can't believe you got hurt. Do you need something for the pain?"

"They gave me something. It's not bad. I'm not going to give up, because I have you."

Her eyes twinkled with laughter as she said, "Really?

You feel it, too? Our connection? I thought…" Another sob. "Oh, Sasha, I've been afraid to say anything and then when we fought before, I thought you didn't care about me."

"Of course I care. Getting matched with you was the luckiest day in my life."

"You mean that?"

"You're my girl."

"Oh, Sasha."

She covered her mouth to hold in a giggle, then climbed into the bed next to him.

"I don't want to hurt you," she told him.

"You couldn't. Just being next to you makes me know everything is going to be all right."

"I want to kiss you," she said, while sticking a finger down her throat and silently pretending to gag.

He had to swallow hard to keep from laughing. "Yes, baby," he murmured. "Just holding you makes it all better."

They began to kiss, going more for noise than passion. Sasha heard the sound of metal hooks on a pole as the privacy curtains were opened enough for the camera to get a shot of them.

He kept his eyes closed and thought about what he would do with his half of the money. How every woman would want him and every man would want to be him. Then he flipped Lani onto her back and put some tongue into it.

FINN WATCHED THE LIVE FEED of the show. The blend of what was happening on stage and taped pieces was interesting. Someone had to plan all that—figure out what to put where. Some of the taped pieces showed a contest with the various couples putting together bookcases. The kind that came in long flat boxes, with too many pieces and instructions written in awkward English.

Sasha and Lani laughed more than they worked and didn't finish in the allotted time. Stephen and Aurelia came in first. They worked together quickly and easily, sharing the tasks and ending up with a project that actually looked like a bookcase.

After the taped piece about Sasha and the Fire Poi, viewers were asked to vote for their favorite couple. The results would be announced in a couple of hours.

When the show ended, Finn knew Sasha and Lani would be staying. He had a feeling that building a bookcase wasn't enough to entice viewers, so Stephen and Aurelia might be at risk.

Dakota walked over to him. "How did it go?" she asked.

"Sasha and Lani are going to clean up this week," he told her. "I'm less sure about Stephen and Aurelia."

"Still think it's too soon for him to want to go home?"

"I'm sure of it."

"Have you asked Stephen what he would do?"

"I'm a guy," he said. "So is he. We don't have conversations."

"That's part of the problem."

"It must be nice to always have the answer," he said, annoyed by her certainty.

Dakota raised her chin slightly. "I'm not the bad guy here. I'm on your side."

"Then why are you always telling me what I'm doing wrong?"

"Because you're reacting as if you're trying to reason with yourself instead of your brothers. You're not looking at the situation from their point of view."

"I know them a hell of a lot better than you do."

"Which isn't the point. Your way hasn't changed their mind. Maybe another point of view would be helpful."

"But only if it's yours, right?"

She exhaled sharply. "I didn't say that. I care about you and them. I want you to stay close with your brothers so the family unit remains intact. I'm not sure why you can't see that. You're so determined to protect them from the world. And you can't."

"I can sure try."

"They're not seven. You keep saying that the twins are the ones who have to grow up, but maybe you're the one who can't let go of the past."

He glared at her. "Is this advice free or am I expected to pay for it? Because it's not worth shit."

She looked at him for a long time. "Fine. I thought that you wanted my opinion. My mistake. I can see you're only interested in being right."

With that, she turned and walked away.

Finn let her go. He didn't need her. He didn't need anybody. Only he knew he was lying. If he really didn't care, he could get on the next plane to Alaska and leave his brothers to their fate. If he didn't care, he wouldn't be wondering how badly he'd messed up with Dakota and how he could fix it without getting deeper into a relationship that wasn't meant to be.

CHAPTER NINE

"You've got to give me something to work with," Karen said. "I think you're a cute couple with a lot of potential, but there's nothing there. No fights, no kissing and certainly no making up. There's nothing interesting to film. You know how Geoff is. You two came in second to last on the voting. That means you're at risk of being voted off."

"Do we have to come in last before we're let go?" Stephen asked. "Is that decision based on numbers or does Geoff make it?"

Karen sighed. "Technically you have to go if you come in last on the viewer voting. My point is, if you want to stay on the show, you have to give us something. Otherwise you're gonna be gone."

"Thanks for letting us know," Aurelia said.

She was doing her best to accept the information in the spirit in which it was given. But it was very difficult not to feel even more romantically inept than usual. Here she was, failing at a fake relationship. If she couldn't make this work, when it wasn't even real, how was she supposed to ever find a man and fall in love?

"I think you two like each other," Karen said. "Maybe

you should think about that and stop worrying about the cameras."

Aurelia nodded. She knew that a lot of the couples had no trouble being around the cameras. But she was always aware of them, afraid of how she looked. Afraid of what people would say. After the show first aired, her mother called with her critique. It was not kind. She didn't like her daughter's clothes, or her hair or what she said. She also didn't like how young Stephen was but agreed there was nothing to be done about it. It wasn't as if Aurelia had picked him.

The only bright spot was the fact that Aurelia wasn't expected to visit her mother as much.

"I need to get back to the office," Karen said. "Please don't say anything. I'm not supposed to tell you, but I wanted to."

"We won't say anything," Stephen promised. "We'll do better next time."

Aurelia waited until the production assistant had left, then turned to him. "I guess we're done," she said. "The twin factor helped us the first couple of weeks, but the thrill is probably wearing off."

Or it was her. A conversation she didn't want to have with Stephen.

They were sitting on the grass in the large park in the center of town. The live portion of the show had been the previous night, and now they were on their own for a couple of days. For Aurelia, that meant going back to work. Show or no show, she still had clients.

"I'm not ready for this to be over," Stephen told her. "Do you want to be finished with the show?"

"No, but we're not like your brother and Lani. Do you want to play with Fire Poi to get more votes?"

"I would prefer to get out of the show unscarred," he said with a grin. "But we could do something."

"What I should do is grow a spine," she murmured. "Stand up to my mother. I'm a lot more afraid of her than I am of Geoff."

Stephen sat across from her. His blue eyes darkened with concern. "Why does she scare you?"

"Scared isn't exactly the right word. When I'm with her, I feel bad about myself. I feel guilty. Like I'm always doing something wrong. When I was a kid, it was just the two of us. We felt like a team. We did everything together. But then something changed. I'm not sure exactly when, but one day there were expectations. Rather than going off with my friends, I was supposed to come home and hang out with her. In high school, I didn't date. Some of it was me. I was bookish and not very pretty. Some of it was her, though. When I did get asked out, she always had a dozen reasons as to why I couldn't go."

"Because she wanted to keep you for herself?"

Aurelia hesitated. "I'm not sure. Although she's always complaining I'm not married or giving her grandchildren, I'm not sure she would be happy if I was. She has a sense of entitlement. She believes that it's my responsibility to take care of her."

"Is she sick?"

"No. She works, but she expects me to pay most of her expenses. It's as if I only exist to serve her. She doesn't like that I have a life. And somehow I've let that be okay. She talks about all the things she did for me and tells me over and over again that I should be grateful. I am. It's just, when do I get to have a life of my own?"

Stephen leaned toward her and took her hands in his. "Now," he said softly. "You get to have a life now. The longer you let her do this to you, the harder it's going to be to break away. Don't you want more?"

What she wanted was someone to look at her the way he was looking at her now. With caring and concern. With an intensity that made her fingers tremble.

She must be dehydrated or something. This was Stephen. He was young enough to be her baby brother. Nothing about him should make her tremble or even see him as anything but a friend. He was practically a teenager.

"I do want more," she said. "I want what most women want. A husband and children."

"That's not going to happen until you're willing to stand up to her. So which is bigger—your fear of her or your desire for your dreams? Because that's what it comes down to."

In the space of a few minutes, he'd managed to articulate everything she'd been thinking for the past five years. "You're right," she whispered. "I do have to confront her." She looked at him, then bit her lower lip. "Does it have to be today?"

He laughed. "No, it doesn't."

"Good. I need to work on my courage a little bit."

"So you're not ready for the show to be over yet?"

She shook her head. Even just another week with Stephen would be wonderful. He was so easy to be with, someone she could really talk to. He was…safe. Not a description he would like, but to her it meant the world.

"Then we're going to have to work on giving the camera something," he said, moving toward her. "I suggest we start with this."

Before she knew what he was talking about, he'd taken her in his arms and pressed his mouth to hers.

She didn't know which shocked her more—the kiss or the fact that they were outside, in the middle of the afternoon, where anyone could see. She wasn't a middle-of-the-day kind of girl. Not that she had a whole lot of kissing experience. There had been a few boys in college, but still. Those had all been night kisses.

Yet she couldn't seem to summon the indignation to protest. Not when he had one hand on her shoulder and the other on her thigh. Not when she could feel the heat from his body and feel how her heart bumped around in her chest. Not when his lips on hers felt so good.

Tentatively, she raised her arm so it rested on his shoulder. She slowly, very slowly, tilted her head and let her lips soften. She found herself straining toward him, wanting more than just a simple kiss.

Then it happened. Somewhere deep inside of her a

small, cold, empty space came to life. Instead of feeling inadequate, she felt powerful. Instead of wondering what everyone else was thinking, she found herself thinking about what she wanted. Instead of holding back and being scared, she leaned in and touched his bottom lip with her tongue.

Stephen responded by wrapping both arms around her, lowering her to the grass, then kissing her with a passionate intensity that stole her breath away.

She met him stroke for stroke, enjoying the warmth that poured through her, feeling long-numb parts come to life. At that moment it didn't matter that he was nine years younger or that she was a wallflower who hadn't been on a date in six years. In his arms, with the bright sun blessing them, she was a woman and he was a man and everything about this moment was right.

DAKOTA WALKED THROUGH the production offices, looking for Finn. She hadn't seen him in a couple of days and felt badly about their last conversation. In truth, he should be the one coming to look for her, but she wasn't going to wait for that to happen. She liked Finn and wanted to make sure they stayed friends.

She found him in one of the empty offices, working a column of numbers with a calculator.

"Hi," she said as she leaned against the door frame. "How's it going?"

He looked up. "Things are good." He grinned. "I talked to your boss about the flying school."

"How did that go?"

"Great. He had a lot of information on starting a non-profit business. It's going to take a hell of a lot of money, but he gave me some ideas on where to start."

"You sound excited."

"I am. I've been playing with the idea for a while, but never thought anything could come of it."

"See what happens when you come down to the lower forty-eight?"

"Yes, I do. I have a lot to figure out. My charter business, the twins, this damn show. But I'm thinking I want to seriously consider the flight school. I'm not sure what the focus would be right now, or where I'd start it, but I know it's important."

He was enthused and not worrying as much about his brothers. At least not the way he had before. The flight school idea had some interesting consequences. As he'd mentioned before, there weren't a lot of inner-city kids in South Salmon. Which meant Finn had to be considering moving. Maybe Fool's Gold would make the list.

"I wondered if you wanted to come over for dinner," she said. "I have another chicken recipe that's pretty good."

He rose, shoved his hands into his jeans pockets, then rocked back on his heels. "Thanks for asking, but I'm going to pass."

"Oh. Okay. Sure."

The refusal surprised her. She told herself not to take his words personally, that she couldn't know everything going on in his life. Saying no wasn't a personal rejection. But psychological training didn't make it any easier to avoid feeling hurt.

"I guess I'll see you around," she said and turned to leave.

"Dakota, wait."

She faced him again.

"This isn't a good idea." He pulled one hand free of his jeans and motioned between them. "Us seeing each other. I'm not staying, which means this isn't going anywhere."

He was dumping her? They hadn't technically been dating. How could he be dumping her?

"I didn't expect it to go anywhere," she told him, doing her best to keep her voice even. So much for the hopes he would settle here. "I know that you're heading back to Alaska or wherever, and I'm staying here. This was always just going to be for fun."

"I thought you might be getting more involved."

"What gave you that idea?"

He shrugged.

She moved from hurt to pissed. This was so like a man. "I wasn't," she said coolly. "I was very clear on the parameters. Please don't worry about my feelings."

"I won't."

"Good."

Her anger grew. She wanted to scream or throw something, then told herself to keep breathing and take the high road. She might not like it now, but she would feel a whole lot better about herself later.

"Have a good night," she said between clenched teeth and left.

Once outside, she started home, then changed direction a block later and walked toward Jo's Bar. Tonight was definitely a margarita night. She would drink tequila, have a salad and watch HGTV. Later, when she was at her place, she would take a bath, go to bed, all the while reminding herself that Finn Andersson was an annoying jerk and that she was well rid of the likes of him.

In a couple of days, she would even believe it.

NEVADA'S INVITATION to dinner came at exactly the right time. Dakota appreciated the chance to get out of her house and spend time with her sisters. Three grilled steaks and one bottle of red wine later, they were all feeling pretty good. Dakota hated to upset the mood, but she knew it was time to come clean.

Her sisters were sprawled on the red sectional sofa. There was a fire in the fireplace and the soundtrack from *Mamma Mia* playing in the background. Montana had already mocked her sister for her choice in music, so Dakota didn't bother. But she did wait until the song about money was over, before introducing the topic of her infertility.

"I need to tell you something," she said in the brief silence between songs.

"We already know you're sleeping with Finn," Montana told her. "I can't decide if I want details or not. On the one hand, at least one of us is getting some. On the other hand, I don't know that I want to be made aware of how pathetic I am. It's a tough decision."

"I don't want to know," Nevada said. "I don't want the reminder of what I'm missing."

Eventually she was going to have to tell them that Finn had dumped her. But it wasn't what she wanted to talk about tonight. Instead, she had to figure out a way to explain that she would probably never have children. At least not the old-fashioned way.

Montana sat up and looked at her. "What's wrong?"

"What is it?" Nevada asked, at almost exactly the same moment.

It was as if they were reading her mind. One of the unique realities of being a triplet.

"I saw Dr. Galloway last fall." There was no reason to explain who the doctor was. All three of them saw her. Dakota would guess most of the women in town had Dr. Galloway as their gynecologist.

"The pain during my periods was getting worse. She did a few tests and it turns out I have some problems." She went on to explain the ramifications of having both polycystic ovarian syndrome and pelvic endometriosis.

"I actually have a better chance of being struck by lightning than getting pregnant the old-fashioned way," she said, keeping her tone light. "Even intervention is unlikely to help. I'm thinking of trying for the lottery instead. The lightning thing doesn't sound very fun."

Nevada and Montana moved as if one. They crossed the small living room and crouched in front of her chair.

"Are you okay?"

"Why didn't you tell us?"

"Can we do anything? Donate anything?"

"Will it get better over time?"

"Is this why you want to adopt?"

The questions overlapped. Dakota didn't worry about the turn the conversation was taking. What she felt, what healed the lingering ache in her soul, was the love that comforted her like an embrace.

"I'm fine," she told them. "Seriously. I'm perfectly fine."

"I don't believe that," Nevada said flatly. "How can this be? You've always wanted kids. A lot of them."

"Which is why I'm adopting. I'm on the list. I could get a call any day now."

That was a slight exaggeration. So far, her adoption experience had been less than perfect, but it could change. She refused to give up hope.

Montana hugged her. "There are other ways to get pregnant, right?"

"I'll definitely need help if I want to carry my own child."

Because of the scarring, there might not be any good eggs. And getting them out would be more difficult than for most women. But there was no point in getting into that.

"Have you given up?" Montana asked.

"On having a kid? No. I'll get there." She didn't know how, but it would happen. She had to hang on to that.

"This doesn't change anything," Nevada told her. "You're great. Smart and beautiful, with a great personality. Any guy would be lucky to have you."

She appreciated the vote of confidence, especially because she happened to know Nevada didn't think of herself as very attractive. An interesting mental schism. If Nevada thought Dakota was pretty and she and Dakota were identical triplets, how could she not admit the same about herself? Perhaps that should have been the topic of her thesis.

"Guys seem to be amazingly blind," Montana said. "It's very annoying."

"Who have you liked who hasn't liked you back?" Dakota asked.

Her sister's mouth twisted. "I can't think of anyone right now, but I'm sure it's happened." She sat on the carpet and rested her chin in her hands. "What's wrong with us? Why can't we find 'the guy' and fall in love? Everyone else seems to be in a relationship. Even Mom is thinking of dating. But here we sit—alone."

Montana looked at Dakota. "Sorry. I didn't mean to rant off topic. We can talk about the baby thing more."

Dakota laughed. "I'm okay with being done with it. As to the man question, I don't have an answer."

"You don't need one," Nevada grumbled. "You have Finn."

Not as much as they thought. "He's only here temporarily. As soon as he gets his brothers to go back home or figures out it's time to let go, he'll return to South Salmon."

"What about a long-distance relationship?" Montana asked.

Dakota shook her head. "Finn and I want different things. He's tired of being responsible and I want to get serious. In fact, he told me he's concerned I'm getting too attached, so I don't think we're going to see each other anymore."

Both her sisters stared at her.

"He didn't," Nevada breathed.

"He did."

"Butthead," Montana grumbled. "I liked him. Why do all the guys I like have to be jerks?"

"Max isn't a jerk," Nevada said.

"Would you lay off Max? He's old enough to be my father and while he's nice and everything, um, ick. He's my boss."

"The boss-secretary romance is very popular," Dakota said, her voice teasing. "What about that 'Ms. Jones, you're so beautiful' moment? That could be fun."

"I don't want to have sex with Max. Ever!"

Nevada looked at Dakota. "I hope she makes up her mind soon. All this indecision exhausts me."

Dakota sighed as she leaned back in her chair. "Me, too."

"I'm ignoring you both," Montana grumbled.

Nevada laughed.

"We'll all find someone," Dakota told her sisters. "Statistically, it's bound to happen."

"I love math as much as the next girl," Nevada said, "but I don't find it very comforting when it's applied to my love life."

"You could go to South Salmon with Finn," Montana suggested.

Dakota shook her head. "First, he hasn't asked." If anything, he'd made it clear he wasn't interested in keeping things going for the next two days, let alone twenty years. "Second, I don't want to. I'm sure it's a wonderful place to live, but my life is here. I love Fool's Gold. My family is here. My history, my friends. I belong here. When Geoff's show wraps up, I'm going back to work for Raoul and develop the curriculum for the program we want to start."

She was also thinking of opening a private practice. Just part-time, seeing a few patients a week.

"His loss," Nevada said firmly. "I'd thought the guy had a brain, but I was wrong."

"I wish I had a dog that liked to bite people." Montana wrinkled her nose. "A really big, scary, biting dog. That would show him. Maybe I could train one of the dogs to bite on command."

Dakota leaned forward and hugged them. "I love you both," she whispered.

"We love you, too."

She was lucky, she reminded herself. No matter what, she would never have to deal with the dips in her life alone. There were people who cared about her. People who would always be there for her. And eventually, because she refused to give up hope, she would have a child. And that would be enough.

CHAPTER TEN

FINN FOUND SASHA AND LANI playing volleyball in the park. His brother had recovered from his minor burns and seemed to be doing just fine. Sasha spotted him and waved but didn't break away from his game.

After watching for a few minutes, Finn wandered away. It was Saturday afternoon on a warm spring day. Much of the town seemed to be outside taking walks, running errands. He saw parents with small children, old ladies walking little dogs. The fire department had pulled one of their trucks up to the park. Children scrambled over the shiny rig. Restaurants and coffee shops had set up tables outside, taking advantage of the mild weather.

Two of the other couples on the show were away on dates. Finn thought they might have gone to Lake Tahoe. Regardless of their destination, there was no filming in town today.

He walked through the park, remembering that Stephen had told him he and Aurelia were going to have a picnic by the lake. Twenty minutes later he found them on a blanket in the shade of a tall tree. Aurelia sat cross-legged while Stephen lay on his stomach, looking at her.

Their expressions were intense, as if they were talking about something important.

Finn hesitated, torn between the normal polite response of not wanting to interrupt and the need to come between a sophisticated older woman and his brother. Then Aurelia spotted him and waved him over.

"How's it going?" he asked, hovering at the edge of the blanket, not comfortable sitting down.

Stephen sat up. "Good. We were just talking."

"I have an overbearing mother," Aurelia admitted. "We're strategizing. I'm going to stand up to her and tell her to get off my back." She wrinkled her nose. "That sounds so brave. I'm fearless, right up until I see her. Then I crumble." She looked at Finn. "Any suggestions for gathering courage while facing a private demon? Not that my mother is a demon. She has her reasons for running my life. I'm the one with the problem."

Finn was having a little trouble following her conversation. "I'm sure you'll be fine."

Stephen laughed. "Typical guy response to an emotional situation. When in doubt, distance yourself, then run."

"You're not running," Finn said. "Why is that?"

"I like Aurelia. We have a lot in common." Stephen sat up. "We're both the quiet ones in our family, we like the same movies, we enjoy reading."

"I finished college and you didn't," Aurelia said with a quick smile. "Oh, wait. That's a difference."

Her teasing but effective dig surprised Finn.

"You're taking my side on the college thing?" he asked, incredulous.

"It does seem a little shortsighted to go all the way to your last semester and then quit." Instead of looking at Stephen, Aurelia looked at him. "Stephen's been majoring in engineering."

"I know," Finn told her. He didn't understand. She seemed to think the words were significant. He was Stephen's older brother. Of course he knew what he was studying.

Stephen shot her a look that silenced her. When she ducked her head, he reached out his hand and touched her arm.

Finn stood there, feeling like the odd man out. There was an undercurrent he didn't understand and made him uncomfortable. Which made him miss Dakota. She would get it and smooth the situation over. She did that kind of thing.

"I, ah, have to get going," Finn said quickly. "You two kids have fun today."

He hurried away, not sure where he was going but wanting to get far away.

What was up with those two? As for Aurelia supporting the idea of Stephen finishing college, he couldn't tell if that meant she was an okay person, as Dakota had claimed, or if this was all part of her cougar game.

He kept walking. The park was filled with residents and tourists. Young children offered bread to the ducks by the pond. He caught sight of someone with blond hair and a familiar build. Dakota!

He turned toward her, frowning when the family between them moved. No. Not Dakota. One of her sisters walking several dogs wearing service vests. He stood in place until she was out of sight. His cell phone rang.

He checked the screen and recognized Bill's number. "How's it going?"

"Great. The new guy's a terrific pilot. There's no bullshit. He does the work and then he goes home. I like that. We've already got sixty boxes delivered."

"That's fast," Finn said, surprised they were doing so well.

"Tell me about it. If this guy wants to stick around, you can stay there as long as you'd like."

"Good to know. I didn't like leaving you short-handed."

"Plenty of hands now," Bill told him. "I gotta run. Talk to you later."

Finn listened to his partner hang up, then stood in the center of the park and realized he had nothing to do with the rest of his day. He stepped into the sunlight and looked around at the bustling town. Everyone had somewhere to be. Everyone had someone to be with. Except for his brothers, the only other person he wanted to spend time with was Dakota. The problem was, the last time he'd seen her, he'd acted like an ass.

It hadn't been her at all, he admitted to himself. It had been him. He wanted to say he'd acted the way he had because he'd known the relationship wouldn't last and he was only trying to protect her. But that would make him a liar. Instead, he'd felt himself getting closer to her. The realization had scared the crap out of him. So he'd acted or, rather, reacted. He'd rejected her and sent her on her way.

Now he was left with the consequences.

Knowing that, whether or not she was willing to forgive him, he had to apologize, so Finn walked the short distance to Dakota's house. When he reached the front door, he knocked, then waited. If she wasn't home, he'd come back later.

The door opened a few seconds later. Dakota raised her eyebrows when she saw him but didn't say anything. She was wearing jeans and a T-shirt. Her feet were bare. Her blond hair tousled. She looked good. Better than good. She looked sexy and only slightly pissed at him.

"I should probably talk first, huh?" he said.

She leaned her shoulder against the door frame. "Sounds like a good idea."

"I have a good excuse for acting like a jerk."

"I can't wait to hear it."

He cleared his throat. "Would saying it's because I'm a guy be enough?"

"Probably not."

It had been worth a try, he thought. "I was frustrated and angry about my brothers. And starting to get involved with you. That last part wasn't supposed to happen. You know I'm leaving and I know I'm leaving."

"So you decided on the mature response," she said.

"I'm sorry. You didn't deserve that. I was wrong."

She stepped back and held the door open. "Come on in."

"As easy as that?"

"It was a good apology. I believe you."

He stepped into the house and she shut the door behind him and faced him.

"Finn, I have a good time with you. I like talking to you and the sex is pretty good, too." She smiled. "Don't let that last part go to your head."

"I won't," he promised. Although he wanted to take a second and enjoy the praise.

Her smile faded. "I'm very clear on the fact your stay here in town is temporary. When you leave, I'll miss you. Despite that, I'm not going to get crazy and try to make you stay."

"I know," he said quickly. "I shouldn't have said all that before. I'll miss you, too."

"Having cleared up how much we're going to miss each other, do you still want to spend time together while you're here?"

He hadn't dated much in the past eight years. Once his parents had died and he'd become responsible for his brothers, there hadn't been time. So he wasn't sure if her direct attitude was about dating a woman who was more mature, or if she was incredibly special. He had a feeling it was the latter.

"I'd like to see you as much as I can," he said. "And

if you want to beg me to stay, I wouldn't mind that, either."

She laughed. "You and your ego. I'm sure you would love that. You in your plane, ready to fly away. Me sobbing on the edge of the runway. Very 1940s and going off to war."

"I like war movies," he said.

"Let me put on some shoes." She walked across the living room and slipped her feet into sandals. "I'll show you the town and later you can stay for dinner." She turned back to him. "And if you're very lucky, I might just use you for sex."

"If there's anything I can do to encourage that last one, just let me know."

"I'm sure there's something," she said with a smile. "Let me think on it."

DAKOTA SPENT THE AFTERNOON showing Finn around town. They explored Morgan's Books, got a coffee at Starbucks and watched the last two innings of a Little League game. Around five, they headed back to her place.

"Want to get takeout?" he asked.

"I still have the ingredients for that chicken dish," she said, enjoying the soft breeze and the feel of his hand in hers.

"Who taught you to cook?" he asked. "Your mom?"

"Uh-huh. She's a great cook. We always had a tradition of big family dinners. We were all expected to show up every night, regardless of what else might be going on. As a teenager, I hated the rules, but now I appreciate them."

"Sounds like you were part of a close family."

She looked at him. "From what you said earlier, it sounds like you were, too."

"It wasn't the same. Dad and I were always flying off somewhere. We didn't have a lot of meals together. But you're right. We were close."

They'd reached her house and went inside. While he browsed through her music selection, she got the chicken ready to put in the oven. Once she'd slid it into place, she grabbed a bottle of wine and joined him in her living room.

They sat together on the sofa.

"How old were you when you learned to fly?" she asked.

"Seven or eight. Dad started taking me up when I was about four. He would let me take the controls. I got serious about studying to be a pilot when I was ten. There's a lot of written material, but I got through it."

She shifted so she was facing him on the sofa. "Why do you love it?"

"Part of it is growing up in Alaska. There are lots of places that you can only get to by boat or plane. Some of the towns in the far north are only accessible by plane."

"Or dogsled," she teased.

"A dogsled only works in the winter." He put his hand

on her leg. "Every day is different. Different cargo, different weather, different destination. I like helping people who are depending on me. I like the freedom. I'm my own boss."

"You could be your own boss anywhere," she said.

"I could," he agreed. "As much as I like Alaska, I'm not one of those guys who can't see himself living anywhere else. There are things I like about being in the city. Maybe not a big one. But there's something to be said for tradition. My grandfather started the business. It's been in the family ever since. Sometimes there's a partner, sometimes it's just us."

Dakota knew all about belonging to a place. "My family was one of the original families here in town. Being there from the beginning can make you feel like a small part of history."

"Exactly. I don't know what's going to happen with the company," he admitted. "Sasha's not interested in flying. I always thought Stephen would take it over, but now I don't know. Bill, my business partner, has a younger brother and a cousin. They both want in. Right now they're flying for regional carriers. That's why he couldn't hire them to help while I'm down here."

He leaned forward and picked up his wine. "Sometimes I think about selling out. Taking the money and starting over somewhere else. It used to be important for me to stay in South Salmon, for my brothers."

"Less of an issue now?" she asked.

He nodded.

Dakota told herself not to read too much into the conversation. Finn was just talking. The fact that he wasn't determined to stay in Alaska forever didn't change their circumstances. He'd made it clear several times he wasn't going to stay in Fool's Gold. When a man spoke like that, he was telling the truth. It wasn't code for "try harder to change me."

But there was a part of her that wanted it to be. Which made her foolish, and Dakota didn't like being a fool.

"You don't have to make a decision today," she said. "Even if you don't stay in South Salmon, there are other parts of Alaska."

He glanced at her. "Trying to make sure I don't change my mind about leaving? That sounds a lot like 'don't let the door hit you in the ass.'"

She laughed. "I would never say that."

He chuckled. "Thinking it counts."

He put down his wine, then pulled her against him. She went willingly, enjoying the feel of his body against hers. As always, the combination of strength and gentleness aroused her. The man could make her melt without even trying. How fair was that?

He brushed his mouth against hers. "Dinner's in the oven?"

"Uh-huh."

"How long do we have?"

She glanced at her watch. "About fifteen minutes. I was going to make a salad."

"Or you could spend the next fifteen minutes making out with me."

She wrapped her arms around him and drew him closer. "Salad is very overrated."

He pressed an openmouthed kiss against her lips. She parted for him, enjoying the slow, enticing strokes of his tongue. Wanting grew. He put his hand on her knee, then moved it steadily up her body until his fingers caressed her breast.

Her nipples tightened and the pleasure began. Between her legs, she was already wet and swollen.

Were they really that hungry, she wondered. Couldn't she pull the chicken out of the oven and let it finish cooking later?

She drew back slightly, only to have the phone interrupt the question. Finn reached across to the receiver on the end table and handed it to her.

She sat up.

"Hello?"

"Dakota Hendrix?" an unfamiliar woman asked.

"Yes."

"I'm Patricia Lee. We spoke a few months ago about your adoption application."

"What?" She quickly cleared her thoughts. "Oh, yes. I remember." The international agency had been quick to approve her application. Unlike several of the others she'd tried, this one hadn't minded that she was single.

"I heard about what happened with that little boy,"

Patricia said. "I'm so sorry. I don't know if they told you, but there was a mix-up in the paperwork."

Dakota had been told the same thing, although she'd never been sure if it really was a mix-up or if the agency had preferred sending the child to a married couple. Either way, it was an odd thing to call about on a Saturday night.

"Of course I was disappointed," Dakota admitted.

"Then you're still interested in adopting a child?"

"Of course."

"I was hoping you would say that," the other woman said. "We have a little girl. She's six months old and quite adorable. I wonder if you would be interested in her."

Dakota felt the blood rush from her head and wondered if she was going to faint. "Do you mean it? You have a child for me?"

"Yes, we do. I'm emailing you her file right now. There are a couple of pictures, as well. I was wondering if you would call me back after you look at the pictures. We have one of our workers returning home late tomorrow. If you want to take the child, she can get on the same flight. Otherwise it might be a couple of months until you can have her. I know this is quick, so if you want to wait we all understand. It won't change your application status."

Dakota's head spun. They were offering her what she'd always wanted. The chance for a family of her own. And six months old. That was so young. She was somewhat familiar with the developmental problems of a child raised in an orphanage. The younger the child, the more easily those problems were overcome. The little boy she'd been offered before had been five.

"When would you need to know?"

"In the next couple of hours," Patricia admitted. "I'm sorry it's such short notice. Our contact has been called home with a family emergency. We try to send a child with every adult going home. But again, it's up to you. We're not trying to pressure you. If you're not ready, we'll call the next family on the list."

Dakota walked into the kitchen. She picked up a pen and some sticky notes, then sat at the kitchen table. "Give me your number," she said. "I'll look at the file and call you back within the hour."

"Thank you," Patricia said.

Dakota took the information, then hung up. She sat in her kitchen. She knew she was in a chair with her feet on the floor, but part of her felt as if she were flying. Flying and shaking and emotional beyond tears. She had to still be breathing because she was conscious, but she couldn't really feel her body.

Somewhere in the background there was a dinging sound. Finn walked into the kitchen and took the casserole dish from the oven. Then he turned to face her.

"You're adopting a child?" he asked, sounding stunned.

She nodded, still unable to focus on anything. "Yes. They have a little girl for me arriving in L.A." She looked at him. "She's from Kazakhstan. Six months old. They're sending me a file. I need to go turn on my computer."

She stood, then couldn't remember where her computer was. This wasn't happening, was it? She laughed. "They're going to give me a little girl of my own."

"I know you wanted kids…" His voice trailed off, then he nodded slowly. "You have a lot to deal with. Why don't I get out of your way?"

"What? Oh."

So much for their romantic dinner, she thought sadly. So much for him. Finn had more than made it clear he wasn't looking for another family.

"Thanks," she said. "I have to make a decision pretty quickly."

"No problem." He started to leave, then paused. "You'll let me know what you decide?"

"Of course."

"Good."

She watched him leave. There was a whisper of sadness, but it quickly faded as she hurried to her spare room and turned on her laptop. The machine seemed to take forever to boot, but when it finally did and she was able to open the file, she saw the picture.

And she knew.

CHAPTER ELEVEN

MAKING THE DECISION was easy, Dakota realized the next morning. The details, on the other hand, threatened to drown her. She'd barely gotten any sleep. Every time she'd closed her eyes, she'd thought of something else she had to do. Even putting a pad of paper and a pen on her nightstand hadn't helped very much.

It was barely after eight in the morning, and she was exhausted. She had lists, including supplies, and the names of who she was going to call. The last big issue to be resolved was whether to drive to Los Angeles or to fly.

Although flying would be faster, she had to face the reality of dealing with the six-month-old baby she barely knew. What if her new daughter cried the whole way? Dakota wouldn't know how to handle that. So driving made more sense. Except it was probably an eight-hour drive and wouldn't that be stressful on the child, as well?

Dakota tapped her pen on the paper, not sure what was the best solution. In a few minutes, she would call her mother. She wanted to tell Denise the good news and ask her advice on the transportation issue.

In the meantime, she could review her shopping list. Not only would she need diapers and a couple of blankets, there was the issue of formula. Dakota didn't know very much about babies, but she was relatively sure switching formula could cause an upset stomach. Hopefully, the person traveling with the little girl had brought plenty.

She crossed to the phone by the sofa, but before she could pick up the receiver, there was soft knocking on her front door. She changed directions and opened it, only to find Finn standing on her small porch. He had take-out coffee containers in each hand.

"What are you doing here?" she asked. "It's early."

He handed her the coffee. "Nonfat, right?"

"Yes. Thank you." She stepped back and shook her head. "Sorry, I'm a little fuzzy this morning. Why are you here?"

"You're keeping the baby."

"How do you know?"

He smiled. "I know you. You talked about the fact that you can't have kids and you're a kid person. Given the chance to adopt, you will."

"Oh, you're right." Unexpected insight, she thought. But nice.

He followed her into the house.

"I don't know what I'm doing," she admitted. "I didn't get much sleep and it seems like there are a thousand things to do."

He followed her into the kitchen. "Sure there are.

Most people get nine months to figure out what to do about a baby. You've had what? Nine hours?"

All of which was true, she thought. But she was still surprised to see him. He'd taken off so quickly the previous night.

"I'm doing the list thing," she said, pointing to the pages on the kitchen table. "I'm going to call my mom in a few minutes. She's had six kids. If anyone knows what to do, it's her."

"Have you picked a name?"

She smiled. "I was thinking of Hannah. It's the name that came to me when I saw her picture."

"Hannah Hendrix. I like it."

"Me, too," she said. "Everything is so surreal. I don't know what to think even."

"You're going to be fine," he told her.

"You can't know that."

"Sure I can. You're the kind of person who cares about other people. And isn't that what you're always telling me? That kids want to know you're there for them?" He smiled. "I'm really happy for you, Dakota."

His support was unexpected, but very nice. She was close enough to the edge that it could've made her cry, but she was determined to maintain control.

"For a guy who isn't interested in having a family," she said, "you're pretty sensitive and understanding."

He winced. "Don't let word get out. I have a reputation to uphold. How are you getting to L.A.?"

"To pick up Hannah? I can't decide. That's what I

was going to talk to my mom about. Flying is faster, but I'm afraid to take an unfamiliar baby on a plane. Which means driving makes more sense, but it's kind of long. I don't know how she'll feel or what she's like. She could be really scared."

"Let's fly," he told her. "I'll rent a plane. She's coming into the international terminal, right?"

"Yes, but you can't fly me to Los Angeles."

"Why not? Don't you trust me?"

Her concern wasn't about his flying abilities. She was sure he was very good. "Isn't renting a private plane a big deal? And expensive?"

"Not that big a deal. It's going to cost more than flying commercial, but I'm talking about a four-seater plane. Not a jet. It'll be faster than a car, and when you consider going through security and having to get there two hours before your flight, faster than flying commercial. There's an executive airport just east of LAX. We'll land there and take the shuttle to the international terminal."

"That sounds perfect," she said, relieved to have her problem solved. "Thank you. This is a huge relief. How do I pay for the plane? Do you want my credit card number?"

"We'll work that out later," he told her. "Let me go arrange for the rental."

They decided on what time they were leaving in the morning, then Finn kissed her lightly. "Congratulations," he said.

"Thank you for everything."

"I'm happy to help."

After he left, Dakota stood in the center of the room, holding her coffee. She was still surprised by his offer of help, although very grateful. She wasn't sure why he was getting involved, but she knew better than to ask questions.

A quick glance at the clock told her it was time to call her mother. She only had one day to get her entire life rearranged. In less than forty-eight hours, she would be a mother.

BY NOON, her house was overflowing with well-wishers. Dakota had called her mother. Denise had called her other daughters, along with most of the people they knew in Fool's Gold.

Nevada and Montana had shown up first. Then her mother had arrived minutes later. Liz and Jo were joined by Charity and her new baby. Marsha, the town mayor, arrived with Alice, the chief of police. Friends and neighbors filled Dakota's small house.

She'd already printed out the pictures of Hannah the adoption agency had emailed, and they were passed from hand to hand.

"Are you excited?" Montana asked. "I would be terrified. The dogs take the best of my maternal skills. I'm not sure I could manage more."

"I am terrified," Dakota admitted. "What if I screw up? What if she doesn't like me? What if she wants to go back to Kazakhstan?"

"The good news is, she can't talk," Nevada told her. "So asking to leave is out of the question."

"Small comfort," Dakota muttered.

Her mother joined her on the sofa and put her arm around her. "You're going to do just fine. It's going to be difficult at first, but you'll get the hang of it. Your daughter is going to love you and you're going to love her."

"You can't know that," Dakota told her, fighting panic.

"Of course I can," her mother said. "I guarantee it. And the best part of all is I finally get a granddaughter."

Nevada smiled. "Because it's all about you?"

"Of course." Denise laughed. "Not that I don't love my grandsons, but I'm dying to buy something pink and frilly. Please don't turn my only granddaughter into a tomboy, I beg you."

"I'll do my best," Dakota promised.

She looked around her crowded living room. Most of the women had brought food for the impromptu gathering. A few had brought casserole dishes that she could use later in the week. That was the way of life here. Everyone took care of their own.

A very pregnant Pia and her husband, Raoul, Dakota's boss, moved toward her.

"So typical," Pia said hugging her as tightly as her huge belly would allow. "Jumping to the front of the line. Here I am nearly two months away from giving birth and you're getting a baby first."

"Congratulations," Raoul said, kissing her cheek, while managing to keep his arm around Pia. "How you holding up?"

"I'm in a panic. I need to go shopping," she said. "I need diapers and a bed and a changing table." She knew there was more, but she couldn't think of what. One of those baby books would help, she thought. Didn't they have lists of what you needed? "Are there baby things that you don't need when the kid is six months old?" she asked.

"Not to worry," her mother told her. "I'll go shopping with you. I'll make sure you have everything you need for the flight home. You're going to give me your house key. By the time you get home tomorrow, everything will be waiting."

If anyone else had told her that, she wouldn't have believed her. But this was her mother. Denise knew how to get things done. You couldn't have six kids and not be an expert at management.

"Thank you," she whispered, then hugged her mother. "I couldn't get through this without you."

Emotions threatened to overwhelm her. None of this felt real, yet she knew it was happening. She was going to have a baby. A child of her own. Despite her broken body, she was getting her own family.

As she looked around the room, at all the friends and family who had dropped everything to stop by and wish her the best, Dakota realized she was wrong. She wasn't getting her own family. Her family had always existed. What she was getting instead was a wonderful, unexpected blessing.

DAKOTA HAD NEVER BEEN in a small plane before. But even flying in something roughly the size of a tin can was nothing when compared with the reality of becoming the mother of a six-month-old child she'd never met.

As Finn flew them southwest toward Los Angeles, she frantically flipped through the book she'd bought the previous day. The authors of *What to Expect the First Year* deserved some kind of award. And perhaps a house on the beach to go with that. Thanks to them, she at least had a place to start.

"Diapers," she muttered.

"You okay?" Finn asked.

"No. Yesterday Pia went on and on about different kinds of diapers. I thought she was silly. I mocked her. But what do I know about diapers? I can't remember the last time I diapered a baby. Any babysitting I did in high school was with older kids."

She looked at him, trying to breathe through her panic. "This is crazy. What are those people doing, leaving me alone with a child? Shouldn't they have investigated me more? There were only two home visits. Should I have to take some kind of practical evaluation? I don't know what formula to give her or if she's had shots. Kids get shots, don't they? Shots are a big deal."

"Calm down," Finn said soothingly. "Diapers aren't

that hard. I changed them when my brothers were babies. The disposable kind make it really easy."

"Sure. They were easy twenty years ago. Things could be different now."

He turned his attention back to the view out the front window. One corner of his mouth turned up. "You think they've made it more difficult to diaper a baby in the past twenty years? That doesn't make for a very good marketing plan."

Her chest felt tight. She told herself she was fine, but it seemed more and more difficult to breathe. "Don't use logic on me, mister. Do you really want me to get hysterical? Because I can."

"I don't doubt you," he said. "Dakota, you're going to have to trust yourself. As for the formula and shots, whoever has Hannah now will give you all that information. What did they tell you when they called?"

"Not that much," she muttered. "You heard most of the conversation."

"Didn't you have other interviews before?"

"Yes. Several. There was paperwork and we talked and they came to Fool's Gold and checked out me and my family. The process was very lengthy."

"So they've checked you out thoroughly. If they trust you, then you should try trusting yourself."

"Okay." She inhaled. "That could work."

"Remember, you have your mom for help. Your sisters and your friends. You can ask me anything you want."

She clutched the book tightly against her chest. "Would you please turn the plane around?"

"Anything but that. You know you want this baby."

He was right. Sure, it was going to be tough in the beginning, but she would learn. Mothers had learned for thousands of years. She was considered to have above average intelligence. That had to help.

She opened the parenting book and tried to read. The words were a blur. The illustrations frightened her, and the lists made it difficult to keep from screaming.

"I need more time. Can't I have more time?"

"We'll be landing in about forty minutes. Is that enough?"

She glared at him. "That's not funny."

"I wasn't trying to be funny." He clicked on the microphone and spoke to the tower.

Dakota didn't know much about flying, but she realized Finn had been telling the truth. As she looked out the window she saw the vastness of Los Angeles spread out before them.

She could do this, she told herself. She wanted to do this. She glanced at the notes her mother had given her. She knew she had the right supplies, even if she didn't know what all of them were. She was prepared for Hannah to be tired and cranky. There were soft blankets and diapers and stuffed animals in the baby bag. A couple of changes of clothing in different sizes, in case Hannah's clothes were damp.

Finn had promised to help her with the first couple

of diaper changes. There would be a family restroom in the airport terminal. Everything was going to be fine. She just had to keep telling herself that.

As promised, forty minutes later the plane rolled to a stop. Finn grabbed the diaper bag and stepped out of the plane. Dakota followed. She felt light-headed, and if her heart pounded any harder, it was going to jump out of her chest. That wasn't going to be pretty.

Finn checked in with the office and explained they were only going to be on the ground about an hour. Dakota had already called on the flight from Europe. Hannah and her escort were probably clearing customs right now.

They took the shuttle from the chartered airport over to the LAX international terminal. Finn had the diaper bag over one shoulder and held on to her hand. She clung to him, aware she probably looked pathetic, but not caring.

The main floor of the terminal was crowded with waiting families. People from dozens of countries spoke different languages. She wasn't sure how they were supposed to find a woman they'd never met, carrying a baby she'd never seen in person.

"I wish they'd sent me her picture as well as Hannah's," she said. "That would have made this easier."

"Dakota Hendrix?"

Dakota turned and saw a small nun with gray hair holding a crying baby. The little girl was the same one in the picture, she realized. Her face was flushed and she was much smaller than Dakota had expected. Even so, everything inside her went still, as if each cell in her body knew this was one of those extraordinary moments out of time.

"I'm Dakota," she whispered.

"I'm Sister Mary and this is your little girl."

Instinctively, Dakota held out her arms and took the child. Hannah didn't struggle. Instead her slight weight settled into Dakota's arms, and she gazed up at Dakota with dark brown eyes.

Hannah wore a pink jumper with a T-shirt underneath. Both were wrinkled and had a few stains on them. Not surprising, given how long she'd been traveling. Her dark hair was cut in an unflattering bowl style, but she was still beautiful.

Her full cheeks were deep red, and her mouth moved as if she were gathering her energy to cry. Even through her clothes, she felt warm.

Finn led them to a relatively quiet corner of the terminal. As people bustled around them, Sister Mary checked Dakota's identification. They both signed paperwork, and then it was done.

"Someone from the agency will call you in a couple of days, to set up an appointment," Sister Mary said. "Have you named her?"

"Hannah."

"A beautiful name," the nun said. "She's had a difficult journey. She has a low-grade fever and you'll want to get her ears looked at. I think she has an ear infection."

The other woman sighed as she passed over some baby Tylenol. "This is all we have. Money is so limited. There are so many children and so few resources. The doctor cleared her for the trip but that was more so she could come here. She's due for another dose in an hour."

Hannah's eyes had closed. Dakota stared at her, torn between the beauty of her daughter and the fear that she might be sick.

"Is she small for her age?"

"Not compared with some of the other children. I've brought a supply of her formula, a few diapers and her clothes." The nun glanced at her watch. "I'm sorry but I have a flight to catch."

"Yes, of course," Dakota said. "Please feel free to go. I'll get Hannah into a doctor as soon as possible."

"You have all the numbers for the agency," Sister Mary told her, handing Finn a small suitcase. "Call anytime, day or night."

"Thank you."

Finn stood and shook hands with her. When the nun had left, he turned to Dakota. "Are you okay?"

"No," she said softly. "Did you hear what she said? Hannah might be sick." The baby's eyes were closed. Her breathing was regular, but her skin was so red. It burned Dakota's fingers when she stroked her cheek. "I need to get her to a doctor."

"Do you want to do that here or do you want to go home?"

"Let's get her home." Dakota checked her watch. She

already had an appointment with the pediatrician late that afternoon. Better to take care of things there.

They went back the way they'd come. Fortunately, the shuttle driver had waited for them. It only took Finn a few minutes to check the plane and then get clearance. Less than an hour after they'd landed, they were airborne again.

This time, she sat behind the passenger seat with Hannah strapped into a car seat next to her. Dakota watched her anxiously, counting every breath.

"You doing okay?" Finn asked.

"I'm trying not to freak."

"She'll be okay."

"I hope so." She kept her gaze on her daughter. "She's so small." Too small. "I know she comes from a very poor part of the world, that the orphanage doesn't have much money or many resources. I knew there could be problems. They warned me about that."

When she'd first applied, there had been several live interviews where she'd seen videos of the different orphanages the agency worked with. She'd also spoken with other parents. They'd told her about children who were small for their age, but quickly caught up. They'd glossed over any initial difficulties.

Now, as Dakota felt her daughter's fiery cheek, her own eyes burned.

"I don't want anything to happen to her."

"You're taking her to a doctor. It's only a few hours."

She nodded because it was impossible to speak. Her

new daughter might be desperately ill, and she didn't have any way to make her better. Not medicine or even the experience to know how to make a poultice.

"Do you know what a poultice is?" she asked Finn.

"No. Why?"

"I thought it might help."

"Dakota, you have to relax. Wait until there's a reason to get upset, okay? You're going to need your energy to keep up with Hannah once she's crawling around."

"I hope you're right," she said, her voice oddly thick. It was only then, she realized she was crying.

She dropped her head into her hands and gave in to the tears. A couple of seconds later, Hannah woke up and started crying, too. The baby rubbed at her ears, as if they hurt her.

"It's okay," Dakota said quickly. "It's all right, sweetie. I have some medicine right here."

She dug out the Tylenol and measured the dose. The plane was amazingly steady, for which she was grateful.

"You're saving my life," she told Finn. "I couldn't have done this on my own. I don't know how to thank you."

"Just hang on."

She nodded, then offered Hannah the baby spoon. The little girl turned her head.

"Come on, sweetie. Take the yummy medicine. It will make you feel better."

After offering it a couple more times, Dakota lightly touched the girl's nose, then stroked her cheek. Hannah parted her lips, Dakota slipped the medicine inside, and the girl swallowed.

But whatever bothered her was too much for an over-the-counter remedy. Or the child was tired, or maybe scared. After all, she was surrounded by strangers. Whatever the reason, she cried louder and harder, her whole body shaking with her sobs. Dakota tried rocking the car seat and rubbing her tummy. She sang to her. Nothing helped.

Through the rest of the flight and the car ride to the pediatrician, Hannah screamed. The sound wrenched at Dakota's heart and made her feel nauseous. She didn't know what to do and knew that her ignorance could put an innocent child at risk. What had the agency been thinking—giving her a child?

Finally they pulled up in front of the pediatrician's office. She got Hannah out of her car seat, wrapped her in a blanket and carried the still-screaming infant into the waiting room, Finn close behind her.

Dakota, crying as well, could barely speak her name. The receptionist took one look at the two of them and motioned to the door on her left.

"Vivian will show you right into a room."

"Okay. Thanks."

Dakota looked at Finn. "I don't know how to thank you," she said over the baby's crying. "You don't have to wait. I'll call my mom and she'll come get me."

Finn brushed her cheek with his fingers. "Go. I'll

wait. I'm not going to leave you now. I have to see how this all ends."

"You're a good man. Seriously. I'll talk to someone about getting you a plaque."

One corner of his mouth curved up. "Nothing too big. You know I'm all about it being tasteful."

Despite everything, she managed a smile, then turned and followed the nurse into the examination room.

CHAPTER TWELVE

"THE KEY TO GOOD PARENTING is to keep breathing," Dr. Silverman told Dakota. "Seriously, if you pass out, you're no good to anyone." The pediatrician, a petite blonde in her late thirties, smiled.

Dakota wanted to shriek at her. Did the doctor think this was funny? Nothing about this was funny. It was horrifying and potentially life threatening, but not funny.

As soon as Dr. Silverman had walked into the examining room, Hannah had stopped crying. She'd submitted to the detailed exam with barely a sound and now lay in Dakota's arms, her hot body limp.

"She's exhausted," the doctor said. "That trip wouldn't be easy on anyone. I'm sure she's scared and confused. Her life hasn't been easy. Adding to that are the other problems."

Dakota braced herself for the worst. "The fever?"

The doctor nodded. "She has an infection in both ears and she has her first tooth coming in. She's way too small for her age, which isn't surprising given her circumstances. I don't love the formula they've been using, either."

She looked at the can of powder Dakota had given her. It was the same one Sister Mary had left with Hannah's things.

"All right," the doctor continued. "We're going to start her on a course of antibiotics. I don't like to use them for ear infections, but under the circumstances, she needs the jump to get better."

Dr. Silverman explained how to administer the medicine and told her what to expect with the combination of fever, first tooth and potential digestive upsets. They went over how to slowly transition Hannah to a more easily digested formula, and she offered suggestions on how much to feed her and how often.

"Normally at six months she'd be starting on solid foods, but I want you to hold off on that for at least three weeks. Let's get her healthy and her weight up a little. Then you can begin the process." Dr. Silverman explained how to make sure Hannah didn't get dehydrated.

"Do you have someone to help you?" the doctor asked. "The first few days will be the most difficult."

"My mom," Dakota said, trying to absorb all the information. "I have sisters and friends." Not to mention all the women in town who would step in.

"Good." The doctor pulled a business card out of her white coat pocket. "I'm on call this weekend. If you need me, the answering service will be able to get in touch with me."

Dakota took the card and sighed. "Thank you. Is there

any way I could convince you to move in with me for the next couple of years?"

Dr. Silverman laughed. "I think my husband would object, but I'll ask him."

"I really appreciate all of this."

The doctor touched the top of Hannah's head. "From what I can tell, she's basically healthy. Once we get her ears cleared up and her baby teeth in, your life will calm down. Try to stay relaxed and sleep when you can. Oh, and keep breathing."

They discussed when Dakota should bring her new daughter in for a follow-up visit, what circumstances would require a phone call to the doctor and what to look for that could be dangerous.

"I think you're going to be fine," the doctor told her. "Both of you."

Dakota nodded. "I understand and I appreciate all the information." Now if only she could figure out a way to keep it straight in her head.

She carried Hannah back into the waiting room. Finn stood when he saw her and closed the distance between them.

"What did she say?" he asked.

"Hopefully not more than I can remember." Dakota walked to the receptionist and made her follow-up appointment.

As she and Finn walked to his car, she told him about the visit and what the doctor had said. "I have to get a prescription filled," she said. "And change her formula, but I'm supposed to do that over time. Otherwise she could get really sick. Right now tummy trouble is the last thing she needs."

Getting overwhelmed seemed easy enough, she thought. Talk about going from zero to sixty without a whole lot of warning. Everyone was encouraging her, telling her she could do it, but at the end of the day, she was going to be the one left with the baby.

"I'll take you home," Finn told her. "Then I'll go get the prescription filled. One less thing for you to do."

Dakota finished strapping Hannah into her car seat, then closed the back door and straightened. "You've already done so much for me. I don't know how to thank you."

"I'll send you a list."

The drive back to Dakota's place didn't take very long. She kept looking over her shoulder, checking on Hannah. Exhaustion seemed to have set in, and the baby was sleeping.

She told herself that once Hannah started on the medication, everything would be better. At least that was her hope. There were—

"Somebody's having a party," Finn said as he pulled into her driveway.

She followed his gaze and saw there were at least a dozen cars parked on the street. She recognized a few of them and had a feeling she knew the owners of the others.

Warmth and relief chased away a good portion of

the fear. She really wasn't alone. How could she have forgotten that?

"It's not a party," she told him, then got out of the car. "Not in the way you're thinking."

He faced her across the roof of the vehicle. "Then what is it?"

"Come see."

She collected Hannah from her car seat. The baby barely stirred. Finn grabbed the diaper bag and followed her into the house.

She'd seen all the cars, but was still surprised by the number of people in her living room and kitchen. Her mother was there along with her sisters. Mayor Marsha and Charity, a very pregnant Pia. Liz and the feuding hairdressing sisters, Julia and Bella. Gladys and Alice, and Jenel from the jewelry store. There were women everywhere.

"There she is," Denise said, hurrying toward them. "Are you all right? How was the trip? How's your sweet little girl?"

Dakota handed her daughter over to her mother. But that was all she could do. Anything else was impossible. Her throat was too tight, her heart too full.

From where she stood, she could see stacks of presents. The packages were yellow and pink and white, topped with ribbons and bows. There was a high chair in the dining room and stacks of diapers on the chairs. She could see two steaming crockpots on the counter in her kitchen, a large basket of fruit and a bouquet of balloons.

As Denise rocked her new granddaughter in her arms, Nevada and Montana led Dakota into the spare room. Her small computer desk had been pushed to the far wall. Once-white walls had been painted the softest of pinks. New curtains hung at the windows. A thick rug covered the hardwood floor.

A crib sat in the center of the room. The linens were a cheerful yellow and white background with ballerina rabbits. A mobile of bunnies and ducks spun lazily overhead. There was a changing table and a dresser. The closet doors were open and tiny clothes hung on white hangers.

"It's some special paint," Nevada said. "There aren't any fumes, so it's safe for the baby. Everything else is organic or nontoxic."

Dakota didn't know what to say, so it was good that her sisters simply hugged her. She'd seen the town in action before, had been a part of it several times, but she'd never been on the receiving end of Fool's Gold love. The sense of connection and belonging nearly overwhelmed her.

"I didn't expect any of this," Dakota whispered, fighting her happy tears.

"Then our work here is done," Nevada teased.

Finn walked into the baby's room. "You people know how to throw a party," he said. "I'm going to get the prescription filled. I'll be back as soon as they're finished."

She nodded, rather than speak. From her perspective, she'd already spent much of the day crying. If she tried to thank him, she would only resume the waterworks. The man deserved a break.

Dakota allowed her sisters to lead her back to the living room. Her mother still held Hannah, and the baby seemed more relaxed in experienced arms. Several of the women jumped up to make room for her on the sofa. Dakota collapsed onto the cushions. A plate was put in her hands and a glass of something that looked like Diet Coke was placed on the coffee table in front of her.

"Now start at the beginning and tell us everything," her mother said. "Is Hannah all right? Finn mentioned he had to go out for medicine."

"She's going to be all right," Dakota said poking her fork at the pasta salad on her plate. "It might take a little while for us to get there, but Hannah is going to be just fine."

AURELIA STOOD on the sidewalk in the warmth of the early evening. Some people were just plain gifted. As she watched, Sasha and Lani stood in the park, fighting. They weren't just having an argument, they were yelling and waving their arms. At one point, Sasha grabbed Lani by her upper arms, hauled her close and kissed her.

Lani resisted at first. She twisted away, then raised her hand as if she were going to slap Sasha. He held her in place and kissed her again. This time, she surrendered. Her body went limp against his, and her hands drew him closer. From several feet away, it looked as though the young lovers had averted a crisis.

Aurelia knew better. She knew the fight was staged, a little scene for the cameras. "You have to admit they're really good," she told Stephen. "Whether or not they make it to the end of the show, they obviously have what it takes to be successful actors."

Stephen rested his hands on her shoulders. She wasn't sure why, and thinking about the possible reasons made her head hurt. He was a good guy. He was smart and fun to be with and really caring. Being with him was easy, even though it didn't show on camera. Every time she and Stephen were filmed together, the situation became awkward.

She couldn't say what was wrong. Her nature was to accept all the blame, but if that were true, then their time on camera should only be half bad. Instead it was, as Geoff had said the previous morning, truly awful.

"Hello, Aurelia."

Aurelia turned at the sound of her name and saw her mother walking toward her. Between work and the show, there hadn't been much time to visit. She'd called regularly, although her mother explained that was hardly the same and not nearly enough.

"Your mother, I presume," Stephen whispered in her ear.

Before she could agree, he stepped past her and

introduced himself. They shook hands. While keeping her mother's hand in his, Stephen thanked her for insisting Aurelia go on the show.

"Your daughter speaks of you frequently," he continued. "I can see how much she cares about you.

"No, she doesn't." Her mother sniffed, then withdrew her hand and glared at them both. "If she really cared about me, she would stop by to see me more."

"She's busy with her job and the show."

Aurelia stepped between them. She could see where the conversation was going, and while she appreciated Stephen looking out for her, she knew it was time for her to stand up for herself.

"Stephen, could you give us a minute?"

He nodded and moved back.

She led her mother over to a bench. But before she could speak, her mother jumped in.

"I can't believe how young he is. I'd hoped they were exaggerating, but now I've seen him in person. Obviously, they weren't. It's humiliating. Do you know what my friends are saying? The people at work? Don't you care about me at all?" Her mother sighed and shook her head. "You've always been selfish, Aurelia. And while we're on the subject, where's my check for this month?"

Aurelia stared at the woman who had raised her. It had always been just the two of them, and for so long, that had been enough. She had been brought up to believe that family was everything and that taking care of her mother was her responsibility. She'd told herself that her mother's bitterness could be excused, if not explained. Now that she thought about it, she wasn't exactly sure why her mother was so angry all the time.

Stephen didn't appreciate Finn's interference and saw it as nothing more than irritation. She knew better. Finn had put his life on hold because he was worried about his brothers. He wanted nothing for himself. Everything he did was for them. It had never been that way with her mother.

In Aurelia's family, her mother came first. Her mother was the important one. Somehow Aurelia had allowed herself to be manipulated. Part of the blame lay with her mother, but part of it lay with her. She was nearly thirty years old. It was time for her to change the rules.

"Mom, I really appreciate you encouraging me to go on the show. You were right—I haven't been doing anything to move on to the next stage of my life. I want to get married and have children. Instead, I hide myself at work and I spent all my free time with you."

"Not recently," her mother snapped.

"I'm sorry you feel that I haven't been paying enough attention to you. The time on the show has allowed me to get a little perspective. I'm your daughter, and I will always love you, but I need to have my own life."

"I see," her mother said icily. "Let me guess. I no longer matter."

"You matter very much. I don't want it to be an either/or. I think I can have a life, and you and I can still be close." Aurelia sucked in a breath. Now came the hard part. There was a knot in her stomach, a ball of fear and guilt.

"You have a really good job," she said slowly. "The house is paid for, as is your car." She should know. She paid off both loans herself. "Obviously, if there's an emergency, I want to help. But otherwise, you need to be responsible for your own bills."

Her mother sprang to her feet and glared at her. "Aurelia, this is not how you were raised. I'm the only mother you'll ever have. When I'm dead and gone, your selfishness will haunt you forever."

Aurelia watched her walk away. She knew her mother expected her to run after her, but she couldn't. The relationship they'd had before had been twisted and difficult. If she wanted it to change, she would have to be strong.

Stephen walked over to her and put his arm around her. "How do you feel?"

"Nauseous." She pressed her hand to her stomach. "We're not done. She'll be back. But I feel like I've taken the first step and that's something."

"It's great."

She looked up at him and smiled. "Great is healing some freakish disease. All I did was stand up to my mother."

"When was the last time you did that?"

"I was probably five."

"Then it's a big deal."

"You're too nice to me."

"Not possible."

They walked through the park, going away from the direction her mother had chosen. Aurelia told herself to ignore the guilt, and that in time, it would fade.

The reality was her mother was more than capable of supporting herself. But for some reason, she wanted to be taken care of.

"Maybe she thinks that having me pay for things proves that I love her," she said, thinking out loud.

"Or she wants to be able to tell all her friends. That gives her status with them. After all, what do their kids do?"

"I hadn't thought of that," she admitted. "On my good days, I tell myself to feel sorry for her rather than be angry or resentful."

"Does it work?"

"Sometimes."

They stopped by Lake Ciara. The sun had set and the sky was dark. She could see the first stars appearing. As a little girl, she'd wished on the stars, wanting them to make her dreams come true. Back then, most of her dreams had been about a handsome prince who would rescue her.

Now, looking back, she realized the rescue was about escaping her mother. While she'd appreciated having someone to care about her, that relationship had too many rules and strings. Even as a child, she'd felt the need to be loved for herself.

That desire was still there, but she knew it wouldn't come from the stars. Instead she would have to grow enough as a person to be able to accept that kind of love. Tonight had been a good first step. If her mother returned and tried to suck her back into their old relationship, she would do her best to stand strong.

"You're looking serious about something," he said.

"Reminding myself to stay strong."

He gazed into her eyes. "I really admire you."

She blinked. "Excuse me?"

"You've had to deal with so much. You're standing up to the only family you have. You're on this show."

While she appreciated the praise, she didn't feel especially worthy. "I'm nearly thirty years old. It's long past time for me to take on my mother. Besides, you stood up to your brother. I think you inspired me."

He shook his head. "It was just the two of you. Changing that relationship isn't easy." He grimaced. "I didn't stand up to my brother, in fact. I ran."

"That's different."

Without warning, he leaned in and kissed her. The feel of his mouth against hers made every part of her weak with longing. She kissed him back, knowing she shouldn't, telling herself she would stop any second now.

He wrapped his arms around her and pulled her hard against him. She went willingly, surrendering to a force bigger than her doubts. He was tall and strong and made her feel safe. Stephen always made her think that, as long as he was there, nothing bad could happen.

When his tongue touched her bottom lip, she parted for him. She met him stroke for stroke, feeling the heat grow. His hands moved up and down her back, then dropped to her hips. She surged toward him and felt his erection against her stomach.

The physical proof of where this was going shocked her into pulling away. She stepped back, her breathing ragged, and stared at him.

"Stop," she gasped, then shook her head and held up a hand. "You have to stop. *We* have to stop. This is crazy."

His blue eyes were bright with passion as he reached for her again, but she stepped back.

"I mean it," she said as forcefully as she could. It was difficult to be stern when all she wanted was to throw herself at him, to be held by him, to make love with him.

"I don't understand," he told her. "I thought..." He looked away. "My mistake."

"No." She grabbed his arm to keep him in place. "I'm sorry. I'm saying this all wrong. Stephen, this isn't about you. It's about me and us and where we are in our lives." She stared at him, willing him to understand.

"You're twenty-one years old. You need to finish college and go live your life. You have so many firsts, so many new experiences ahead of you, and I don't want to get in the way of that."

He didn't look the least bit understanding or appreciative of her attempt at self-sacrifice. "What the hell are you talking about? You're acting like you're a hundred years older than me. What first do I have in front of me that you don't have, too? Sure, you're a couple of years older, but so what? I like being with you. I thought you felt the same."

He liked being with her? It was hard to focus on what was important and not revel in that information. As for the firsts… "What about falling in love for the first time? You need to do that with someone your own age."

He stared at her with the expression of a confident male. At that moment there wasn't nine years between them. They were equals—or maybe he was a little in charge.

"Who have you been in love with?" he asked.

"Um, well, technically I haven't been in love, but we're not talking about me."

"Your point is that you have a whole world that I haven't experienced. But that's not true. You told me that even during college you were coming home every weekend. It's not like you had a great love affair. And since then, you've been involved with work and dealing with your mother."

Aurelia began to regret all the things she'd told Stephen. She hadn't realized he would use the information to win an argument.

"You're not a virgin, are you?" he asked.

She flushed but managed to keep looking at him. "No.

Of course not." She'd had sex. Once. Back in college. The night had been a disaster. For once, she hadn't gone home for the weekend. She'd stayed on campus and gone to a party where she'd gotten drunk for the first time in her life. Not to mention the last time.

She remembered going to the party and meeting a guy. He'd been cute and funny and they'd spent a couple of hours talking. Then he'd kissed her and... She'd never been sure what had happened next. Events were blurry. She remembered him touching her everywhere and being naked and that sex had hurt a lot more than she'd thought it would. But there were no details, just vague images.

She'd spent the next three weeks sweating whether or not she was pregnant, and the next few months waiting to see if there was anything else she had to worry about. She'd managed to escape relatively unscathed, but nothing about the encounter had made her want to repeat it. Until now. Until a twenty-one-year-old boy held her and kissed her. Suddenly there were possibilities.

Life was nothing if not unexpected, she thought sadly. She'd finally found someone she could care about, and everything about him was wrong. She supposed it could be worse. He could be married or eighty or gay.

"I know what I want to do with the rest of my life," she said. She had to do the right thing. "I have an established career and something resembling a life. Yes, I have issues with my mother, but I'm working on them. I'm going to keep working on them. You need to go finish college and find out what you want to do with the rest of your life. You need to find a girl your own age and fall in love and get married and have beautiful babies."

It was difficult to talk. Her throat tightened, and her eyes began to burn. "You're really special, Stephen. I want the best for you."

"This is bullshit. You think I care what other people think? What does age have to do with it? Why can't you be that girl? As for what I want to do with my life, why can't I figure that out with you?"

"Because you can't."

"There's an argument." He grabbed her by the shoulders. "You're the one that I want."

"You say that now. But you could change your mind tomorrow."

"So could you," he told her. "I should trust you because of your age?"

What she wanted to say was that he could trust her because he knew her. But she knew he would tell her the same applied to him. The part that scared her was that she knew he could be right. Which left her exactly where?

"You scare me," she admitted in a shaky whisper.

He immediately dropped his hands and took a step back. "I'm sorry. I didn't mean to—"

"Not that way," she said quickly. "I'm not afraid *of* you. I'm afraid of what I feel when I'm around you. I'm afraid of what I want." She shook her head. "I don't want to see you again privately. We'll go out on our dates for the show but that's all. I can't do anything else."

"Aurelia, no!"

She turned and walked away. It wasn't easy, but it was the right thing to do. She heard him start to come after her, then he seemed to change his mind. It was for the best, she told herself. It didn't feel like it right now, but eventually she would get over him and move on. He needed to be with someone else. As for what she needed, she'd always been very good at thinking about others first.

FINN HELD the front door open as the last of Dakota's guests left. When he'd returned with the prescription, the house had still been full of helpful friends. As he watched, they'd shown her the best way to feed the baby. That had been followed by a diapering demonstration and lots of other advice.

Denise, Dakota's mother, had offered to stay, but her daughter had refused.

"I need to know if I can do this," Dakota said, sounding brave.

"Call me if you need anything," her mother said. "I can be here in ten minutes."

Dakota looked like she was going to change her mind and ask her mother to stay, then shook her head. "We'll be fine."

Finn led Denise to the door.

"If things look desperate," Denise whispered, "you call me."

"I will," he promised. Although if things looked

desperate, his plan was to stay the night. It might have been a long time since his brothers were babies, but Finn remembered the drill.

He returned to the living room only to find it empty. Making a logical assumption, he went down the short hallway and into the baby's room.

Hannah lay in her crib. Earlier, Dakota had changed the baby's clothes. Everyone had agreed that she could wait on the bath. There had already been enough new experiences for one day.

Hannah stared up at the gently turning mobile. She was mesmerized by the rotating bunnies. But even as she stared, her eyes slowly drifted closed.

"I didn't expect her to be so beautiful," Dakota whispered as she brushed her daughter's cheek.

He came up behind her and put his hand on her waist. "In about fifteen years, you're going to have guys lined up around the block."

Dakota smiled at him. "Right now I'd settle for getting through the night."

"She's on her medicine and seems to be feeling better. Her tummy is full, you know how to change a diaper."

She stepped away from the crib. He followed her into the living room.

"You're right," she said brightly. "I've had a crash course in parenting. I'm going to be fine." She smiled, which didn't fool him. "You've been great. I really appreciate all your help. It's been such a long day, you must be exhausted."

She was working the program, he thought. Faking it with the best of them. He could see the terror in her eyes, but she was determined to be brave. At least on the outside.

This was where he told her he was leaving, he reminded himself. What they'd had before had been great. Fun and uncomplicated. Hannah changed everything. Dakota was now a mother. There were new rules, and he wasn't going to screw with them. Getting out while he could made the most sense.

Except he couldn't seem to leave. Her pretend bravery touched him. Her willingness to throw herself into a situation for which she was desperately unprepared made him admire her. Add that to the fact that he already liked her, and there was no way he could walk out. Even though it was the smart thing to do.

"I'm staying," he told her. "You can't change my mind, so don't bother trying. You're stuck with me for the night."

"Really?"

He nodded.

She sank to the sofa and covered her face with her hands. "Thank God. I was trying to make everyone think I know what I'm doing. I don't have a clue. I've never been so scared in my life. She's completely dependent on me and I don't know what I'm doing."

He sat down next to her and pulled her against him. "Here's what we're going to do. You're going to get the baby monitor and put it in the bedroom. Then we're going to get ready for bed. I'll be here, so you're going to sleep as much as you can."

"I'd like to sleep," she admitted, leaning her head on his shoulder.

"Then here's your chance."

She raised her head. "Thank you for everything. You're my hero."

"I've never been anyone's hero before."

"I doubt that."

He stood and pulled her to her feet. Together, they walked toward the bedroom.

Inside of him, a voice screamed that this was trouble, but he silenced the words. He wasn't getting involved. He was staying for one night and then things would go back to the way they'd been before.

CHAPTER THIRTEEN

"WE NEED TO MAKE THE SHOW more interesting," Geoff said. "I want to use one of the festivals as a backdrop. This town has them every other week."

"Sometimes more," Dakota agreed. "I think the Tulip Festival is next. I'll talk to the mayor and see what she says about you filming there."

She had a feeling Mayor Marsha would be less than amused at the idea but would still probably agree to it. After all, keeping Geoff in plain view was safest for everyone.

"Good," Geoff told her. "We need to add some drama to the show. I've been getting complaints from the executives. I'm not sure the festival is going to be enough. Do you think we could get a police band radio and follow the cops? Maybe if there was an explosion or something."

"We don't have an explosion rate here," she told him, doing her best not to roll her eyes.

"Too bad," he muttered.

Dakota wasn't sure what to say to that.

Geoff glanced at the pad in his hand, as if checking to see if there was more. Just then, Hannah made a cooing sound.

The producer turned toward the noise and saw the baby in her playpen. Hannah was on her back, staring at the mobile Dakota had attached to the side of the crib.

"Is that a baby?" Geoff asked.

"Uh-huh."

"Yours?"

She hid a smile. "Yes."

He turned to leave, then looked at her again. "Were you pregnant and I missed it?"

"She's six months old."

"So that's a no?"

The smile escaped. "I wasn't pregnant before."

"Okay. Because I've been told that I'm not very observant when it comes to anything other than the show. But I would have noticed if you were pregnant."

"I'm sure that's true."

He looked at Hannah. "She's yours, right?"

Dakota thought about explaining about the adoption, but decided he really wasn't that interested. "She's mine."

"Okay, then. You'll ask about the explosion?"

"No, but I'll ask about the festival."

Geoff sighed. "I guess that will have to do."

"I guess it will."

He left.

Dakota laughed, then crossed to the playpen and picked up Hannah. "What a silly man," she said, holding her daughter in her arms. She felt the girl's forehead and was pleased that it was cool. The antibiotic was working quickly.

Her mother had stopped by that morning to check on her and warn her that Hannah's fever could climb during the day. Dakota was prepared with Tylenol drops. So far, though, everything was going well. Hannah had been eating and seemed less frightened of all the new experiences.

While Dakota sat in her chair, holding the baby, she called the mayor and explained about the festival.

"If I say no, will he take his show and go away?"

"Probably not."

"Then I suppose he can film it. How's Hannah?"

"Doing well. She slept for a few hours last night. She's eating well."

"Good. You know you can call me if you need anything."

"Yes, I know. Thanks."

Dakota made a couple more calls, then walked around the production office with her daughter. No one seemed overly interested in the child, which was fine. These people didn't know her.

When they got back to her desk, she put the baby in her car seat and placed her so that she could see the morning filming out the window. Dakota did her best to work but found herself glancing at Hannah every few seconds.

She had a baby. A child of her own. The true miracle of it all had yet to sink in.

A few minutes later, Bella Gionni, one of the feuding Gionni sisters, walked into her office.

"I wanted to see how things were going," the dark-haired, forty-something woman said. "We were all worried about your first night. How was it?"

"Good," Dakota told her. "Hannah slept relatively well. She's doing better. I don't think her ears are bothering her as much."

What she didn't admit was that Finn had spent the night with her. Every time Hannah had whimpered, Dakota had jumped to her feet and raced into the baby's room. Finn had been right there with her, helping with the formula, getting her settled in the rocking chair. She couldn't have done it without him.

"Can I hold her?" Bella asked.

"Of course," Dakota said. The doctor had told her to make Hannah's life as normal as possible. In Fool's Gold, that meant knowing lots and lots of people.

She took the baby out of the car seat. Bella held out her arms, and Hannah seemed to lean into her. From what Dakota could tell, the little girl was enjoying the attention. Perhaps there hadn't been enough at the orphanage.

"Who's that beautiful little girl?" Bella asked, cooing softly. "That's you. Yes, it is. You're going to be a heartbreaker."

Dakota knew this was the first of many visits. Not only would Bella come back again, but there would be others. The women in town would take care of them both.

While she appreciated the support and knew she could depend on it, she knew that last night it had been Finn who had kept her sane. Having him stay had meant everything to her. It had been better than sex. Not that she would say so if he asked, because the sex was amazing. But last night had been about taking care of her. About being the man she needed.

She'd never been able to depend on a man before. The experience was new, and she found she liked it. Still, it wasn't something she should get used to. After all, Finn was leaving. He'd made that very clear.

Even so, she was determined to enjoy what she had while it lasted.

AURELIA KNEW there was a problem when three more days passed and she hadn't heard from her mother. Normally they didn't go an entire day without speaking at least twice. While she knew she had to learn to stand on her own, there was no reason she also had to lose contact with the only relative she had. After work the following Friday, she went by her mother's house.

Her mother answered the door right away.

"Hi, Mom."

"Are you here to see me?" her mother asked, feigning surprise.

"Yes. We haven't spoken in a few days. I wanted to check on you."

"I can't imagine why. You've made it clear that you

care nothing about me. I could drop dead in the street and you would simply step over me."

Aurelia told herself to be patient. She had established new boundaries that her mother didn't like, and they were going to be tested. If she respected herself, her mother would learn to respect her, as well.

Instead of getting angry or frustrated, she smiled. "You have such a way with words. You always create the most amazing visuals. I wish I'd inherited that ability from you." With that, she slipped past her mother and entered the house.

"Have you made tea yet?" she asked as she made her way to the kitchen. Her mother always made tea after work, unless she was going out with friends.

There was no kettle on the stove, which meant her mother was going out that evening. Good. Conversation couldn't drag on for hours.

Her mother followed her, then came to a stop in the middle of the kitchen. Her arms were folded tightly across her chest and her mouth was pinched.

"Did you come here to mock my poverty?"

Aurelia raised her eyebrows. "There you go again. Mom, have you ever thought of writing fiction? You'd be so good at it. Maybe short stories, you know, for those women's magazines?"

"I don't appreciate you making fun of me."

"I'm not," Aurelia said gently. "I wanted to check on you and make sure everything was all right. I'm sorry you don't feel comfortable calling me. I hope that will change."

"It will change when you stop acting so selfishly. Until then, I want nothing to do with you."

There it was. The gauntlet. In the past, Aurelia had always given in. The thought of being abandoned by her mother had crushed the little spirit she had left. But today was different. Sure, she felt like throwing up, but that would pass. She meant what she'd said before. She was happy to help in an emergency, but she was done being a financial and emotional convenience.

She'd had plenty of time to think about her actions. Stephen had respected her wishes. She hadn't heard from him once. Why did her mother find it so easy to ignore her while Stephen found it so easy to do exactly what she asked? A dilemma for another time, she told herself.

"I hope you have fun tonight with your friends," she said quietly. "It was nice to see you, Mom." She turned to leave.

Her mother caught up with her in the hallway. "You're leaving? Just like that?"

"You said you didn't want to have anything to do with me unless I went back to the way I was. I can't do that. I'm sorry if you think that makes me selfish. I don't think it does."

"I'm your mother. I should come first in your life."

Aurelia shook her head. "No, Mom. I need to come first in my own life. I need to take care of myself."

Her mother put her hands on her hips. "I see. Selfish

to the end. I know what you're saying to yourself. When in doubt, blame the mother. I suppose this is all my fault."

"I didn't say that and I'm not thinking that. But if you're first in your life and you're first in my life, where does that leave me?"

She didn't expect an answer, but she waited for a few seconds anyway. It seemed polite. Her mother opened her mouth and closed it.

"I'll talk to you soon," Aurelia said, then left.

On the walk home, she replayed the conversation in her head. For once, she was happy with what she'd said. She might not be where she needed to be, but she was making progress.

She found herself wanting to call Stephen and tell him what had happened. Only she couldn't. They were seeing each other on the show and nowhere else. She knew she'd made the right decision, but that didn't make the loneliness any easier to bear.

DAKOTA WRAPPED the towel around Hannah. Her daughter was warm and rosy after her bath. Denise stood at the end of the changing table and gently tickled her granddaughter's toes.

"Who's a beautiful baby girl?" Denise asked in a singsong voice. "Who's special?"

Hannah waved her fingers in the air and laughed.

"She's feeling much better," Dakota said. Knowing her daughter was healing was such a relief. Getting used to dealing with a baby was hard enough, but when that baby was sick, it was a nightmare.

She and Hannah had been together nearly a week now. They'd established something of a routine. The follow-up visit to the pediatrician had been much better than that first encounter. The doctor had said Hannah was doing well. Her weight was up, and her ears were clear. Hannah had to finish the course of antibiotics and there was still teething to get through, but all that was doable.

"She's eating well," Denise said. "I can tell she's feeling better. Do you have her on the new formula?"

"Yes. We were lucky. Her tummy handled the change well. The doctor said to start her on solid food in another week, which is a whole week sooner than we expected. That will help her gain more weight and catch up with her age group."

She finished drying the little girl, then put a new diaper on her and slipped her into her pajamas. By then, her daughter was half asleep. Her eyes sunk closed and her body relaxed.

"Go ahead," she told her mother. "You put her to bed."

Denise smiled at her. "Thanks," she whispered, and picked up the baby.

Hannah snuggled close. Denise crossed the room and settled the little girl on her back in the crib. After starting the mobile, they dimmed the lights and stepped out of the room.

"I'm so lucky with her," Dakota said, as she adjusted the volume on the baby monitor. "Hannah enjoys being with people. I've heard that some of the children from orphanages are cautious around anyone new. In this town, that would be a problem."

They settled on the sofa. Her mother looked at her.

"You're doing well," her mother told her. "I know you're terrified half the time, but it doesn't show. Soon you'll be terrified only a quarter of the time, which is something to look forward to."

"Thanks," Dakota said. "You're right. I am scared. It's getting a little better. Knowing that she's healing helps a lot. As does all the company. Ethan and Liz stopped by a couple of days ago and I'm getting lots of visits at work." She smiled at her mother. "You're helping a lot, too."

"I love having her here. Finally a grandchild who lives close to me. You'll have to tell me if I become one of those annoying, interfering grandparents. I'm not saying I'll change my behavior, but I will at least feel guilty about it."

Dakota laughed. "As long as you feel guilty, then I guess it's okay."

"So you're handling the stress? You're sleeping?" her mother asked.

"Better than I was." Finn had stayed with her the first couple of nights. Just having him around had made everything better. But she'd realized that at some point she had to face motherhood on her own. She hadn't slept at all the first night he'd been gone, but since then she'd been sleeping more and more.

"Sometimes I freak out for no reason," she admitted. "Does that get better?"

"Yes and no," her mother said. "You freak out less and then they become teenagers. That's when the real nightmare begins." Denise smiled brightly. "But that's some time away. Enjoy Hannah while she's still young and rational."

"We weren't that bad," Dakota told her.

"You didn't have to be that bad. There were six of you."

"I guess you have a point there."

Her mother studied her. "At the risk of interfering, how are things going with Finn? I haven't seen him around. Or is he here when I'm not?"

"Finn has been a great help with Hannah," Dakota admitted. "Which has been wonderful. But romantically…"

It was difficult to explain the relationship, mostly because she didn't understand it herself.

"He's a great guy, but we want different things. We were having fun together, only it started to get complicated. He's here about his brothers and…" She shrugged. "I don't actually have an answer to that question."

"I got that," her mother said. "I'd wondered if it was getting serious with him."

"It wasn't," Dakota assured her, then wondered if she was lying.

She thought about Finn a lot and missed him. She knew he was working at the airport and told herself that was why he hadn't been around. There were plenty of tourists to keep him busy. And Raoul had mentioned he'd had another meeting with Finn about starting a nonprofit program.

"I see." Her mother studied her. "None of my girls are married. Sometimes I think it's my fault."

"As much as I would love to put all this on you," Dakota told her, "I don't think I can. I've never been in love. I've always wanted to be, I always thought I would be. There were guys in college who were great but I couldn't see myself spending the rest of my life with them. Maybe it's me."

"It's not you. You have a warm and giving heart. You're completely adorable. I think the men in this town are stupid."

Dakota laughed, then leaned close and hugged her mother. "Thank you for your unwavering support. As for the men in this town, I don't have an answer for that, either."

"And you're sure about Finn?"

"He's looking for less responsibility, not more. Once he gets his brothers settled, however that works out, he's going back to his regular life. Even if I'd been tempted before, having Hannah changes everything."

Dakota was very aware of the fact that having a baby, being a single mother, was only going to make the man thing more difficult. But they were two different animals—she didn't want to give up one kind of love for another.

"I want what you had," she told her mother. "I want a great love. A love that will sustain me for the rest of my life."

"Is that what you think?" her mother asked. "That we only get one great love?"

"Do you think differently?"

"Your father was a wonderful man and I loved him very much. But I don't believe there is only one man for each of us. Love is all around us. Maybe I'm foolish and too old to be thinking that, but I would like to be in love again."

Dakota did her best to keep from showing her shock. Dating was one thing, but falling in love? She'd always assumed there wouldn't be anyone for her mother but her father.

Now, looking at Denise, she saw her for what she was. An attractive, vital woman. There were probably a lot of men who would be interested in her.

"Do you have anyone in mind?" she asked.

"No, but I'm open to the possibility. Does that bother you?"

"It makes me envy you," Dakota admitted. "You're willing to take a chance again."

"You've taken a chance on that little girl. The right man will come along. You'll see."

"I hope so."

She wanted to fall in love, too. The problem was,

thinking about being in love made her think about Finn.
Was she truly interested in him? Or was it just easier
to distract herself by wanting the one man she couldn't
have?

CHAPTER FOURTEEN

DAKOTA SAT ON THE FLOOR with her daughter. They were on a blanket, in the middle of her living room. There were several age-appropriate toys scattered around. Dakota had a large picture book in her hand and was slowly reading the story to Hannah.

"Lonely bunny was happy to have found a friend." She pointed to the drawing on the page. "See the bunny? He's not lonely anymore. He has a friend now." She pointed to the fluffy white kitten, nose to nose with the formerly lonely bunny.

"See the kitten?" She pointed to the kitten. "He's white."

From all that she had read, Hannah needed plenty of verbal and visual stimulation. Hannah seemed interested in the story. She would look where Dakota pointed, and the bright colors of the picture book kept her attention. Dakota was about to turn the page when someone knocked on her front door.

She stood and collected Hannah. She felt her breath catch in her chest as she saw Finn standing on her small front porch.

He looked as sexy as ever, especially when he gave

her a slow grin that made her thighs heat. "Hey. I should have called first, shouldn't I? Sorry. I've been doing a lot of flying and this was my first break. How are you?"

"Good. Come on in."

He stepped into the house, then reached for Hannah. "How's my best girl?" he asked.

The baby reached toward him. He pulled her against his chest, and she settled in as if she, too, had been missing him.

"You're growing," he murmured, kissing the top of Hannah's head. "I can see the difference already." He turned his attention to Dakota. "You look good, too, by the way."

She grinned. "Gee, thanks. I appreciate the compliment, even if it is an afterthought."

She led the way into the living room. Finn settled on the blanket, with Hannah on his lap. Dakota sat across from him.

He'd always had the kind of looks that made her think of tangled sheets and late mornings spent in bed. But there was something about seeing a strong, confident man holding a baby. She'd never experienced it before but now she totally got the appeal.

"How are things on the show?" he asked. "I talked to Sasha a couple of days ago and he was complaining that they needed to go on a hot date."

"Bad choice of words. After the fire incident, I'm thinking even Geoff is hesitant to let those two loose."

"I think that's why they're staying close to home.

Nothing's been scheduled with Stephen and Aurelia. I don't think they're interesting enough for Geoff."

"Probably not. He's getting frantic about keeping the ratings up. He mentioned he would love an explosion at the Tulip Festival. I told him there was no way that was going to happen. So how's the flying? Miss those Alaska mountains?"

"Not as much as I would have thought. There are plenty of people who would rather fly to Fool's Gold than drive. I don't get it—the drive is beautiful, and I say that as a pilot. Still, it's keeping me busy. I've flown a few cargo flights and had an interesting afternoon taking a whooping crane from San Francisco to San Diego. The bird I flew is supposed to be a hot breeder." He chuckled. "He didn't look any different to me, but I'm not a girl whooping crane."

As he talked, Hannah reached toward one of the small stuffed animals on the floor.

"Do you want that?" Finn asked. He picked up the small pink stuffed elephant and handed it to her.

"Ga ga ga."

Dakota stared at the little girl. "Did you just say ga?" She turned to Finn. "You heard that, right? She spoke."

Finn rolled onto his back and held the little girl up in his arms. "Look at how smart you are. You can say ga."

Hannah squealed with delight as Finn continued to hold her in the air. When he rolled back to a seated position, she reached for her elephant. He handed it to her.

Dakota couldn't stop grinning. "I know I had nothing to do with it, but I feel so proud."

"It's a parent thing."

That's right. She was a parent now. "I need to remember what this feels like so that when she's fourteen and driving me crazy, I have something to fall back on."

He chuckled. "You are a woman with a plan."

They watched the little girl. She seemed mesmerized by her pink elephant.

"One of the guys I flew in told me there's talk of building a casino just north of town," Finn said.

"I heard about that. Apparently it's going to be a very upscale facility. More tourists are always a good thing."

"I also heard plenty of talk about the man shortage. You know the world thinks Fool's Gold is filled with desperate women."

Dakota winced. "It's been an ongoing problem. I told you about the grad student who wrote about the man shortage in her thesis. The media picked it up and went crazy. That's why we have Geoff here, doing his show. Demographically, men might be outnumbered, but we are hardly desperate women." She looked at him. "Although it does explain my attraction to you."

"You'd want me no matter how many men were in town."

"There's certainly nothing wrong with your ego."

"Or any other part of me."

He was right about that, Dakota thought, remembering the feel of his body against hers. But she wasn't going to admit it.

"There seem to be plenty of guys in town," he said. "Is there still a shortage?"

"I'm not sure. They were coming in by the busload last fall, but I don't know how many of the men stayed. Still, the town is fine. That's what made all the media attention so frustrating."

"It's a good town," he told her. "You'll get through this."

"Mayor Marsha is counting the minutes until Geoff and his production company leaves. She's afraid of what they'll want to do next. I'm pretty sure Geoff finds Fool's Gold quiet and boring. We don't want him writing our tourist brochure, that's for sure."

As they were speaking, Hannah started to lean more heavily against Finn. Her eyes began to close in that familiar way.

"Someone's getting sleepy," Dakota said, scrambling to her feet. She glanced at the clock. "It's a little past time for her nap. I don't want to put her down too late. She's nearly sleeping through the night."

Finn handed her the baby, then stood. "Not something you want to mess with."

"Exactly. Sleep is still precious. More so for me than for her."

Dakota headed for her daughter's room. Finn trailed

along behind her. She checked the baby's diaper, then put her in her crib and turned on the mobile.

Finn moved next to her and touched Hannah's cheek. "Sleep well, little girl."

The baby sighed and then drifted off to sleep. Dakota picked up the monitor and stepped out of the room. Finn closed the door behind them.

"How long does she sleep?" he asked.

"About two hours. Then we have dinner and I read to her some more. The evenings are—"

She had more she was going to say but never got the chance. They were barely in the living room when Finn put his hand on her waist and drew her to him. She went without thinking and was glad she did when his mouth settled on hers.

Her first thought was that it had been too long between kisses. He'd been busy with flying, and she'd been adjusting to being a mother. But when she felt his tongue on her bottom lip, her thoughts faded as she lost herself in the fiery passion that lurked whenever he was near her.

He tasted of coffee and mint. His body was strong and hard against hers. She wrapped her arms around his neck, trying to get closer, to feel all of him. His heat surrounded her.

More, she thought hungrily. She wanted more.

Still holding on to the monitor, she led the way into her bedroom. She put the monitor on her dresser and checked the sound, then turned to him.

Neither of them had said anything. She suspected neither of them had planned this moment. But if the desire in his eyes was anything to go by, he wasn't going to object, and she knew she wanted everything he had to offer.

He stepped toward her. She moved into his arms.

Perhaps this wasn't the smartest decision she'd made that day, but she was okay with that. There might be consequences for giving herself to Finn when she knew that eventually he would leave. She would worry about that later, she promised herself, getting lost in his kiss and the feel of his hands on her body. For now, there was only the man and the way he made her feel.

FINN WAS AWARE of Dakota's even breathing. It might only be four in the afternoon, but she was exhausted. He would like to take credit, but an hour of passionate lovemaking was nothing when compared to caring for a six-month-old baby.

He doubted she slept for more than four hours at a stretch. So when he heard the sound of Hannah stirring, he got up from the bed and turned down the monitor.

After pulling on boxers and jeans, he walked barefoot into the baby's room. Hannah smiled when she saw him and raised her arms, as if she wanted to be picked up. He obliged her and held her tiny body against his bare chest.

"Did you sleep well, pumpkin cheeks? Your mama is

getting some rest right now. So we're going to be very quiet."

He walked over to the changing table. After taking care of her diaper, he carried her into the kitchen and checked the refrigerator. Knowing Dakota as he did, he wasn't surprised to see several bottles already prepared.

"You have to admire a woman who knows how to take care of business," he told the baby.

A pan of water sat on the stove. He turned on the burner and waited for the water to heat. He briefly glanced at the microwave. A pan of water might be old-fashioned, but it was more reliable.

While they waited, he rocked the baby in his arms. She kept eye contact with him and offered a tentative smile.

"You are going to be a heartbreaker one day," he told her. "Just like your mother."

Dakota was more than that, he thought, remembering the taste of her, the feel of her skin. She was a temptation. Not just because of how she got to him in bed, but because he enjoyed her company. She was the kind of woman a man looked forward to coming home to. Under other circumstances...

No, he told himself firmly. She was not for him. He had a life, and it didn't include a woman and a baby. He'd been the responsible guy for the past eight years. Now that his brothers were nearly grown, he was going to be free. And he had plans. A new business to build. The last thing he wanted was to be tied down.

When the bottle was heated, he tested the milk. Assured that the temperature was correct, he returned to Hannah's room and settled in the rocking chair.

The little girl latched on to the bottle eagerly. As she ate, he watched her watch him. There was something about her big brown eyes. He smiled at her. She raised her hand and grabbed on to his little finger, holding tight. Deep inside, he felt something shift, almost as if making room.

Ridiculous, he told himself.

When she'd finished eating, he grabbed a towel from the pile by the rocker, put it on his shoulder and burped her. She snuggled close. He held her as he rocked, humming tunelessly.

"Your mom said that she reads to you now. I saw the book about the bunny. I guess that's more appropriate than *Car and Driver*. Although you might be into cars. It's probably too soon to tell. And we should check on your mom. Last I saw, she was naked." He grinned. "She looks good naked."

"I'll have to take your word on that."

Finn looked up and saw Dakota's mother standing in the doorway. He stood, then wondered if that was a mistake. He was wearing jeans and nothing else, holding Dakota's baby in his arms. Dakota was in her room, probably still asleep. And naked, as he'd so helpfully pointed out.

Although he was usually good on his feet, he couldn't think of a single thing to say.

Denise approached and took the baby. "I suppose I should have called first. Dakota's asleep?"

He nodded.

He felt like a seventeen-year-old caught making out with his girlfriend. Except he wasn't seventeen, and they'd done a whole lot more than kiss.

Getting dressed seemed to be the first priority, he thought, wondering how he could get around Denise without being obvious. Then he heard a sound in the hall.

"Did you take care of Hannah?" a very sleepy Dakota asked, walking into the room.

She'd pulled on a robe and nothing else. Her hair was mussed, her mouth swollen from his kisses. She looked rumpled and satisfied, and then completely shocked when she spotted her mother.

"Mom?"

"Hello. I was telling Finn that I should have called first."

"I, ah…" Dakota grinned. "At least you didn't show up two hours ago. That would have been awkward."

Her mother laughed. "For all of us." She stepped out of the way. "I think Finn was trying to get past me without being obvious."

"I thought I'd get dressed," he murmured.

"Don't put on a shirt on my account," Dakota's mother told him and winked.

"Mom, you're going to frighten him."

"I can handle it," he said, wondering if he was telling the truth.

He excused himself and escaped into Dakota's bedroom. Once there, he dressed quickly. He was stepping into his boots when Dakota showed up.

"Sorry about that," she said. "She didn't have a habit of stopping by before I had Hannah. I didn't think she would today."

"It's okay."

She shrugged. "It's embarrassing."

"I'll survive." He pulled on his boots, then straightened and kissed her. "You okay?"

"Uh-huh. Thanks for letting me sleep."

"You needed it. Hannah is fed."

"I could tell. She has that look of happy contentment."

He touched her cheek. "So do you."

He was a good man, Dakota thought, as she walked Finn to the door.

Her mother was hiding out in the kitchen, which Dakota appreciated. Saying goodbye in private would be a lot easier. Of course, she still had to face her mother and explain what was going on.

"I'll see you soon," Finn said.

She nodded and hoped he was telling the truth.

Dakota returned to the kitchen where she found her mother playing with Hannah.

"I'm glad you got some rest," her mother told her. "I know how tired you've been."

Dakota waited, but her mother didn't say any more. "You have to want to know about Finn."

"I think I know enough already. He's the kind of man who looks good holding a baby. Should I worry about you?"

"No. I'm protecting my heart." For a moment, she allowed herself to wish that she didn't have to. That, in addition to looking good holding a baby, Finn was the kind of man who stayed. But she knew the truth.

"Are you sure you're not already in love with him?"

Talk about a crazy question. "Of course I'm sure. I would never let that happen."

Aurelia stood awkwardly on the sidewalk. Karen, one of the production assistants, had emailed her the time of her next date with Stephen. Aurelia had hoped everyone would just forget about her and Stephen, but that was too much to ask. Now she had to not only go on a date with him, but she had to do it in front of the camera crew and who knew how many people watching on television.

If only they'd been voted off sooner, she thought, shifting her weight from foot to foot. But that was the coward's way out.

In truth, she owed Stephen an apology. Not that they would ever be right for each other, but that didn't excuse how she'd handled the situation. She hadn't been very nice. Probably because there was a part of her that didn't want to give him up. There was a part of her that didn't care about the age difference or the fact that he deserved someone who was where he was in life.

Somehow everything had gotten so complicated, and she didn't know how to make it simple again.

"Aurelia?"

She turned toward the voice and found Stephen standing behind her. Despite her best attempt, he'd still managed to sneak up on her. For a single heartbeat, she felt only happiness at the sight of him. So tall and strong, so handsome. She smiled and knew he could read everything she was thinking.

Then reality returned and, with it, the realization that she could never be right for him.

"I guess we have a date to get through," she said. "If we continue to be the most boring couple, I'm sure we'll get voted off this week."

"Is that what you want?" he asked.

"It makes the most sense."

She found it difficult to talk. When she was that close to him, her brain didn't work right. She could only think about him holding her and how she felt when he kissed her.

Why did it have to be like this? Why couldn't he be older or her younger?

"I didn't want to hurt you," she blurted. "I never wanted to be someone you would regret. I'm not afraid for me. I'm afraid for you."

She clamped her hand over her mouth and wished

there was a way to call back the words. She should never have told him that, never have admitted the truth. He would think she was an idiot. Or worse, he would feel sorry for her.

Without thinking, she started walking away. She had no destination in mind, just a burning need to escape the situation. But before she could go anywhere, he was in front of her, his hands on her shoulders, his intense blue eyes staring into her face.

"I could never regret you. Us."

How she wanted that to be true. In this moment, it probably was, but one of them had to think beyond today.

"Let's say I believe you," she said. "So what happens next? What are you going to do?"

He grinned. That happy, easy grin that made her toes curl.

"Go back to college."

She stared at him. "Excuse me? Go back to college? That's what your brother wanted all along. Why would you agree to it now?"

"Because I know it means you'll take me seriously."

She opened her mouth, then closed it. "Really?"

He nodded. "I liked college. I enjoyed studying engineering. I've been taking classes in bioengineering, with an emphasis on alternative fuels. It's a growing industry. College was never the problem—it was Finn. He knows Sasha isn't interested in the family business, so he's expecting me to be the one to join him." He shrugged. "I like flying, but I don't want to make it my career. I've never wanted that."

"I know that, but Finn doesn't. You have to tell him."

His mouth twisted. "Would you tell him if you were me? Finn has a bug up his ass about the business and college. I think it has more to do with our parents dying and him having to raise us. He's done a good job, but he's gotten too used to running our lives. I knew he expected me to go into the family business. I didn't know how to tell him I didn't want that. So I did something drastic—I came with Sasha to be on the show. I never expected to find you."

She stared at him. "I don't understand." Her voice was a whisper.

"I thought I was looking for something. Now I get that I was looking for some*one*. You. I'll go back to school and get my degree because it will make you happy. But also because it will make me the kind of man you want. This is all about you, Aurelia. Don't you get that?"

All she heard was a faint buzzing sound. The world seemed to move around her, and it took her a second to realize she was on the verge of passing out. She couldn't catch her breath, but then Stephen was kissing her and little things like breathing didn't matter.

She kissed him back, losing herself in the feel of his mouth on hers. The moment was everything she'd ever wanted. Better than that, the man was everything she'd ever wanted.

He raised his head and stared at her. "I love you, Aurelia. I think I have from the first moment I saw you."

"I love you, too."

She hadn't been sure she would ever get to say those words to a man. Now, as she spoke them, she knew the rightness of each syllable.

Sure, there were complications. Things to be worked out. Explanations to be made. But that was for later. Right now there was Stephen and the fact that he loved her.

He kissed her again. She moved closer and—

"Now that's what I'm talking about," Geoff said. "This is good television."

Stephen straightened, looking as shocked as she felt. She stared at him, horror growing inside of her. The cameras. How could they have forgotten about the cameras? They weren't having a private conversation. They were on television.

Stephen swore softly. "I'm sorry. I forgot they were there."

"Me, too."

There was no point in going to Geoff. He wouldn't understand the concept of keeping a private moment private. He was interested in ratings. The boring couple had just given him a blockbuster of a teaser.

It wasn't just that Geoff and the crew had seen it all. Soon everyone would be a witness.

Stephen cupped her face. "Want to change your mind?"

"No."

"Me, either." He smiled. "We should probably brace ourselves for the worst. What's that line from that movie? If you jump, I'll jump."

"It's a long way down."

"Don't worry. I'll catch you."

CHAPTER FIFTEEN

DAKOTA AND FINN SAT on her sofa, watching that week's installment of *True Love or Fool's Gold*. The teaser right before the commercial break was of Aurelia and Stephen, standing somewhere in town, looking intense.

"I didn't know they were going to be featured this week," Dakota said. "They didn't have a date, did they?"

"Not that I know of," Finn said, passing her the bowl of popcorn.

He'd come over for dinner. She'd made steaks and salad. They'd sat at her table and laughed and talked, taking turns holding Hannah. A good evening, she thought, telling herself not to read too much into it. Sure, she enjoyed Finn's company, but as a friend. What was that phrase? Friends with benefits?

Hannah had gone to sleep, and Dakota was hoping that after the show, she and Finn would also go to bed. Although the sleep part wasn't what interested her.

The commercial ended, and the show resumed. A long shot of Aurelia and Stephen made her think the camera was some distance away. The sound seemed enhanced, too, as if the two of them hadn't been miked.

It took Dakota a second to realize what Aurelia was saying. Something about not wanting to hurt Stephen, that she didn't want him to have regrets. The look on his face when he said he could never regret their relationship stunned Dakota.

"I didn't realize," she began, then pressed her lips together. Oh, crap. So much for them being the quiet couple. When no one was looking, they'd gone ahead and gotten involved. If she didn't know better, she would swear they'd fallen in love.

Finn wasn't going to be happy about that.

She glanced at him out of the corner of her eye and saw him staring intently at the screen. Before she could figure out what to say, or even if she should say anything, the topic of the conversation shifted.

"I knew Finn expected me to go into the family business. I didn't know how to tell him I didn't want that."

Finn handed her the popcorn bowl and stood. "Well, hell."

Dakota set the bowl on the coffee table and rose. "Take a breath," she said. "This can't be news."

Finn glared at her. "Of course it's news. We've been talking about this for years. When Stephen finishes college he's coming into the family business. That was always the way it was going to be."

She didn't actually believe that. From what she could tell, Stephen had never shown any interest in the family business. He was majoring in engineering in college. If he wanted to join forces with his brother, wouldn't he have been studying business or something flying-related?

"You're not upset because he doesn't want to be in the family business," she said gently. "It's that he didn't tell you himself. You had to find out this way."

"Sure, that's some of it. Why the hell couldn't he come talk to me? I'm his brother. Why wouldn't he tell me the truth?"

She put her hand on his arm. "Maybe because you're not interested in the truth. You only want to hear the story you want to hear. I suspect both your brothers have been telling you things for a long time. They didn't decide to come here on a whim. They've been looking for a way out for a while. The show offered them that in an easy way."

"You don't know as much as you think you know." His voice was low and angry, although she had a feeling he was more angry at himself than at her.

"I know you're pushing them. I know you've been pushing them for a long time. You want to run their lives because you believe it's the only way to keep them safe." She drew in a breath. "Finn, you've done an amazing job with your brothers. Everyone can see it. There is no arbitrary line that you cross that says it's okay to stop worrying. That it's okay to stop taking care of them. That's what you're looking for. Someone somewhere to tell you it's okay to let go."

He shook off her hand and backed up a couple of steps. "You don't know what you're talking about."

"Yes, I do. Let them be. You've given them everything they need to be successful. Trust yourself and trust them."

"Even if that means not finishing college?"

"Yes."

"Not possible." He shoved his hands into his jeans pocket.

"So what are you going to do?" she asked. "Force Stephen into the family business? Are you going to guilt him into it? That's not you. You don't want him living a life of duty, doing things because he has to."

"That's what I had," Finn growled. "Nobody asked me what I wanted. Nobody gave a damn about my life. One day my parents were alive and everything was fine. The next they were dead. I was there. Did you know that? I was flying the plane when it crashed. There was a storm and my mother didn't want to fly, so we were going to wait. But she was worried about my brothers, so we took off anyway. The plane was hit by lightning and we went down. They were both injured. I had to hike out, and by the time I got back with help, they were dead."

He'd never told her how his parents had died beyond the fact that it had been a plane crash, and she hadn't thought to ask for details. She'd assumed it had been some kind of accident but nothing this bad. Nothing he'd been a part of. No wonder he held himself together so tightly. No wonder he didn't want to get involved or have more responsibility.

Everything made sense now. His intensity with his

brothers. His concern about their future and safety. He was trying to control fate, and that wasn't possible.

She stepped in front of him and stared into his dark blue eyes. "You did what you had to do. You took care of your own. Your parents would have been very proud of you."

He started to turn away, but she grabbed the front of his shirt and held him in place.

"You're right," she said. "No one asked you if you wanted to take on that responsibility. You did it because they're your family and it was the right thing to do. You understood that. Just like you know, deep in your heart, that you don't want Stephen in the business if he doesn't want to be there."

Finn stared at her for a long time, then opened his arms. She stepped into his embrace and hung on as if she would never let go.

"He should have told me," he whispered. "He should have told me himself. I would have understood."

She doubted Finn would have made the conversation very easy. Even so, his point was a good one. This was not how he should have found out.

She could argue that Stephen was still a boy, although that wouldn't help her case of Finn letting them grow and live their lives. Besides, she understood his pain, even if she couldn't feel it herself. He had given up so much, and now he felt betrayed.

Families were hard. They were great, but they were

hard. Or maybe it was just loving someone that made things complicated.

As she held on to him, she realized that her mother had been right. Falling in love with Finn would be easy. Too easy. She was going to have to be very, very careful.

DAKOTA AND HER SISTERS lay sprawled on several blankets in the backyard. Hannah sat between them, laughing at their various antics. The sun was warm, the sky was blue, and Buddy, one of Montana's rescue dogs, a pale cream labradoodle, monitored them anxiously.

"I can't believe you're really a mother," Nevada said. "It happened so fast. Last month you were single and now you have a kid."

"Tell me about it," Dakota said, rolling on her side and facing her daughter. "Obviously I've been thinking about adopting ever since I found out how difficult it would be for me to have children. But that was a theory. This is real." She grinned. "Of course, I'm still single."

Hannah reached for her pink elephant. It was slightly out of reach, and she tumbled to her side as she stretched. Montana scooped her up and held her in the air. The baby laughed while Buddy whined nervously.

"It's okay," Montana told the dog. "She's fine."

Montana put the little girl back on the blanket. Buddy crawled toward her. When he was next to her, he angled his body to provide support and maybe protection.

"He's really good with her," she said.

Montana nodded. "He does great with little kids. Although he's a bit of a worrier. He gets crazy when they fall. But he's so patient. He doesn't mind if little kids crawl all over him and pull his fur and tail. Some of it is the training, but most of it is his personality. He's a nanny dog." She leaned over and rubbed Buddy's head. "Aren't you, big boy?"

The dog kept his attention on the baby. He whined a little, as if concerned they weren't paying enough attention to what was going on.

"I want a baby," Nevada murmured. "At least I think I do, but not like this."

"You wouldn't consider adopting?" Dakota asked, a little surprised by her sister's reaction.

"Sure I would, but not so quickly. Yes, this was a deliberate act, but you had to make the final decision quickly. Didn't that scare you?"

"It terrified me, but that's part of the process. I suppose if I'd been picked by a woman who was pregnant, I would have had more time to get used to what was going to happen." She touched her daughter's soft, dark hair. "Except I wouldn't change any of this."

"You're braver than me," Montana admitted. "The dogs are about all I can handle. Besides, I don't think I'd be a very good mother."

"Why not?" Dakota thought her sister would be great. "You're caring and nurturing. You give everything you have. Look at how you are with the dogs."

"That's different."

"I don't think it is," Nevada said. "You're not as flaky as you think."

Hannah dropped her elephant again, then reached to pick it up. Buddy nudged it toward her, as if wanting to make sure she was careful.

"How is Finn taking all this?" Montana asked in a not-so-subtle attempt to change the subject. "He flew you to Los Angeles to pick her up. That was nice."

He'd done plenty of other nice things, she thought. And they weren't all about transportation.

"He's a good guy. The baby thing doesn't freak him out. His brothers are a lot younger and that helps. He remembers the baby stage."

He was also careful not to get too involved, she reminded herself. That kept stress at a minimum for him.

As she watched her daughter laugh, she wondered what it would be like if Finn weren't the kind of man who planned to walk away. Having him want to settle down would be pretty amazing. Especially if he wanted to do that settling with her.

"Dakota?"

She looked up and saw her sisters staring at her.

"You okay?" Nevada asked.

"Fine. Just daydreaming."

"About a certain handsome pilot?" Montana asked with a grin. "He looks like he's a great kisser."

"He is, but we're just friends. Anything else would be foolish."

"On his part or yours?"

"You know why he's here," Dakota reminded them. "When he figures out his brothers are doing fine on their own, he'll leave. After all, he has everything he needs in Alaska."

"You're not there," Montana said loyally. "Or Hannah. Plus he has to like the town. Who wouldn't want to live in Fool's Gold?"

"I'm sure there are hundreds of people," Nevada murmured.

Dakota decided she was tired of talking about herself. "Anyone know if Mom's been on a date?"

"No," Nevada said. "There are a couple of guys I know—contractors who are really nice. They're about her age. I suppose if I were a better daughter, I would offer to set her up. Only I can't seem to do it."

"Do you think it's a bad thing?" Montana asked, frowning slightly.

"No. I want her to be happy and it's been over ten years since Dad died, so I'm not thinking it's too soon."

"Then what?" Dakota prompted.

Nevada grinned. "I think I'm afraid she'll find someone in thirty seconds. That would be so depressing. I can't remember the last time I was on a date."

"Tell me about it," Montana said with a sigh.

"What about those contractors?" Dakota asked. "Any of them young enough to be interesting?"

"I work with them. It's not good to date someone you work with."

"Why not?" Montana asked. "If you work with them, then you get the chance to see them in all kinds of circumstances. You'll know a lot about their character. Isn't that a good thing?"

Nevada shrugged and turned to Dakota. "I suppose you're not interested in dating."

"I have a new baby."

"And a man." Montana flung herself on Buddy. "Admit it. The sex is pretty fabulous."

Dakota didn't hide her grin. "It's even better than you could imagine."

FINN DID HIS BEST to avoid his brother. There was nothing Stephen could say that he wanted to hear. But two days after the broadcast, his brother cornered him out at the airport. He looked up from loading boxes into the plane and found Stephen standing there.

"I'm busy," Finn said brusquely.

"You have to talk to me sometime."

"I haven't seen you in a week. Don't make it sound like you've been dogging my heels for days."

"You know what I mean," his brother said, glaring at him. "You're pissed."

Finn put the box in place, then straightened. "Because you went on national television and told the world I was a jerk? Why would I be pissed?"

"I didn't say that. I said…" Stephen shook his head. "Forget it," he said, turning away. "It doesn't matter.

You're not going to listen. I don't know why I bother trying."

Stephen started to walk away. Finn's instinct was to let him go. The kid was acting like a spoiled brat. He'd made one attempt to get his point across, and when that didn't work, he gave up. So much for Dakota's theory that his brothers were ready to be on their own.

Except he was supposed to be the mature one in the relationship.

"All you had to do was tell me," he said.

Stephen came to a stop but didn't turn around. "You wouldn't have listened. You would have told me to get my ass back to college and to plan on being in the family business. You always knew Sasha wasn't interested, and that left me."

Finn felt frustration building, but he did his best to ignore it. Communication, he reminded himself. That was the point of a conversation. Not to yell. Not to win.

"I wouldn't want you to do something that made you unhappy," he said. "I thought you were studying engineering because it was interesting, not because you wanted to be an engineer."

His brother faced him. "I took an introductory class my freshman year and got hooked."

Stephen shoved his hands into the front pockets of his jeans. "Don't take this wrong, but I don't want to be you. I like flying. It's fun and it gets me places, but it's not my life. Not wanting to be part of the business doesn't mean I don't appreciate what you've done. You gave up a lot when Mom and Dad died. You were there for us. I'm only a couple of years younger than you were when it happened and I can't imagine doing what you did."

Finn shifted uncomfortably. "You don't have a couple of kid brothers depending on you. That changes things."

"You took care of us," Stephen said earnestly. "I really appreciate that. We both do." He gave him a halfhearted smile. "Me more than Sasha."

Finn found himself relaxing his shoulders. "Dad wanted the business to stay in the family. Bill's always on me about selling and I didn't want to, because of you two."

"I thought you loved flying. I thought the business was everything."

"I do love flying, but carrying cargo back and forth isn't my idea of a good time. I want to start a charter company and take people places. Maybe teach flying to kids." Finn drew in a breath. "Sometimes I've thought about going somewhere else. Starting over. The world doesn't begin and end in South Salmon."

"I didn't know you realized that."

"I have my days."

Stephen's humor faded. "I'm sorry about what happened on the show. We didn't know the cameras were there. We were just talking."

"I kind of figured that out," Finn admitted. "I just

wish you'd come to me before and told me. It might have changed things."

"You're right. I'm sorry."

Words he didn't hear very often, Finn thought. Good words. "I'm sorry, too. I didn't mean to push you into something you didn't want to do."

"Thanks. I guess it worked. I'm going back to college."

Finn stared at him. "Since when?"

"That's how the conversation with Aurelia started." Stephen looked confused. "I said I was going back to college and then we were discussing engineering."

"Okay. I remember that."

"Let me guess," his brother said, rolling his eyes. "You heard the part about me not wanting to go into the family business and got mad. Did you hear anything else?"

Finn shook his head. "Apparently not. I guess I should've listened harder."

Stephen looked uncomfortable again. "About Aurelia," he began.

"I'm really grateful to her," Finn told him. "I don't know how she got you interested in school again, but I'm glad she did."

"It's more… You're right," his brother said. "She, ah, has really been talking to me about the importance of an education."

There was something else. Finn could tell Stephen

was either hiding something or trying to distract him. What he didn't know was what the something was.

He thought about pushing, then decided to let it go. Dakota was right. His brothers were grown-ups. They could handle their own lives. At least Stephen was going back to college. Finn knew Sasha was headed for Los Angeles or maybe New York. But Stephen would complete what he'd started, and that was a win.

WHAT HAD BEGUN as a quiet lunch with her sisters had somehow grown into a chickfest. It seemed that nearly every woman Dakota knew in town had come into the Fox and Hound that day for lunch. Tables had been pushed together in the center of the restaurant. The tourists sat in booths, watching the loud group.

Dakota sat at one of the square tables. She and Hannah were the center of attention. Actually, it was mostly Hannah. The baby was passed from arm to arm. She was cuddled and cooed at and rocked and held.

"At least you're not dealing with baby weight," Pia said. As she spoke, Pia shifted in her chair. She was about six or seven months pregnant, with twins. Just looking at her made Dakota uncomfortable.

"How do you sleep?" Dakota asked.

"Restlessly. If I can get comfortable I sleep really well. The problem is getting comfortable. That and wanting to eat Cincinnati. I'm hungry all the time. What is it about being pregnant and wanting food? Sure, I'm eating for three, but two of them weigh less than five pounds. You'd think I was giving birth to linebackers."

"It will be worth it," Mayor Marsha told her.

"I'm excited about the babies," Pia said. "It's the baby weight that has me nervous. I've been doing some reading. I think if I breast-feed, that helps."

"Breast-feeding twins is going to be a challenge," one of the women said with a laugh. "But it will help you lose the weight. Plus it's better for the babies. Something about the immune system and bonding. Everybody gets to bond."

"Raoul is already bonded," Pia muttered. "I wish he could breast-feed."

Dakota grinned at the thought of the former football player nursing a child. "He can be supportive in other ways."

"He's certainly trying," Pia admitted. "He loves these babies and they're not even born yet."

"And you love him," Nevada told her from across the table.

Pia smiled slowly. "I do. He's pretty amazing. I got so lucky when he fell in love with me. Of course, I tell him he got lucky when I fell in love with him. I think it helps to keep him humble. I just know it would be so hard to be doing this alone."

"Twins are a challenge," the mayor said. "Still, you would have had all of us. Just like Dakota does."

Dakota nodded. "I definitely don't feel alone in this." Which was true. While it would be nice to have a man

around—a partner to be there and pick up the slack—
she knew she could always ask for help and it would be
there.

Although she had to admit to a twinge of envy when
Pia talked about Raoul. Her friend's eyes lit up, and her
mouth curved into a special smile. Her mother looked
the same way when she talked about her late husband.
Being in love did wonderful things to a woman, Dakota
thought wistfully.

She'd always told herself that she would find that special someone eventually. Now she was less sure. Hannah
was wonderful, and she was so grateful to have her, but
being a single mother would make the whole "falling in
love" thing more complicated.

Had she been holding her baby, she would have whispered that she was more than worth it. As it was, Hannah
was on the opposite side of the table with Gladys, one
of the older ladies in town.

"So, does breast-feeding keep you from getting pregnant?" Pia asked.

"I think so," Denise said, then tilted her head. "Or
is it not breast-feeding? It's been too long for me and
tragically, I'm not having sex with anyone."

"Tell me about it," Gladys said, reluctantly passing
Hannah to Alice Barns, the police chief. "Sure there are
more men than there were, but they're all too young.
How about shipping in a few older guys?" She grinned.
"But not too old."

Everyone laughed.

"I know you don't get your period for a while after you're pregnant," Denise said. "I remember that much. But I think you can get pregnant before it starts. It seems to me that at least one of my boys was the result of that lack of information." She chuckled. "Not that I'm complaining."

"About the boy or the sex?" Gladys asked.

"Both."

Dakota leaned back in her chair and enjoyed being with the women she loved. This town was special. Whatever happened, there was support and understanding. Look at her situation. Everyone was there for her as she adopted Hannah. If she'd chosen to become a single mother the old-fashioned way, they would have been there for that, too.

Not that it was likely, she reminded herself. One in a hundred. It might as well be one in a million. If she ever did get pregnant, she should go buy a lotto ticket. There was absolutely no way—

Dakota sucked in a breath. Everything inside of her went still as she realized she hadn't had her period in a while. Certainly not since she'd gotten Hannah and even some time before that.

Thoughts swirled as she tried to figure out what was going on. The obvious answer was that she was pregnant—except she couldn't be. Her doctor had been very clear on that. She could still hear Dr. Galloway delivering the harsh news.

"It's very unlikely you'll ever conceive through

intercourse. I won't say it's impossible, but statistically the reality is it's not going to happen."

She placed her hand on her belly and wondered what on earth was going to happen if the doctor was wrong.

CHAPTER SIXTEEN

"I DON'T UNDERSTAND," Dakota murmured, despite having said the same thing about six times already. "I can't be pregnant. I can't. It's supposed to be impossible."

Dr. Galloway, an older woman with a sensible haircut and a kind smile, patted her leg as she removed Dakota's feet from the stirrups and helped her sit up.

"I would say it's a miracle," she told her patient. "Or is this not good news?"

Dakota took a deep breath, trying to clear her spinning head. The home pregnancy test she'd used the previous evening had confirmed what she'd begun to suspect. Driving to the next town to buy it had taken more time than waiting for the results. As she'd played with her daughter, she'd watched the time, then had read the clear message.

Pregnant.

A single word that was difficult to misunderstand, although she was having a whole lot of trouble absorbing it. Pregnant? Impossible. And yet, she was.

"It's good news," she said slowly. "Of course I want

more children." Hannah and her sibling would be close in age. But now? "I just didn't think…"

"You didn't think it would happen," Dr. Galloway told her. "That's life. I've seen it many times in my office. Although I should lecture you on the foolishness of not using a condom, young lady. Pregnancy isn't the only reason for protection."

"You're right, of course." Dakota wanted to grab her head and scream, more from the surreal nature of the conversation than because she was upset. "You're really sure?"

"I'll do a blood test to confirm, but I'm sure. Based on my exam, I would say you're about six weeks along."

Dakota opened her mouth, then closed it. Six weeks ago? That would mean it had happened the first time she and Finn had made love. They'd been so frantic for each other, so lost in passion. If any event was going to defy the odds, it made sense that was the one.

"I'm in shock." She shook her head, wondering if she would ever feel normal again. "I didn't think this could happen. I thought if I were to get pregnant I'd need medical intervention."

"So did I. When I said it was unlikely for you to conceive naturally, I was being kind. I thought it was impossible. Yes, there was the smallest of chances, but I never thought I would see it happen." She smiled. "Your young man must have impressive swimmers."

"I guess." Dakota looked at her. "I just adopted a baby girl. She's six months old."

"Good for you. This is excellent news. I've always thought siblings should be close in age. Harder for the parents, but better for the children." Dr. Galloway wrote on a pad. "What about the father?"

"I have no idea what he'll think," Dakota said honestly, wondering if the swirling she felt in her stomach was nerves, panic or hormones. "Finn isn't looking to get involved seriously or to take on more responsibility." He'd nearly gotten his brothers on their way. A baby would completely freak him out.

"Men often talk that way, but when faced with a child of their own, they come around. You're going to tell him, I hope?"

"Yes." Eventually. First she had to be able to grasp the information.

Even now, sitting in her doctor's office, naked from the waist down after peeing on a stick and having a pelvic exam, the information wasn't real to her. She could say the word *pregnant,* but she couldn't feel it in her heart.

Dr. Galloway opened a drawer and pulled out several brochures. "Some information to get you started. Pick up some sample prenatal vitamins and a prescription for more on your way out." She rose. "You're a healthy young woman. The problem was never about your carrying the baby. Now that you've conceived, we'll do everything we can to make sure you have an uneventful pregnancy. Enjoy your blessing, Dakota."

"I will."

Dakota waited until the doctor had left to stand and then reached for her clothes. She set the paperwork on the exam table and drew on her bikini briefs. As she picked up her jeans, her gaze fell on a drawing of a pregnant woman. The side view showed a sketch of how the near-term baby was positioned inside of her.

As she studied the simple picture, she touched her own still-flat belly. Her heart began to beat faster, and her breath caught in her throat.

She was pregnant! After all the pain and heartache, after thinking she was broken and could never be like anyone else, she was pregnant.

She stood in the center of the examining room and laughed, then felt tears burning her eyes.

"Happy tears," she whispered. "Happy, happy tears."

She dressed quickly, eager to tell her mother, who was watching Hannah. Denise would be thrilled. Dakota hung on to the happiness, knowing the freak-out at the thought of being a single mom to two small children would hit her any second.

Could she do it? Handle it? Did she have a choice?

There was so much to think about, to consider. She had to go by the airport and…

And what? Tell Finn?

She sank onto the edge of the examining table and shook her head. This wasn't going to be good news for him, she thought sadly. There was no way he wanted to take on a baby.

Sure, he was good with Hannah and very supportive,

but not in a way that meant he was interested in more than a temporary "uncle" relationship. He enjoyed the baby, but being a guy who liked kids did not a father make.

Finn had been clear about what he wanted from the first second they'd met. He'd never tried to convince her he was interested in anything but getting gone. If she wanted more, then she was only fooling herself.

Thinking that made her remember the name of the show. *True Love or Fool's Gold.*

She knew which she wanted. That was easy. But finding it was more complicated. As for the fool's gold—an artificial and unsatisfying substitute for the real thing—maybe she'd accepted a little of that, too. Allowing herself to believe there was more between her and Finn than there really was.

He was a great guy, and she knew she was in danger of losing her heart to him. But she also knew he'd been honest with her, and that, when he said he didn't want to stay, he meant it. Which left her in an uncomfortable dilemma.

How and when did she tell Finn she was pregnant?

She didn't think he would believe she'd lied about her condition to trick him, at least not when he'd had a chance to think about it. But she wouldn't be surprised if he went there at first, so she had to be prepared.

There was also the issue of coparenting. Did he want to? If so, how would they manage? Would he fly in from South Salmon? What about the winter, when the small town was practically cut off from the world? What would happen later if one or both of them fell in love with someone else? It wasn't anything she could imagine for herself, but Finn was the kind of man nearly every woman would want.

Too many questions, she told herself as she stood and picked up her purse. She took a cleansing breath. They didn't all have to be answered today. She was about six weeks pregnant. That meant she had months and months before any decisions had to be made. She could take her time and figure out the best way to tell Finn what had happened. As for his part in raising their baby—if she had to do it alone, she would. She might not have a life partner, but she had family and a town, and they both loved her.

Sensible words, she thought as she walked toward the reception desk to pick up her samples and prescription. Words that should have made her feel better and stronger. Instead there was an emptiness inside, a sense of longing for the very thing she couldn't have.

Finn.

SASHA LEANED BACK on the bench. "I thought I'd hear from an agent by now," he grumbled. "What if none of them are watching the show?"

Lani sat on the grass in front of him. She looked up and smiled. "They're watching."

"You can't know that."

Most of the time Sasha liked Lani. She was easy to

get along with, and, because neither of them wanted to sleep with the other, there was none of that tension between them. It was like hanging out with his sister. If he had one.

But sometimes she really bugged him. Especially when she acted as if she knew everything about being on TV and he knew nothing. Maybe he hadn't been to Los Angeles for pilot season, but that didn't mean he didn't read and talk to people. He'd studied a lot on the internet.

Lani rolled onto her stomach. Her long, dark, wavy hair brushed against the grass. She was beautiful and all, he thought. But not his type.

"I told you," she said, her voice sounding smug. "I sent notices to all the best agents in L.A. Well, to their assistants. I suggested they watch us."

He'd forgotten about that. "You don't know that they're watching."

She rolled her eyes. "Don't be so negative. You have to believe. You have to see what you want in every detail and then do the work to make it happen. That's how we're going to become stars. Do you think I like being on this stupid show? It's a great concept, but Geoff's a pain in the ass. He has no vision. But it gets me in front of people. It gets me seen. That's why I'm here."

Lani was so sure of herself, Sasha thought. She had a plan. All he had was a dream and the need to get out of South Salmon. That was the difference between them, he realized. Instead of complaining about her, he should learn from her.

"So what do we do now?" he asked.

"Close your eyes."

He looked at her. "I don't think so."

She pushed up into a kneeling position. "I'm not going to do anything bad. Trust me. Now close your eyes and start breathing real deep. Like from the bottom of your stomach."

He did as she instructed, leaning back against the bench and closing his eyes. He consciously slowed his breathing and felt himself start to relax.

"Okay. Now picture your dream house in L.A. It's on the beach right?"

"Malibu," he said with a smile, still keeping his eyes closed. "I can see the ocean." What he could see was girls in bikinis, but he didn't say that to Lani. "And I know how to visualize."

"You know how to daydream," she said. "There's a difference."

He wanted to push back but reminded himself she wasn't playing at any of this.

"Okay," he said, his eyes still closed. "Go on."

"Now imagine your house has a deck and there are stairs down to the beach. Ten stairs. They're wood. Your feet are bare. It's warm and sunny. You can feel the railing in your hand and you can feel the wooden deck below your feet. There's a light breeze."

Sasha was surprised to realize he actually could feel

the deck. The wood was smooth and warm from the sun. He could feel the loose sand under his toes. The light breeze she described blew against his face. He felt his hair move.

"Now imagine yourself walking down the stairs," she said, her voice low and soothing. "You're getting closer to the beach. You can smell the ocean and hear the sound of the surf. You can see people on the beach." She laughed. "Let's change that. You can see girls on the beach."

"Maybe just a couple," he said with a chuckle. "Okay. I'm walking down the stairs."

"Go slow," she said. "Imagine everything about it. The railing. Don't forget that. You're walking down and down. There's only one more step and then you'll be on the beach. So stop at the last step. Can you see yourself there?"

He nodded. He could see everything, and he could feel it, too. The moment was so real, he could taste salt on his lips.

"Now step onto the sand," she said. "Feel the warm sand. It's just the right temperature. Not too hot, but warm on top and cooler underneath. Three of the girls see you. They whisper to each other and then start running toward you. They know exactly who you are and they are so excited to meet you. Because you're on their favorite show. One of them is holding a copy of *People* magazine. And you're on the cover."

Sasha grinned. Everything about it was real, right

down to the picture of him on the magazine. With his eyes still closed, he squinted, then laughed. There it was, in bold print. *Sexiest man alive.*

He opened his eyes and looked at Lani. "That was great. How do you do that? I want to do it more."

"You're such a baby. Why aren't you visualizing every day? It's the best way to get what you want. Sure, you have to do the work, but this allows you to be in the right place at the right time. When you visualize and practice, you prepare yourself for success. I've been visualizing myself winning an Oscar since I was fourteen years old."

She stood and walked over to the bench, then sat next to him. "I don't know anyone in the business," she told him. "I don't have a lot of experience or friends I can ask. I'm doing this all on my own. This is how I make it real. This is how I get through the day. If you want it, Sasha, you have to believe in yourself. Most of the time no one else will believe in you."

"I get it. I need to come up with what I want and then imagine it already happening."

"Yes. But do it every day. That's what makes it powerful." She sighed. "I imagined myself on a reality show. I should have been more specific. I can't get anyone to tell me ratings numbers. Have you heard anything?"

"What are you talking about?"

She groaned. "How is the show doing? Are the advertisers happy with the number of viewers? That kind of information is important. We want the show to be successful."

"What does it matter if it isn't? We'll be gone."

"It's important because if we're going to put it on a resume somebody has to have heard about it. There is no point in claiming stardom on a show no one saw." She stared at him. "You make me crazy, and not in a good way."

"Part of my charm," he told her and grinned.

"You are not all that." She looked past him. "For all we know, one of the camera guys followed us. We should probably make out for a little bit just in case."

While there wasn't any chemistry between them, kissing a pretty girl was never bad. But instead of thinking that he wanted her, he found himself remembering her lesson on visualization. He would get started on that right away. The first thing he was going to visualize was his big brother flying back to Alaska and leaving him the hell alone.

FINN PICKED UP his two bags and left the grocery store. He barely made it onto the sidewalk when a tall older woman stopped him.

"You're that man," she said, peering at him. "The one dating Dakota."

He wasn't sure if she was telling him or asking a question. Either way it wasn't her business. Except this was Fool's Gold and he'd learned that people got involved whether you wanted them to or not.

"I know Dakota," he admitted.

"How is she doing? Her baby is just so precious. Hannah—that's her name, right?"

"Um, yes." Finn wanted to hurry her along to ask her why they were having this conversation, but he knew better. This stranger would get to her point when she was good and ready. His job was to wait and listen.

"Do you know if she still has a lot of food in the freezer?" the woman asked. "I always prefer to wait before bringing over a casserole. In the beginning of any family crisis, everyone rushes in with food and it all has to be frozen. It's never as good when it's thawed and heated. I think we should make a schedule. People could sign up and bring food on an ongoing basis. But no one listens. So I do it myself. I wait a couple of weeks and then bring by food. So do you know if she has enough?"

"Olivia."

Finn turned and saw Denise, Dakota's mother, approaching. Her smile looked amused rather than friendly, as if she knew he were trapped and she was trying to decide if she was going to help him escape. As he had been practically naked in her daughter's house, he understood her need to make him squirm. He could only hope that in the end she helped set him free.

"Hello, Denise," the older woman said. "I was just talking to Dakota's young man here to find out if I should bring over a casserole."

"Olivia is known for her casseroles," Denise told Finn.

"She's a member of another of the founding families here in Fool's Gold. Olivia, this is Finn."

"We've met," Olivia announced. "He doesn't say much, does he? I can respect that. I, too, enjoyed a quiet man. I assume he has other attributes that recommend him."

Finn couldn't remember the last time he'd worried about blushing. He figured he had to have been in his teens. But here he was, standing on the streets of Fool's Gold, trying not to turn red.

Denise's brown eyes danced with amusement. "I'm sure he does. Not that Dakota discusses them with me. Perhaps if you ask one of her sisters."

Finn nearly choked and started to inch away. Denise grabbed him by the arm to hold him in place.

"Perhaps I will," Olivia said. "In the meantime, if you think she would enjoy something to eat, I'll take Dakota a casserole."

"I wish you would," Denise said. "I know you'll enjoy meeting Hannah. She's wonderful. An adorable little baby girl. She was small for her age when Dakota got her, but she's growing fast. She's starting to eat solid food."

"I remember what a mess that was," Olivia said with a smile. "All right. Thank you for the information. If you see Dakota, please let her know I'll be by later today."

"I will," Denise promised. She waited until the older woman had walked away, then turned to Finn. "I wasn't sure you were going to make it," she said.

"I respect your need to torture me."

"A mother's prerogative. But it really wasn't that bad. Most everyone in town is nice, if a bit inquisitive." The dancing humor was back in her eyes.

He found himself smiling. "People don't go through many things alone around here."

She took one of the bags from him, and they started walking toward his rented room.

"We don't believe in self-sufficiency," she told him. "But you grew up in a small town, so you understand."

"We were always ready to help a neighbor, but we were expected to manage pretty much on our own."

"When I gave birth to the girls, I had some complications." Denise shook her head. "I was pretty sick. I don't remember very much. My husband, Ralph, didn't want to leave me alone in the hospital. But he had three little boys at home and a business to run. Not to mention triplet infants and it was Christmas. It was a stressful time. When I finally came home, I was weak. It took me a couple of months to recover. The women in town took care of us. Someone was in the house every single day for the first six months. I don't think I changed a diaper until the girls were at least three months old."

"Impressive."

"I want you to know that we take care of our own. If you choose to stay here, then you would become one of us, and we would take care of you, too."

"I don't need a lot of taking care of."

"I'm sure that's true. I'm just letting you know how

it would be. But from what my daughter tells me, you're not thinking about staying."

He glanced at her, wondering what was coming next. As he wasn't sure what Denise thought of him, he couldn't guess her preference. Did she want him to stick around? Or would she prefer he left sooner rather than later?

"I'm not looking to add more responsibility to my life," he admitted. She might not like the truth, but he wasn't going to lie to make her happy. "Dakota is great, though. I like her a lot."

"But not enough to stay." Denise wasn't asking a question. "You don't have to worry. If you wanted to stay, that would be great. But if you don't, she'll be fine."

She was giving him permission to walk away. There wouldn't be any guilt or games. In a way, it was the perfect situation. So why didn't he feel better about it?

They had reached his motel room. Finn felt funny about inviting her in but wasn't comfortable standing in front of the door. Denise solved the problem by handing him back his second bag.

"I hope you find what you're looking for," she told him.

"What makes you think I'm looking for anything?"

"Because you don't seem very happy." She tempered her observation with a gentle smile.

With that, she turned and left. Finn watched her go, then let himself into his small room and shut the door.

He put away the groceries, filling the tiny refrigerator. Then he paced restlessly in the room.

He wanted to go after Denise and tell her that she was wrong. Of course he was happy. He'd spent the past eight years raising his brothers, and his job was finally done. He could go home, knowing they would be okay in the world. Why the hell wouldn't he be happy?

He flung himself on the bed and stared at the ceiling. Who was he kidding? He wasn't happy. He hadn't been for a long time. He wanted to blame his brothers but knew it was more than that. It was him.

A next step seemed logical, he thought. If only he knew what it was.

His cell phone rang, saving him from the pain of introspection.

"It's Geoff," a familiar voice said when he answered. "You'll want to watch the show tonight. I think it will make you happy."

"Not if Sasha plays with fire again," he grumbled.

"It's better than fire," Geoff promised him. "Make sure you watch."

CHAPTER SEVENTEEN

ALTHOUGH DAKOTA HAD SEEN most of the episodes of *True Love or Fool's Gold* with Finn, tonight was different. While he was comfortably sprawled on the sofa, with Hannah on his chest, Dakota found herself restless and uneasy. No doubt it was the secret she was keeping. Being pregnant had a way of changing a woman's perspective. She was thrilled about the thought of having a baby. Two months ago she'd thought she might never have a family, and now she had a beautiful baby girl and another child on the way. What was that old phrase? An embarrassment of riches?

But there was always another side to any situation. In this case, it was telling Finn that *he* was the father of her child. Something she knew he didn't want.

"Have I mentioned Geoff isn't one of my favorite people?" Finn asked. "He specifically told me to watch tonight's episode and so far it hasn't been very interesting. Or maybe that's just me." He glanced at her. "Am I the wrong demographic?"

It took Dakota a second to realize what he was talking about. "I've heard the ratings aren't very good. Karen, one of the production assistants, told me that Geoff was really sweating the numbers. I think it's the show's premise. I'm a big fan of reality television, but this concept doesn't make sense to me. We all want to see people falling in love, but this feels fake."

He raised his eyebrows. "I don't want to watch people falling in love."

She smiled. "Okay, okay. It's a girl thing. A while ago on *Biggest Loser* two of the contestants fell in love. It was just the best. My sisters and I couldn't stop calling each other about it."

"But you don't know them. Why does it matter if they get involved?"

"It just does. It's fun to watch people fall in love. Which should make the show more interesting. I guess that's the problem. No one is falling in love."

She glanced back at the screen and saw Sasha and Lani. "Here they are," she said.

Finn turned his attention to the television. Dakota found herself watching him rather than the show. He was a good man. Kind and responsible. He was also pretty fabulous in bed, but that shouldn't matter. She smiled. Even though it sort of did.

He turned up the volume on the remote with one hand while keeping the other on Hannah's back. The baby was sleeping on his chest, her head on his shoulder, her nose pressing against his neck. It was the kind of image that turned even the most sensible of women's hearts to mush. She wasn't sure how she was supposed to resist.

"This is interesting," Finn said.

Dakota glanced at the screen. Sasha and Lani were in the park. Sasha sat on a bench while Lani sat on the grass in front of him. They were in deep conversation.

"You're such a baby," Lani said. "Why aren't you visualizing every day? It's the best way to get what you want. Sure, you have to do the work, but this allows you to be in the right place at the right time. When you visualize and practice, you prepare yourself for success. I've been visualizing myself winning an Oscar since I was fourteen years old."

She stood and walked over to the bench, then sat next to Sasha. "I don't know anyone in the business," she told him. "I don't have a lot of experience or friends I can ask. I'm doing this all on my own. This is how I make it real. This is how I get through the day. If you want it, Sasha, you have to believe in yourself. Most of the time no one else will believe in you." She sighed. "I imagined myself on a reality show. I should have been more specific. I can't get anyone to tell me ratings numbers. Have you heard anything?"

Dakota blinked. She didn't know a whole lot about the entertainment business, but she was pretty sure contestants on a show weren't supposed to talk about ratings.

"What are you talking about?" Sasha asked.

She groaned. "How is the show doing? Are the advertisers happy with the number of viewers? That kind of information is important. We want the show to be successful."

"What does it matter if it isn't? We'll be gone."

"It's important because if we're going to put it on a resume, somebody has to have heard about it. There's no point in claiming stardom on a show no one saw." She stared at him. "You make me crazy, and not in a good way."

"Part of my charm," he told her and grinned.

"You are not all that." She looked past him. "For all we know, one of the camera guys has followed us. We should probably make out for a little bit, just in case."

As Dakota watched, they went into each other's arms with practiced ease. But little or no romance. It was painfully obvious that they were simply going through the motions to get more show time.

She winced. "Geoff made a huge mistake in showing that. I'm sure he's going to think it will get people talking, but the viewers are going to feel like they've been tricked."

"Which means my brother is about to be voted off," Finn said.

She couldn't tell if he was happy or not. "And then what?"

"Hell if I know." He kissed Hannah's head. "Sorry, little girl." He settled more deeply in the sofa and sighed. "If I had to guess, I would say that Sasha is going to head to Los Angeles. There is no way he's coming back to South Salmon. Stephen told me he was going to finish college. I guess I'm going to have to be happy with one of them getting through school."

Before she could point out that he had a fifty percent

success rate, the scene shifted to Stephen and Aurelia. They were locked in what looked like a very passionate embrace. This wasn't fake, Dakota thought, feeling her mouth drop open. This was hot and sexy and very real.

"Oh, my," she murmured. "I didn't know Aurelia had it in her."

Finn sprang to his feet. She had to give him credit—he held Hannah so securely, the baby didn't even stir. But Dakota saw the fury in his eyes.

"She lied. She made it sound like all she was interested in was getting Stephen back to school. He lied to me, too. Damn him, he never said a word about this." He turned to Dakota. "I'm going to kill them both."

FINN DIDN'T CARE about breaking the law. He knew it was wrong to kill anyone, especially a woman. He knew he would go to jail, and he accepted that. He wasn't sure how this had happened, but he was going to make sure it stopped. And while he was out ravaging the countryside, he was going to find Geoff and put a fist through his face.

In the back of his mind, he acknowledged that for the second time in as many months, he was contemplating murder. In his normal life, the one he liked back in South Salmon, he never had those kinds of feelings. He simply went about his day, fat, dumb and happy. Well, not fat or dumb, but still. He didn't think about crushing another human being.

It wasn't him, he told himself. It was this damn town.

Dakota took Hannah from him. The baby stirred and murmured a protest before falling back asleep. For a second, staring at her sweet face, he felt himself grow more calm. Rational thought took over. Then he looked at the television screen where his brother was making out with some cougar, and the rage returned.

"Don't go out there mad," Dakota told him. "I know you're not happy about this."

"Not happy?"

He did his best to keep his voice level, more for the sleeping baby than because he didn't want to shout. Right now yelling sounded pretty damn good. As did throwing something or maybe putting his fist through a wall. Of course, if he put his fist through a wall, he ran the risk of breaking something and right now the only thing he wanted to break was Geoff's face.

"If I can't imagine hating her, how am I going to kill her?"

"Are you talking about Aurelia?" Dakota's eyes widened. "You can't kill anyone. Not only is it wrong, it's not in your nature."

"It could be. I'm very capable of protecting my own. I knew she was a cougar. I knew it and I should have done something right away. She was so sweet the last time I talked to her, pretending she cared about Stephen going back to college. It was all an act."

"You're going to protect your brother from the woman

he's probably in love with? That makes sense. Finn, sit down. Take a breath. This isn't the end of the world."

"She's nearly ten years older than him. Her life is established. What is she doing with my baby brother?"

"I'm sure she's asking herself the same question. I don't know Aurelia well, but I've met her several times. I saw her in school. She's not aggressive. She has a horrible mother and lives a very small life. I'm sure she's as upset about this as you are."

He deliberately looked at the television screen where the couple in question was still kissing. "Yeah. I can see she's really broken up about it."

Dakota shifted the baby in her arms. "Maybe she's not upset right now, but I'm sure…"

"She wants something from him. Whatever it is, she's not going to get it. She's using him. She's probably been planning this from the beginning."

Dakota didn't look convinced. "Don't do anything rash."

He ignored her request. "Are you going to tell me where she lives?"

"No. And you shouldn't go looking for her or your brother until you've calmed down."

"That's not going to be for a very long time." He started for the door, then turned around and came back. He kissed Dakota on the cheek and Hannah on the top of her head, then stalked out.

Once outside of Dakota's house, he paused, not sure

which way to go. He had no idea where Aurelia lived. He'd have to start with Stephen.

He moved toward the center of town. His brothers shared a room in a small motel opposite the park, just off the lake. Fifteen minutes later, he was knocking on the door to the motel room, but no one answered. No doubt Stephen was hiding from him. A smart move, considering Finn's mood.

He started back across the parking lot, only to see Stephen and Aurelia approaching. The couple was holding hands and came to a stop when they saw him.

He stood his ground, waiting.

About forty feet separated them. Stephen whispered something to Aurelia, then the two of them walked closer. As they passed under a streetlight, Finn could see that Aurelia had been crying.

The information didn't change anything, he told himself. She was a good actress. Too bad she hadn't been paired with Sasha. They could have found fame and fortune together.

"Obviously we have to talk," Stephen said when they were close enough to have a conversation.

"We can have it out here or in your room." Finn glared at Aurelia. "Or we could go back to your place and you could tell me your plan."

Aurelia's eyes widened. More tears slipped down her cheeks. "It's not what you think," she whispered.

"Do I look like I believe that?"

"Don't," Stephen told him, then led the way to

the motel room. After using his key, he pushed open the door.

Aurelia went in first. Finn followed.

The space was small. Two double beds, a long dresser with an old television sitting on top, a chair in the corner and the door leading to an even tinier bathroom. The digs weren't impressive, but then Geoff didn't feel the need to pamper his contestants.

"I know you're upset," Stephen began.

"You think?"

His brother ignored that. "Despite how angry you are, you'll treat Aurelia with respect. If you don't, this conversation is over."

"You're going to make me?"

Stephen stepped between him and Aurelia. "Yes."

There was quiet determination in his brother's voice. A strength in the way he stood. Finn was careful not to let his surprise show. Neither of his brothers had ever tried to stand up to him before. They preferred to sneak off rather than confront him directly. Maybe Stephen was finally growing up.

"All right," he said, folding his arms across his chest. "Tell me why I shouldn't believe the worst."

Aurelia and Stephen looked at each other. Finn was aware of silent communication between them, but he couldn't interpret it.

"We never meant for this to happen," Aurelia said quietly.

"You came on the show," Finn reminded her. "It's a

show about meeting someone. Obviously, you wanted to meet someone. I agree that you probably had no control over who you were matched with."

He could feel his fragile control slipping. The anger returned and with it the need to lash out. "Look at him," he demanded. "He's twenty-one. He's still a kid. His running away to be on this show proves that. If you think there's anything to be gained, any money, you can forget it."

Stephen stepped between them again and put his hand on Finn's chest. "Don't," his brother growled. "Don't push her, don't threaten her, don't make this end badly."

On the one hand, Finn appreciated Stephen's maturity. On the other hand, this was the wrong time for it to show up.

"Stop," Aurelia said. She stepped between them and separated them, holding them at arm's length. "You're family. Try to remember that." She looked at Stephen. "Please let me do this. Finn doesn't mean anything bad. He's worried about you and that's a good thing."

"I'm worried about you," Stephen told her. "I don't want him to upset you."

Aurelia shook her head. "It's not him. It's what's happening around us." She turned to Finn and dropped her arms to her sides. "You're right. I did come on the show looking for something. A lot of it was about my mother, which I'm not going to get into now." She managed a slight smile.

Her whole face changed when she smiled, Finn

thought. She went from plain to pretty. There was an intelligence in her eyes. He could see why Stephen found her so appealing. But that didn't make the relationship right.

"I should have thought this through," Aurelia admitted. "When they first put me with Stephen, I was so embarrassed. He's younger and attractive and outgoing. Everything I'm not. But I was afraid to walk away. It would just be another rejection. I also wanted the twenty thousand. I want to buy a house of my own."

She clutched her hands together in front of her waist. "I know you can't understand. You've always been successful. Look at what you've done with the family business and with your brothers."

She glanced at Stephen, then back at Finn. "I've never had the courage to stand up for myself. I've always been so afraid. Being around Stephen has shown me who I can be if only I'm willing to take the risk. He's taught me to be brave. I didn't know I could be."

"I'm sure this would be very compelling to someone who gave a shit," Finn told her. "But I—"

"I wasn't finished," she told him firmly, staring directly into his eyes. "I would appreciate it if you would let me finish what I have to say."

"All right," Finn said slowly, surprised she was willing to take him on. He was pretty sure he had intimidated her, so this act of courage was unexpected. It was possible it made him like her a little.

"I'm not a cougar. I wasn't looking for a younger man.

I don't know what I was looking for, and maybe that's the problem. I never thought I would find anyone. I never thought I was good enough. But I am. I deserve love as much as anyone else."

She raised her chin slightly. "It was never my intention to be caught in a passionate embrace on television. I apologize for that and any embarrassment it may have brought your family. But I don't apologize for loving your brother. I don't apologize for caring about him and wanting the best for him."

She drew in a breath. "I know he's too young. I know he has a lifetime of experiences waiting for him and I shouldn't get in the way of that. God has nothing if not a sense of humor, because I can't help being in love with him."

Finn had been with her right up until she said she was in love with his little brother. But before he could speak, Aurelia turned to Stephen.

"Your brother is right. You don't belong here with me. Go home. Finish your degree. Get a job doing what you love. Live your life."

She sounded sincere, Finn admitted, if only to himself. Under any other circumstances, he would've believed her and been impressed as hell.

Stephen moved toward her. Finn knew what was going to happen. His brother would yell and stomp and pout until he got his way, his actions proving that he wasn't ready to be in a relationship. But it turned out Finn was wrong.

Stephen cupped Aurelia's face in his hands. "I know that's what you believe. I know you think being with me only hurts me. But you're wrong. You are everything I have ever wanted. I *will* go to college and finish my degree. I *will* get a job. But I'm going to do it here. With you. There is nothing you can say to make me go away. I love you."

Finn could feel the emotion between them. He felt like an outsider caught staring at something intimate.

Stephen turned to him. "I was wrong to run away. Coming here the way I did only reinforced your idea that I wasn't a man. I was acting like a kid and I deserve to be treated like one. I'm sorry for screwing up. I'm sorry you had to come after me. I know you have a business and responsibilities. But I didn't think of any of that. I only thought of myself."

Finn wouldn't have been more stunned if Aurelia had morphed into a squirrel and started dancing. "It turned out okay," he said roughly.

"Not yet, but it will." Stephen faced Aurelia again. "I want to marry you. I know it's too soon, so I'm not asking. I'm just letting you know where I think this is going. I'm going to finish school and get a job. I'm going to keep on seeing you. A year from today I'm going to ask you to marry me. And on that day, I'll expect an answer."

Finn waited for the fury, but there wasn't any anger. There wasn't even a mild annoyance. If he had to name the emotion surging through him, it was regret. Not because his brother had grown up, but because he, Finn, didn't have anything close to what Stephen had with Aurelia. His kid brother had won the prize.

It wasn't that he wanted to be in love. Not exactly. What he wanted was something different. Still, he couldn't escape the sense of having missed out on something important.

"I'll get out of your way," Finn said.

"You don't have to go," Aurelia told him. But she was looking at Stephen as she spoke.

"You two have a lot to talk about."

He thought his brother might want to make sure things were okay between them, but Stephen was too busy kissing Aurelia. Finn backed out of the room, stepped onto the walkway and closed the door behind him. One brother's situation solved, another to go.

He walked down the street, wondering what to do about Sasha. How to get him—

He stopped by Morgan's Books and stared blindly at the display in the window. There was nothing to do about either of his brothers. Dakota had been right all along. His job was done. He'd parented them as best he could, and keeping them safe forever wasn't an option. He had to trust they were ready to make their own decisions. It was time.

DAKOTA STARED at all the clothes spread across the bed. It was as if a department store had exploded in her mother's bedroom.

"I didn't know you owned this many things," she said, putting Hannah into her playpen. "When was the last time you cleaned out your closet? Are those leg warmers? Mom, the eighties were a long time ago."

"You're not funny," her mother snapped. "If you think this is humorous, you're wrong. I'm in crisis here. A really, really big crisis. I feel sick to my stomach, my head hurts, I'm retaining enough water to sink a battleship. I'm a woman on the edge. You need to respect that."

Her mother sank onto the bed where she sat on several outfits, crushing them.

"I'm sorry," Dakota said, trying to keep the humor out of her voice. "I won't be funny again."

"I don't believe you. But that's not the point. I can't do this." Her mother covered her face with her hands. "What was I thinking? I'm too old to do this. The last time I dated, dinosaurs roamed the earth. We didn't even have electricity."

Dakota knelt in front of her and pulled her hands away from her face. "I happen to know nearly all the dinosaurs were extinct and there was electricity. Come on, Mom. You know you want to do this."

"No, I don't. It's not too late to cancel, right? I can cancel. You could call and tell him I have some kind of typhoid fever. Imply that it's very contagious and I'm going to be shipped off to one of those federal medical facilities in Arizona. I hear the dry air is very good for typhoid fever."

Just then, Dakota heard voices in the hall. "Are we too late?" Montana called. "I don't want to miss the fun part."

Montana and Nevada entered the bedroom. They looked around at the array of clothing and accessories.

"I didn't hear about a tornado on the news," Nevada said cheerfully. "Was anyone hurt?"

"I can see I raised you girls with too much freedom and affection," their mother snapped. "I should have repressed you more. Maybe then you'd treat me with more respect."

"We love you, Mom," Nevada said. "And we respect you. I didn't know you had this many clothes."

Dakota chuckled. "Don't go there. She'll bite your head off."

Montana lifted Hannah from the playpen and cuddled with her. "Who's a pretty girl? We're going to ignore all those sniping grown-ups, aren't we?"

"I was telling your sister that I can't do this," Denise said. "I can't go on a date. We were discussing telling him I have typhoid fever."

Nevada rolled her eyes. "Right. Because he'll never guess you're lying if you say that. Come on, Mom. It's one evening. You need to get out there and see if you're interested in dating. Right now it's just a theory. If it's horrible, you never have to go again. Besides, you're making us all nuts. None of us are dating." She glanced at Dakota. "Well, Dakota might be. No one can pin her down on her relationship with Finn. For all we know, they're running off to the Bahamas tomorrow to get married."

"You're getting married?" her mother asked.

Dakota sighed. "Don't pretend to be distracted by something you know isn't true. Nevada is right. Try the date." She carefully avoided asking what the worst was that could happen. That question never went well.

"Who's the guy?" Montana asked, still holding Hannah.

"A friend of Morgan's," Denise said.

"We like Morgan," Nevada said. "That's a good sign."

Denise stood and pressed her hands against her stomach. "His friend may be nothing like him. He may be a serial killer. Or a cross-dresser."

"At least you have enough clothes to support his habit," Montana offered.

Dakota and Nevada laughed. Their mother glared at them.

"You're not helping," Denise informed them. "I'm going to have to ask you three to leave. Hannah can stay. She's very supportive." She looked at the little girl. "Never have daughters. Trust me. They only break your heart."

Nevada walked to the bed and stared at the clothes strewn across it. After a second she reached into the mess and withdrew a white-and-blue floral print wrap dress.

"Wear this," she said. "It will work nearly anywhere. You look great in it and it's comfortable. It's perfect for the season. You have those gorgeous blue shoes. He'll be wildly impressed."

Denise stared at the dress, then at the three of them. "Really?"

Dakota nodded. "You know how I hate to admit that Nevada is right, but this time she is. That dress is perfect. You'll look lovely, and more important, you'll feel good." She walked over to her mom and put her arm around her. "I know this is scary, but it's important. Dad's been gone for nearly eleven years. It's okay for you to move on. You deserve to be happy."

Her mother drew in a shaky breath. "Okay," she said. "I'll go on the date and I'll wear the dress. My makeup is done and this is as good as my hair is going to look. So all I have to do is get dressed." She glanced at the clock. "Oh, God. I have two hours until he gets here. I think I'm going to be sick." She waved her hands in front of her face. "Quick. I need a distraction. Somebody say something that will make me forget I even have a date."

Montana and Nevada looked at each other and shrugged, as if they didn't have anything to offer. Dakota figured this was as good a time as any to spill her news.

"I'll give it a try," she said with a smile. "Mom, I have something to tell you. I'm pregnant."

CHAPTER EIGHTEEN

DAKOTA'S SISTERS looked at her with identical expressions of surprise. Her mother lunged forward and hugged her close.

"Really?" Denise asked, still holding on. "You're not just teasing me to get my mind off my date?"

"I wouldn't do that. I'm pregnant. It's kind of unexpected, given my medical history. I wasn't planning on this, but I can't help but be happy."

"Finn must have some great swimmers," Montana said. "It is Finn, right?"

Dakota laughed. "Yes, it's him. There hasn't been anyone else. I know there're complications and I know this isn't anything he wanted, but I can't help being happy. I'm going to have a baby and I never thought I could."

"You're probably having enough sex to defy the odds," Nevada told her. "Statistically it was always possible. You just needed the right set of circumstances."

Dakota stepped back and turned in a circle. "I don't care whether it was his swimmers or the moon or an alien landing. I'm so excited." She was having trouble grasping the reality of the situation, but so far there was no downside. Sure, having two kids so close together would be a challenge, but other women got through it and she would, as well.

"When you decided to become a mother, you did it in a big way," Denise said with a laugh. "If you're happy, I'm happy."

"I am. Hannah is going to love having a baby brother or sister."

Montana and Nevada exchanged a glance. Dakota knew exactly what they were thinking. She drew in a breath.

"No, I haven't told him," she said, answering their unasked question. "I will. I know I have to. And I know he's not going to take it well. Finn has made it very clear what he wants from life and it isn't more responsibility. He's been great with Hannah, but she's not his. He can walk away at any time. A baby is going to change everything for him."

There was an emotional storm coming. As much as she wanted to believe he would be happy, she knew better. He might even think she'd tried to trick him. Whatever happened, she would get through it. Even if he walked away, she would be fine. Broken hearts healed. Hers would, too. Because no matter what, she was having a baby.

"He might surprise you," her mother said. Although her expression was hopeful, her tone was thick with doubt.

"I don't think so." Nevada looked uncomfortable but

kept on talking. "When it comes to things like this, men tend to tell the truth. If the guy says he's never been faithful, a woman needs to listen. And if a man says he doesn't want a family, he's probably not lying." She turned to Dakota. "I'm sorry. I really want to be wrong. But I don't want to see you hurt more."

"I know." Dakota understood the risks. She and Finn had started their relationship for a lot of reasons that were about attraction and hot sex. Along the way, she had discovered he was a pretty great guy. She'd felt herself starting to fall for him and figured that was the biggest problem she would face. Being in love with a man who only wanted to leave.

Now she had to explain how her claim of being unable to conceive might not have been completely true. Not a conversation designed to go well.

"Maybe he'll surprise you," Montana said. "Maybe he'll be mad at first, but then he'll realize this is what he's wanted all along. Maybe he's wildly in love with you and doesn't know how to tell you."

"If wishes were horses…" Denise said, then sighed. She looked at Dakota. "I'm sorry, honey. Nevada's right. Men tend to tell the truth, even when they don't mean to. I don't think Finn is going to be happy about this."

"I know." Dakota smiled. "I'll be fine, whatever happens. I know I have all of you and the town. I have Hannah. And I'm having a baby. That's the miracle. Whatever else happens, I have my miracle. Most people don't get to say that. Most people go their whole lives without experiencing something like this. Having Finn around would have been an amazing bonus, but I'm okay with what I have."

"You love him," Nevada murmured. "Did I see this before?"

"No, because I didn't want to admit it to myself." Love? Dakota told herself not to be surprised. Considering the man in question, it was probably inevitable.

Love. She turned the concept over in her mind and found that it fit. She loved him. No doubt she had for a long time.

"It will be an unconventional happy ending," she told her sisters and her mother. "I won't get the guy, but I'll get everything else. That's going to be enough for me."

They moved toward her as one, embracing her and holding her close. She felt their love wash over her and through her, strengthening her. There were people who had to go through much worse situations alone. She was lucky. She had her family, and they had her.

FINN CHECKED the cargo manifest against the boxes he loaded. It was a good day to fly. The winds were light, the sky was clear and he was going to Reno. Sure, it was a turnaround trip, with him on the ground less than an hour, but it was always interesting to fly somewhere he'd never been.

He was enjoying the airspace of the West Coast. The weather was more predictable, and there were a lot more airports to be had. Even moderately sized communities like Bakersfield lay sprawled in all directions. There were people everywhere, little towns and big cities. Instead of dodging mountains and arctic storms, he had to find his way through commercial flight paths in the wake of a 757 jetliner. Different challenges, same thrill.

Flying was in his blood. He couldn't escape it, and he didn't want to. He regretted that neither of his brothers were as interested, but he accepted it. He wouldn't have wanted to be pushed into some other career.

He finished the paperwork and started toward the office. If he got back early enough, he could take a second trip that day. That would make Hamilton happy. The old coot reminded Finn of his grandfather. Both men were smart entrepreneurs, patient with honest mistakes and unfailingly generous. They were men from another time.

"Finn?"

He stopped and turned. Sasha was walking across the tarmac. His younger brother had been voted off the show the previous night. Given what he and Lani had admitted on camera, it wasn't a surprise that viewers had been disappointed in them and wanted them gone.

He'd wondered if Sasha would be disappointed. Now as he watched his brother approach, he recognized the other man's excitement. Sasha had good news.

Finn knew without being told that Sasha was not going back to South Salmon. Even so, he paused and waited for his brother to speak.

"Did you see the show?" Sasha asked, sounding more

happy than sad. "I can't believe we got caught like that. We've been so careful." He shrugged and grinned. "I guess not careful enough."

"You don't sound upset."

"I'm going to L.A. I got a call this morning from an agent. One of his assistants has been watching the show and she thinks I'm really hot." The grin broadened. "Hot is good. So he wants me to come down to L.A. We're going to talk. He already has a few ideas of where he's going to send me. There is a show looking to replace an ongoing character and a small part in a movie."

Sasha kept talking, going on about how he and Lani were driving down that afternoon. She knew of a cheap apartment where they could stay. It seemed she, too, had an audition and interested agent.

Finn knew it was time to let go. Sasha no longer belonged in South Salmon. His brother needed to be other places.

"This is what I really want," Sasha told him earnestly. "I know you're disappointed."

"A little," Finn admitted. "But not surprised. You've been heading in this direction for a while."

"That almost sounds like you're not mad."

"I'm not. I won't say I didn't wish this had turned out differently. I would rather you finish college. But you have to make your own decisions and live with the consequences. I hope this turns out for the best. I hope you get to be on TV or in a movie."

"Thanks!" Sasha sounded both happy and surprised. "I thought you'd be furious."

"You wore me down, kid." Finn pulled his wallet out of his back pocket and counted out the money he'd withdrawn from his account that morning. "Here's three hundred dollars and a check for a thousand more. Get yourself a decent place to live. Try to eat regularly."

"I don't know what to say," Sasha admitted, taking the money. "I really appreciate this. It's gonna make a big difference."

"Your brother is going back to college. The money is still there, in your education fund. If you decide to go back, you'll be able to finish whenever you want."

Sasha's mouth twisted. "You're the best brother a guy could have. I know I've been a pain. It wasn't on purpose."

Finn felt his throat tighten. "Most of the time it was."

Sasha laughed. "Maybe fifty percent." His humor faded. "You did a good job with us. Mom and Dad would be proud. I have a plan. You can stop worrying about me."

"That's not going to happen, but I'm ready to let you go."

They moved toward each other at the same time. There was some back slapping and a brief hug. About as much emotion as either of them were comfortable with. Then Sasha put the money in his pocket, waved and walked away.

Finn had come to Fool's Gold to force his brothers to return home. He'd believed the only place they belonged was in college or in South Salmon. He'd been wrong on all counts. Neither brother was coming home, and oddly enough, he was just fine with that.

DAKOTA ARRIVED at work the next morning with a burning need for coffee and a promise to herself that she would tell Finn about the baby before sundown. Or maybe by the end of the week.

She wasn't trying to be a coward or even keep the information from him. It was just that she was so happy. She wanted to stay happy for a little longer. She wanted to have her fantasies about the future and pretend everything was going to work out fine. She wanted to imagine a house with a big tree in the yard and two children playing together and Finn beside her.

Because as much as she wanted this baby, she also wanted to be with that baby's father. The big surprise wasn't that she had fallen in love with him, it was that it had taken her so long to figure it out.

She walked toward the temporary production offices and was surprised to see large trucks pulled up in front of them. As she approached, she saw guys in T-shirts carrying boxes and furniture into the trucks. If she didn't know better, she would say everyone was leaving.

She saw Karen, one of the production assistants, sitting at a table in the middle of the sidewalk.

"What's going on?" Dakota asked as she approached. "Why are you working out here?"

Karen looked up at her. Her eyes were swollen and red, as if she'd been crying. "It's over. The show's canceled." She sniffed. "We were shut down late last night. Geoff called me from the airport. He's already back in L.A."

"Canceled? How can they do that? We're not even through this cycle. Who wins?"

"No one," Karen told her flatly. "No one cares. The numbers suck. We started out okay but then plummeted in the third week. It's a disaster."

Dakota was having trouble taking in the information. "What happens to the contestants?"

"They go home."

"What happens to you?"

Tears filled Karen's eyes. "I work for Geoff. Right now that's not a good thing. I have a lot of friends in the business and they'll help me. I need to get work with another company or producer." She sighed. "I have savings. This sort of thing happens all the time, so if you're going to survive, you have to be prepared to deal with weeks of unemployment. But it's not fun and I know people are wondering if I knew. I didn't. But nobody gives a crap about that."

"I'm sorry," Dakota said, feeling awkward. She didn't know what else to say. She didn't understand how so much money could be put into a show and then the show simply canceled within a few short weeks.

"If you need a recommendation or if I can help in any way, please let me know," Dakota told her.

"Thanks." She glanced at her watch. "You'd better get into your office. If you have anything personal, I'd get it in the next five or ten minutes. Your part of the office is going to be dismantled by nine."

"Okay. I will." Dakota stood there awkwardly for a few seconds, but Karen returned her attention to her work and didn't look up again.

As Dakota walked toward her small corner of the production office, she pulled out her cell phone and left a message for the mayor. She had a feeling that word had already spread all over town. She looked around at the cameras being loaded onto trucks and people getting in cars and driving away. The TV show had tried to take over the town. She had a feeling that in a matter of hours, it would seem as if it had never been there. Maybe that was just the nature of the business. It was all an illusion and nothing ever lasted.

BY NOON, Dakota was back in her old office, ready to tackle the curriculum planning for which she'd been hired. She'd had a quick meeting with Raoul Moreno and, as he put it, a game plan. She let him call her schedule a game plan for two reasons. First, because he was a former NFL quarterback and sports terms made him feel happy. Second, because he signed her paycheck.

Before his summer camp had been transformed into a temporary elementary school, his dream had been to open a facility for kids in middle school. The emphasis would be on math and science. They would come for three or four weeks at a time, have extensive study in either math or science and, in theory, return to their regular schools enthused about what they could accomplish. As the elementary school would need the camp for at least two years, they had ample time to develop their program.

Montana arrived at the office exactly at two. She had a leash in one hand and pushed the stroller with the other. Buddy, the intense and worried labradoodle, kept pace with the stroller. Every few seconds he looked at Hannah, as if making sure she was all right.

"I can't decide if Buddy would make a good dad if he were human," Montana said, "or if he would be on Prozac half the time."

"He's a pretty good-looking guy," Dakota said, rising and coming around her desk. "He'd probably discover women and forget to pick up his kids from day care."

Montana bent down and patted the dog. "Don't you listen to her, Buddy. I know better. I know you'd never forget to pick up your children from day care. Who's that handsome puppy? We'll ignore my mean sister."

Dakota laughed. "I'm sorry, Buddy. I was teasing." She picked up Hannah and pulled her close. "How's my girl?"

Montana straightened. "She was great. She's eating much better. I swear I can see her growing. I can't say I love poopy diapers, but I'm getting good at them."

"I really appreciate you looking after her," Dakota said. "Now that I'm back here, I should be able to bring her to work with me at least three days a week. So I'm not going to need as much day care. Mom's going to take her one of those days and I've had about five calls from different women in town wanting her the other day."

"It must be nice to be popular."

"It's not me. It's Hannah. She's more popular than any of us."

Montana sat on the edge of the desk. "I don't think I could do what you do."

"Plan curriculum?"

"Have a baby by myself." Montana's gaze dropped to her sister's stomach. "Make that two babies."

"It wasn't planned," Dakota admitted, telling herself not to panic at the thought of being a single mom to two young children. "I'll admit I'm scared, but I'm not going to think about that. Both children are a blessing."

"What is Finn?"

A good question and one she couldn't answer.

"I love him," Dakota said quietly and shrugged. "I know it's stupid, but I couldn't help myself. I just…" She smiled. "He's the one."

"Wow. You found him."

"I'm not saying it was an intelligent choice."

"It could work out," Montana told her.

"I appreciate your loyalty, but do you really believe that?"

"He could surprise you."

Dakota gave her a skeptical look. "He's made it clear that he wants his old life back. With his brothers moving on, he's finally free. I know he cares about me, but that's not the same as love or taking on more responsibility."

"So you're not going to ask?"

"I'm not going to make myself crazy wishing for something that might never happen."

Montana started to speak, then stopped. "Tell me what I can do to help."

"What were you going to say?"

Her sister shifted. "That you're giving up without trying. If you love him, if he's the one, shouldn't you at least try to make things work? Fight for him? Only he hasn't said no yet, because you haven't told him. So there's no fight to be had."

"I'll tell him. I'm waiting because I know what's going to happen and I don't want to ruin what we have. Trust me. When Finn finds out I'm pregnant, there will be burning skid marks on the road."

"If you say so."

The conversation wasn't going the way Dakota had intended, and she found herself annoyed. She told herself that this wasn't Montana's fault. She didn't understand. Wanting something didn't make it happen.

"You need to give him the chance to surprise you," Montana murmured. "Maybe he will."

Dakota nodded because she didn't want to fight, but she knew the truth was very different.

THAT NIGHT Dakota felt restless. She couldn't forget her argument with her sister, and she couldn't ignore the voice in her head saying that she was hiding rather than being honest. That both she and Finn deserved better.

When she let him in that night, she had a marinara sauce simmering and soft music playing. Hannah had already drifted off for her dinnertime nap.

"Hey," Finn said, as he walked into her small house. "How was your first day away from TV? Do you miss the excitement of working in the entertainment industry?"

He smiled as he spoke, his blue eyes crinkling slightly. He was tall and handsome and strong. He was someone she could lean on.

Maybe she'd never fallen in love before because she hadn't found the right guy. There had always been a nagging sense of something missing. With Finn, she felt full...complete.

If only.

She waited until he closed the front door, then stepped into his arms. As she wrapped her arms around him, she drew his head down so she could kiss him. Telling him how she felt was a one-way road to disaster, but showing him... That might be different.

She pressed her mouth against his, letting all the frustration, the love, the worry, spill into her kiss. He held on tight, as if sensing she needed to be close. He kissed her back, his tongue tangling with hers, his body surging close.

Hunger flared to life, but it was about so much more

than sex. It was about him and what they could have together.

Wordlessly, she reached for his hand and tugged him through the living room, down the hall and into her bedroom. With the door open, they could easily hear Hannah if she cried.

Once in the dimness of her bedroom, she turned to him. There were questions in his eyes, but he didn't ask anything. Apparently he knew she needed more than conversation.

He put his hands on the hem of her T-shirt and pulled it over her head. She unfastened her bra. When she was naked to the waist, he bent down and drew her already tight nipple into his mouth. He used his hand to tease her other breast.

His mouth was warm. His tongue aroused her, flicking the tip over her nipple. With each deep tug, she felt herself swelling and readying. Only it wasn't enough. She wanted more than this. She wanted all of him, on top of her, filling her, taking her. She needed him. She needed the connection.

Again, he read her mind. He reached for the button on her jeans. She undid it for him, then pushed down her clothes. Immediately he slipped his hand between her legs. She was already wet. With his thumb, he found her center. As he rubbed that sensitive knot of flesh, he pushed two fingers inside of her.

Sensations assaulted her. From his mouth at her breasts to his hand stroking, massaging, pushing. He went in deeper, finding all the places that made her gasp. Even though she hung on to him, her legs began to tremble. She was having trouble staying upright. But she didn't want him to stop. She didn't want anything to distract him from the way he made her feel.

Tension filled her. Tension and pleasure and an unrelenting desire to be swept away into an ocean of satisfaction. She was getting closer and closer, so close that—

He stopped. She cried out her protest, not sure what was happening. Before she could say anything, he'd pushed her back onto the bed. She sat on the edge of the mattress, and then he was on his knees, parting her legs, replacing his thumb with his tongue. He kissed her intimately, even as he thrust his fingers back inside of her.

The feel of his tongue, his breath, the fullness was too much. She barely had time to register the pleasure when she was tumbling into her release. She cried out as her body shuddered.

The waves came again and again until she was limp. Then he was standing and fumbling with his clothes. As he sent his shirt, shoes, socks, jeans and boxers flying, she scrambled up a little higher on the bed. He joined her seconds later.

"Dakota," he breathed, as he pushed into her.

She welcomed him, wrapping her legs around his hips and drawing him closer. Usually she closed her eyes, but this time she kept them open, watching him watch her.

They were connected. She felt what he felt, knew his anticipation, experienced the tension. As he got closer, so did she. The need for more grew until there was nothing to do but come together.

She clung to him as he held on to her. The night closed around them until it seemed as if they had always been together and that they could never ever be apart.

I love you.

She thought the words but didn't speak them. She knew once she said them, she would have to tell him the truth, and then those words would be a trap. A way to make him feel obligated.

If only.

The wish was like a prayer, sent out into the cosmos. Was having the one man she'd waited her whole life to find too much to ask?

Even as the question formed, she heard Hannah's soft sigh and had her answer. She'd already been given so much. There was no way she could have it all.

She might not be able to keep Finn, but she would have his baby, and somehow, she would make that enough.

CHAPTER NINETEEN

"YOU'RE KILLING ME," Bill said, his voice surprisingly clear considering he was twelve hundred miles away. "We're starting our busy season, Finn. You've got to get back here or you've got to cut me loose."

"I know," Finn said, clutching the cell phone. "Just give me another week."

"To do what? You said the show was over. That your brothers were done with it. What more is there to do in that damn town?"

An excellent question, Finn thought. He should be jumping on the first plane back to Alaska. And he wasn't. He kept having this feeling that there was more to do here.

"It's that woman, isn't it?"

"Dakota? Some of it is her." He hadn't meant to get involved. He didn't want to get close to anyone. But there was something about her. Something that appealed to him. Walking away was going to be harder than he'd expected.

"Are you thinking about staying?"

"I don't know. I'm not sure of anything. Look, Bill, I

know this is unfair. I know you're working your ass off. Just give me a week. I'll have an answer then."

His friend sighed. "Fine. A week. But no longer. And you are going to seriously owe me."

"I know. Whatever you want, it's yours."

Bill chuckled. "Like I believe that. Talk to you in a week. If you don't call me, I'm selling your half of the business to the first person who offers me a nickel."

"Fair enough." Finn ended the call.

He stood on the tarmac of the Fool's Gold airport and looked at the planes. He could make a life here, if that was what he wanted. The question was, did he? He'd been responsible for so damn long, and he'd told himself that when he got his brothers raised, he was done. He was only going to think about himself, do what he wanted.

Now that he was free, being alone wasn't quite so appealing. He'd gotten used to being part of the family. Part of something. Did he want to walk away from that? Did it have to be all or nothing?

"What did your partner say?" Hamilton asked.

Finn had mentioned having to phone Bill. "He's not happy I'm still here. I told him I'd make a decision within the next week."

Hamilton raised his bushy gray eyebrows. "You thinking about buying me out? I can have some papers drawn up."

The old man offered him the business nearly every time he reported for work. The price was fair, and there was plenty of potential to grow. Finn had some ideas about scheduled shipping routes and passenger service. If he wanted to stay.

"I'll let you know in the next week, as well."

"What's so special about the next seven days?" Hamilton asked. "You reading tea leaves or something?"

"Not yet. I need to figure some things out."

Hamilton shook his head. "You young people today. Never wanting to make a decision. I know what's keeping you here. It's that girl in town. She seems pretty enough to me, but then what do I know? I've been married nearly forty years." He grinned. "Take it from an old man. Marriage is a good way to go."

Marriage? Is that what they were talking about? He knew in his head it was a logical next step, but the thought of it made him take a step back. Dakota had a daughter. Was he ready to be a father? Hadn't he already done that with his brothers?

He supposed it came down to his feelings for Dakota. He knew he liked her. She had been an unexpected find in what could have been a terrible situation. She was supportive and caring. He liked watching her with Hannah. She was a good mother and a good friend. She would probably make a great wife. The thing was, he didn't think he was looking for one.

"A week," he repeated.

Hamilton raised his arm. "Fine by me. Take as long as you want. I think you like it here. I think you're looking for an excuse to stay. If you were so hot to get back to

Alaska, you'd already be gone. But then I'm just an old man."

Finn grinned. "You say that a lot. That you're an old man and what do you know, but you seem to have an opinion about everything."

Hamilton laughed. "When you're my age, boy, you'll have an opinion about everything, too."

SUNDAY MORNING, Dakota joined her sisters at her mother's house for an informal brunch. It was getting warmer and warmer as they headed for the summer months. Today, Denise had set the table on the patio. There was a bowl of fresh fruit, juice, pastries and an egg casserole. The scent of fresh coffee competed with the delicate aroma of flowers in the morning.

Dakota held Hannah on her lap. The little girl was doing well in her high chair, but this many people would be a distraction. It was easier to keep one arm around her squirming body as she reached out toward her aunt and her grandmother.

"So how was the date?" Nevada asked. She poured herself a cup of coffee, then passed the pot to Montana. "Did you do anything wild and get arrested?"

Denise sipped her juice, then put the glass on the table and leaned back in her chair. "It was fine."

Montana laughed. "I don't think he's going to want your endorsement in a campaign. Fine? Did you have a good time? Did you like him? Start at the beginning and tell us everything."

"He's a perfectly nice man. We talked about a lot of different things. He's funny, sort of. He's well-traveled. It was fine. I wasn't exactly expecting a life-changing event. It was just a date."

Dakota thought about the time she spent with Finn. "Sometimes 'just a date' can be life-changing."

"I'm not sure I believe that," her mother said. "You have to get to know someone. Is there really love at first sight? I'm not sure. Maybe that's only something that happens when you're really young. When you don't have to be cautious and careful."

"Why do you have to be careful?" Nevada asked.

"A lot of reasons. I haven't dated in over thirty years. I don't know how the rules have changed. Plus I'm not a kid. I have responsibilities. I have children and grand-children and a place in the community. I'm not going to run off with some biker just because he sets my thighs on fire."

"I think I'd run off with the biker who set my thighs on fire," Nevada said. She smiled. "Assuming you mean setting them on fire the good way and not with a match."

"Well, of course. I'm not interested in dating a pyro-maniac." Denise shook her head. "It's very complicated at my age. You girls don't understand. You're still very young. The rules aren't the same for you."

"Are you saying you were sexually attracted to him and you're afraid to act on it?" Dakota asked, oddly ter-rified of the answer. She told herself that they were all adults here, and her mother was as much a sexual being as the rest of them. But it was still strange to be having this conversation with a parent.

"No. I was speaking theoretically." Denise picked up her coffee. "There wasn't any chemistry. We kissed." She shuddered delicately. "Maybe I'm too old to have a man's tongue in my mouth."

Dakota did her best not to flinch. Nevada stiffened and Montana shrieked, then covered her ears with her hands.

"I can't," Montana said. "I know it's not mature, but I just can't have you talking about this. It's icky." She dropped her hands. "Not icky exactly, but just too much information."

Hannah clapped her hands and laughed at her aunt's antics.

"At least you're amused," Dakota told her little girl, then kissed the top of her head. She turned her attention to her mother. "While I'm willing to be more mature about this than my sister, I will admit that it's strange to talk about you having a sex life. But as a trained professional, I will listen."

Denise laughed. "You girls are ridiculous. I'm talking about French kissing. It's not like I described twenty minutes of intercourse."

Montana covered her ears again and started humming. Nevada looked like she was ready to bolt.

"It's probably best you didn't have sex on the first date," Dakota said, hoping she sounded calm and reasonable. She was completely with her sisters. Anywhere but here. Parental sex discussions should be illegal. "It's been a long time for you. You were married to Dad for all those years and now you've been a widow for a decade. Starting the dating game slowly makes the most sense."

"That's what I thought," her mother said primly. "The kissing was really just an experiment. I wondered what it would be like with another man. It wasn't that great."

Montana dropped her hands again. "Maybe it wasn't the kissing, maybe it was the guy. Chemistry matters. There has to be that spark."

"Maybe he was a nice enough man," their mother said. "But there was no spark. I'm not going out with him again. I want to say I'm never going out again but it would be silly to make that decision based on a single date. I'll think about it."

She turned to Dakota. "And while we're on the subject about thinking about things—have you told Finn about being pregnant?"

"Is Finn pregnant, too?" Montana asked, grinning.

"I'm ignoring you," her mother said. "Eat your breakfast."

"Yes, ma'am." Montana reached for her fork.

The other two looked at Dakota. She shifted on her feet. "I haven't told him, exactly."

Her mother's expression turned disapproving. "This is not information you keep to yourself. Finn has the right to know he's going to be a father."

"I know, and I'm going to tell him. Soon." She drew in a breath. "Every time I think about telling him, I get a knot in my stomach. He's still here. He doesn't have to be here, but he is. Everything is settled with his brothers and he hasn't said when he's leaving. Which makes me think I might be the reason he's staying."

"You're afraid if you tell him about the baby, he'll run," Nevada said gently.

"Yes," Dakota whispered, knowing it was cowardly and still the truth. "I love him. I want him to stay. Having him go would break my heart."

"Then tell him that," Montana suggested. "Knowing how you feel could change his mind. And you don't know that he won't be happy about the baby. He might surprise you."

Dakota would like to believe that, but she wasn't holding her breath. As for telling Finn that she loved him…

"I don't want him to see my feelings as a trap," she admitted. "I don't want him to think I'm telling him I love him to get him to stay. I'm not sure I can tell him those two things together. But if I tell him I love him and then tell him about the baby, it's still a trap. If I tell him about the baby, I probably won't get a chance to tell him that I love him. I don't know how to fix this."

"That's because it can't be fixed," her mother told her. "There is nothing to be resolved. There is information to be shared and plans to be made." She paused. "As for which you tell him first, I understand your dilemma.

However you choose to handle this, he needs to know that you're pregnant. Every man has the right to know he's going to be a father. Don't wait for the right time, because there isn't one."

It had been many years since her mother had scolded her, Dakota thought. No matter how old she got or how mature she felt, those chiding words still had the power to make her feel small. She wanted to protest that she had her reasons, but she knew her mother was right. She was hiding from the situation, avoiding what had to be done. Whatever the outcome, she had to tell him.

"I'll tell him today."

And by tomorrow he would be gone.

"Sasha called from L.A. He's found an apartment, and sharing it with two other guys. I guess they take turns sleeping. I'm not sure what happened with Lani, but whatever. He sounds happy."

Dakota found it difficult to concentrate on Finn's conversation. While she was usually happy to listen, this was different. The need to tell him the truth pressed in on her. She still hadn't figured out the best words to use, but she was done procrastinating.

"I have to tell you something," she said, interrupting him. "It's important." They were sitting on her living-room floor, Hannah on the carpet between them. The little girl held a set of baby keys in her hand and was delighted by the noise when she shook them.

Finn drew his eyebrows together. "Is everything okay? Is it Hannah?"

Dakota drew in her breath. She just had to say it, she told herself. Just blurt it out. Then hope for the best. "It's not Hannah. It's me." She shook her head. "No, I don't mean it that way. I'm..."

She swore silently. It wasn't supposed to be this hard.

"You've been really great to me," she said, forcing herself to stare into his dark blue eyes. "I know you didn't want to come here. But I'm glad you did. I'm glad I got to meet you and spend time with you. You're really special to me."

She swallowed. There she was—about to say the word she'd never said to a man before. She'd never even come close. She loved her family, but this was different. This was romantic love. And this was the rest of her life.

"I'm in love with you. I didn't mean for it to happen, but it did. And I know you probably don't want to stay here, but you're not gone yet and I'm hoping Hannah and I are part of the reason. There are a lot of complications, your life in South Salmon, my life here, but I thought maybe we could figure it out together."

She couldn't tell what he was thinking. He kept looking at her, but his expression was unreadable. She didn't know if that was good or bad.

Now came the hard part. "There's just one more thing."

Finn wasn't sure what the one more thing could be. Having Dakota spell out her feelings was a surprise. No one had ever been that honest with him. One more point in her favor, he thought, turning her words over in his mind and finding he liked them.

She was right. He'd never planned on staying in Fool's Gold. He'd never wanted to come here in the first place. But he was glad he had. Being here had taught him to trust his brothers. Being here had allowed him to see they were adults and he could let go. Being here had even given him the opportunity to fall in love with Dakota.

His gaze drifted to Hannah. Sure, he didn't want to take on any more responsibility, but this was different. She was a great kid, and he already knew her. Plus the idea of a little girl was fun. There would probably be a whole lot fewer broken windows. He hadn't thought he would get seriously involved for a while, if ever, but life wasn't always tidy.

"I'm pregnant." She bit her lower lip. "I know this is a shock. I know I told you I couldn't get pregnant and it was true. Well, obviously not completely true, but the doctor said it was unlikely and it was a one in one million chance and it's probably because you have really good swimmers and…" She stared at him. "I'm pregnant."

Pregnant.

He knew what the word meant intellectually. He knew where babies came from. He'd known that since he was ten. But pregnant?

He wanted to stand and raise his fist to the heavens.

This was not supposed to happen. She'd told him she couldn't get pregnant, and he'd believed her.

She was still talking, but he wasn't listening. The occasional word slipped through. Something about a small chance. Something about them getting lucky.

He stared at her. "Lucky? You think this is lucky?" Now he did rise to his feet. "This isn't lucky. This is a scam. Was there ever anything wrong with you? Or were you just trying to trick me?"

Even as he asked the question, he already knew the answer. Dakota wouldn't trick him. That wasn't her style. She'd been honest from day one. But damn. Why the hell had this happened?

She scrambled to her feet and pulled Hannah into her arms. The baby gurgled and held out her hands to him.

"I didn't do this on purpose." Dakota's voice was quiet with determination.

He shoved his fists into his jeans pockets and stalked across the room. "I know that," he said, nearly yelling. "But this isn't what I wanted. Not now. Not again. I just got free and now I'm trapped again."

"You're not trapped. You're not anything. Feel free to walk away." She raised her chin. "We don't need you here, Finn. I'm telling you because it's the right thing to do. Not because I want anything from you."

Which sounded good but wasn't the least bit believable. After all, she'd started this conversation by telling him she loved him. Was that even true? Maybe it was all a way to lull him into a false sense of security. Or to make him feel obligated, so when she sprung the pregnancy on him, he would instantly want to be a part of things.

"How do I know this wasn't just a big game to you?" he asked her.

"There are no winners here." She shrugged. "I thought you'd want to know that you're going to be a father. But don't concern yourself. I can see it in your eyes. You want to run. Fine. Go ahead. There's the door and I'm not stopping you."

IN THAT SECOND when he just stood there, Dakota held her breath. She desperately hoped she was wrong, that Finn would want to stay. That somehow he'd realize he loved her back and that they belonged together.

As she watched, she saw the emotional door swing shut and knew that she'd lost. Before he bothered walking out, she knew he was already gone.

CHAPTER TWENTY

TREE-COVERED MOUNTAINS stretched for as far as Finn could see. The sky was blue, the sun bright, even though it was after nine in the evening. This time of year, the northern parts of Alaska got close to twenty hours of daylight.

He'd already completed two flights in the past twenty-four hours. When he flew back to South Salmon, he would rest for a while, then do it all over again. Orders were backed up, and he owed Bill. His partner had been damned understanding about his extended absence.

The controls of the plane were familiar. He didn't have to think to fly—being in the sky, defying gravity, was as natural to him as breathing. This was all he'd ever needed.

In the distance he saw storm heads. The thick, dark clouds could have been a problem, but he knew the weather as well as he knew the sky. The clouds would pass west of him. By the time he was leaving again, the weather would have moved on.

Despite the steady drone of the engine, there was a relative silence. A sense of peace. No one sat next to him. No one waited for him when he landed. He could do what he wanted, when he wanted. He finally had the freedom he'd spent the past eight years longing for.

As he got closer to the South Salmon airport, he reported his approach and headed in to land. When the wheels touched down, he steered the plane toward the hangars he and Bill owned. His partner was waiting for him by the main building.

Bill was a tall, thin guy in his early forties. His father and Finn's father had worked together in the business. There was a lot of history between them.

"How did it go?" Bill asked. "You've been flying a lot of hours."

Finn handed over the clipboard containing the signed delivery receipts, as well as the plane's log. "I'm going to get some rest now. I'll be back about four."

He meant four in the morning. Shifts started early in the summer. They wanted to take advantage of as much daylight as possible. Flying was a whole lot easier when you could see everything.

Bill took the clipboard. "You adjusting okay?"

"Sure. Why do you ask?"

His partner shrugged. "You're not the same. I don't know if you're missing something or someone, or if it's having your brothers gone. There's a lot of new business, Finn. A couple contracts and other folks interested in signing. I've got them for you to look at. The thing is, if you're not going to be here, then I need to hire new pilots. Maybe bring in my cousin."

His partner looked at him. "Do you want me to buy

you out? I can. My in-laws have offered me the money. I could pay about half in cash and get a bank loan for the rest. If you're not sure, this is the time to tell me."

Sell the business. He couldn't say he hadn't been thinking about it. Three months ago he would have sworn everything he wanted was in South Salmon. Now he wasn't so sure. His brothers had left and they weren't looking back. They'd found it surprisingly easy to make a life somewhere else. He had new ideas about what he wanted to do with his life. Run charters, teach kids to fly.

And then there was Dakota. He missed her. As much as he didn't want to, as much as he was pissed and wondering if she'd done her best to trick him—even though he knew in his gut she hadn't—he wanted to be with her. He wanted to see her and hold her and laugh with her. He wanted to watch Hannah grow from a baby to a toddler, then into a little girl with bright eyes and a ready smile.

As for the baby... He couldn't go there. The thought of it overwhelmed him. He'd never considered the idea of more kids. From the day his parents had died, he'd always told himself that when his brothers were finally ready to walk away, he would do all the things he'd missed. He would go where he wanted, do what he wanted. He would be free. He never wanted to "have to" do anything again.

As much as he'd loved his brothers, there had been days he'd resented having to take care of everything. At a time when most guys his age were screwing everything that walked and partying with friends, he was checking homework, doing laundry and learning how to cook. He'd balanced work and parenting. He'd had to be both mother and father, and every single day he'd wondered if he'd been messing it up.

"Finn?"

Finn looked at his partner. "Sorry."

"You were somewhere else."

"The past."

"About the business?" Bill asked. "Can you get back to me by the end of the week?"

"By Friday," he promised.

Bill nodded and walked away.

Finn stayed where he was. There was a post-flight check to be done on the plane and paperwork to finish. But instead of moving on that, he found himself thinking about Dakota and how she would have to be both mother and father to her two children. She'd sought out the adoption, but the baby was as unexpected to her as it was to him.

He was sure she'd meant what she'd told him—that she had no expectations. That he could walk away. She would probably draw up one of those agreements where he gave up all rights to the kid and she gave up all rights to financial support. She wouldn't want him to feel trapped.

Which should have made him happy. It had taken eight long years, but he was finally exactly where he wanted to be. Free. He could go anywhere, do anything. Hell, if he sold the business to Bill, he would have freedom and cash. Life didn't get any better than that.

"I'M FINE," Dakota insisted, speaking the words for the fourth or fifth hundredth time. "Completely and totally fine."

Both her sisters stared at her, as if not convinced. The statement would probably have been a little more believable if her eyes weren't red and puffy from all her crying. During the day she managed to be brave, but as soon as she was alone at night, she kind of lost it.

"You're not fine and you shouldn't be," Nevada told her. "You told Finn you loved him and he left. He didn't say anything, he just walked away. You're left here, pregnant with his baby and completely alone."

"Thanks for the recap," Dakota murmured. "Now I sound pathetic."

"You don't," Montana said quickly. "You sound like you've been through a lot and you have. You're strong. You'll be okay." She and Nevada exchanged a quick look.

"What?" Dakota demanded. She wasn't surprised they'd been talking about her behind her back, but she was concerned that they'd reached a conclusion that hadn't occurred to her.

They were at Jo's bar, with *Project Runway* playing on the big screen and HGTV on the smaller TVs. Denise had insisted Hannah spend the night, probably to give the sisters time to be alone. As the baby adored her grand-mother, Dakota wasn't worried about her daughter.

"It's a big thing, finding out about the baby," Montana said carefully, as if expecting Dakota to blow up at her.

"I know that."

"He probably needs a little time. You needed time."

"I was willing to give him time," she said, doing her best not to clench her teeth as she clutched her glass of cranberry juice. "This isn't a time thing. He *left*. It's the leaving I object to. He stayed in town after his brothers had moved on right up until I told him I loved him and that I was pregnant. That's when he walked out. Left for Alaska that night. No call, nothing."

She'd never been left before. Not like this. The closest feeling she had was when her dad had died. That, too, had been unexpected. There was no arguing, no bargaining. There was just absence and pain.

"It's so like a guy to walk away," Nevada said. "Now you know he's that type."

"What type?"

"He disappears rather than faces responsibility. He only cares about himself."

Dakota shook her head. "That's not fair. Finn doesn't do that. He's spent the past eight years raising his brothers. He had to give up everything to take care of them."

"Look how that turned out," Nevada muttered.

"What do you mean? They're great guys."

"One of them wants to be an actor and the other is dating a woman nearly twice his age."

Dakota straightened. "That's not true."

"Sasha doesn't want to be an actor? He didn't move to L.A., abandoning his college education one semester from finishing?"

"Yes, but—"

Nevada shrugged. "You're better off without him."

"No, I'm not." The unfair assessment startled her. "There's nothing wrong with Sasha following his dream. Should he have finished college? Maybe. But he can go back later. It's not going anywhere. As for Aurelia, she's nine years older than Stephen, as you very well know. She's sweet and they're great together. Stephen is going back to college. He's studying engineering, something you can relate to."

She felt herself getting angry. "Where do you get off being so judgmental? Finn is a good man. He's proven that over and over again. I don't regret our relationship and I sure as hell don't need you making unfounded comments about him and his brothers."

Nevada picked up her drink and smiled. "Just checking."

"Checking what?"

"To see if you're still in there."

Dakota opened her mouth, then closed it. "What does that mean?"

"You're too accepting of this," Montana said, leaning toward her. "You can't be happy Finn left, but you're all

Zen about it. What's up with that? Why didn't you fight for what you wanted?"

"Fight? I can't force him to want to be with me."

"No, but there's a whole ocean between doing nothing and forcing him."

Nevada nodded. "Come on. When you wanted to get into that special grad program so you could get your masters and Ph.D. at the same time, did you just put in your application and wait? No. You pestered the department chair until he nearly put a restraining order out on you. When you needed a classroom of kids for your thesis research, you knocked on teachers' doors for weeks until you found exactly what you were looking for, then you got her to agree."

"When you found out you couldn't have kids without help," Montana added, "you put in your application for adoption, went through all the studies and home visits and adopted a kid. You do things, Dakota. You're quiet about it and you don't expect people to notice, but we do. You've always gotten things done. So why are you being so passive now?"

She felt both praised and scolded. "I'm not being passive. I'm giving Finn time to come to terms with what he wants to do."

"What about what you want?" Nevada asked. "Isn't that important?"

"Sure, but…"

"There are no buts," Montana reminded her. "Remember what Yoda said? 'Do or do not. There is no try.'"

"You can sit on your butt and wait for him to decide," Nevada said. "Or you can take control of your destiny. I know you're scared."

"I'm not scared."

They both stared at her, eyebrows raised in identical expressions of disbelief.

She sighed. "I'm a little scared," she admitted. Confronting Finn did mean taking charge of her life, but it also meant facing the fact that he might tell her he just plain wasn't interested. That she wasn't for him.

She didn't think he was going to walk away from his child. It might take him a while, but eventually he would show up and want to be a part of his or her life. Finn would be a great father, but was he interested in being a husband?

"I thought the people on the show were stupid," she said slowly. "I thought they were desperate and that I should feel sorry for them. But they were simply looking to fall in love. Something nearly everyone wants. At least they did something about it. What have I done?"

She half expected her sisters to defend her, but they were both silent. Talk about truth in communication, she thought, both bemused and a little hurt. Then she reminded herself that it didn't matter what anyone thought but her and Finn. They were the ones this was all about.

She knew what *she* wanted. She wanted a happily-ever-after kind of ending with the man she loved. She wanted to marry him and raise children with him. She wanted a house full of kids and dogs, with a cat or two and carpooling and soccer practice. She wanted a little of what her parents had, with a twist that made it all their own.

But what did Finn want? She knew that eventually he would figure it out and tell her. But was giving him the time he needed being mature or being afraid?

He'd heard her say that she loved him and that she was pregnant, but she'd never had the chance to tell him the rest of it. About how she saw their future and that being responsible wasn't all bad. There were many wonderful rewards.

"I'm not going to wait," she said as she slid out of the booth. "I'm going to South Salmon to talk to him."

"There's an Alaska Airlines flight out of Sacramento at six in the morning," Nevada told her. "You connect with the flight to Anchorage in Seattle." She pulled a piece of paper out of her pocket and handed it over. "I made a reservation earlier. You can pay for it when you get to the airport."

Dakota couldn't believe it. "You planned this?"

"We hoped," Montana told her. "We were also arguing with Mom about who gets Hannah tomorrow night."

Dakota felt tears filling her eyes, but for the first time in days, her crying wasn't about being sad or having lost what mattered most. She waved her sisters out of the booth, then hugged them.

"I love you," she said as she held them close.

"We love you, too," Nevada told her. "Warn Finn that

if he's an idiot, we'll send all three of our brothers after him. He can run, but he won't be able to hide forever."

Dakota laughed.

Montana kissed her cheek. "We'll keep it all together here. Don't worry. Just go find Finn and drag his butt back here."

"COIN TOSS?" Bill asked.

Finn stared out the office window. The first storm had blown through, but there had been a second one behind it. This one was bigger and headed directly for South Salmon.

Storms out here weren't like those down in the lower forty-eight. They were a lot less polite and plenty more destructive. Normally all flights would have been grounded, but a call had come through from a desperate father. His sick child needed to be flown out as soon as possible. The medical planes were all out on other calls. No one else could get there.

Now dark clouds rose fifty or sixty thousand feet into the heavens. There were wind shears and flashes of lightning. Flying in something like that was like daring the hand of God.

"I'll go," Finn said, grabbing his backpack and walking toward the parked planes. "Radio the family that I should be there in about three hours. Maybe a little longer."

"You can't go around the storm." It was too big. There was no "around."

"I know."

Bill grabbed his arm. "Finn, wait. We'll give it a few hours."

"Does that kid have a few hours?"

"No, but..."

Finn knew the argument. People who chose to live outside the civilized world risked situations just like this. Most of the time, the gamble paid off. Every now and then, fate exacted a price.

"That kid isn't going to die on my watch," Finn said.

"You don't owe them anything."

He owed them trying. That's what this job meant to him. Sometimes you had to take a risk.

He crossed to the plane and walked around the outside. The preflight routine was something he could do in his sleep, but today he took extra time. The last thing he needed was a mechanical problem complicating an already difficult situation.

By the time he was ready to take off, the first fingers of the storm were trying to grab him. Wind gusted and there were raindrops on his windshield.

The problem wasn't the flight out. He would be heading away from the storm. It was getting to Anchorage that was going to be the trick.

Six hours later, he knew he was going to die. The parents and the kid were in the plane, the worried father next to him, the mother sitting next to her son. The winds were so strong, the plane seemed to be standing still instead of moving forward. They were buffeted and tossed. A few times they were caught in a small wind shear and dropped a few hundred feet.

"I'm going to be sick," the mother called to him.

"Bags are next to the seat."

Finn couldn't take the time to show her. Not when all their lives depended on him getting them safely landed.

Despite the fact that it was afternoon, the sky was black as night. The only illumination came from the lightning strikes. Wind howled like a monster out to get them, and Finn had a feeling that this time the storm might win.

He watched his warning lights, checked the altimeter and made sure they were on course. Without wanting to, he found himself mentally drifting to another flight very much like this one. A flight that had taken his parents and changed his world.

There'd been a storm, dark and powerful. The lightning had flashed around them, dangerous shards of destruction. Finn remembered one cutting so close, he'd been able to feel the heat. He'd been flying, his father in the copilot's seat. The wind had growled and thrown them around like a kid with a softball.

They'd swooped and bucked, and then a single flash of light had hit their engine. The plane had shuddered as the engine was fired into a useless molten part, and the plane had dropped like a rock.

There'd been no controlling the descent. It had been

too dark to know where to land, assuming there had been somewhere safer than the forest where they'd crashed. Finn didn't remember much about the impact. He'd awakened to find himself lying on the ground, in the rain.

His parents had both been unconscious. He'd cared for them as best he could, then he'd hiked out to get help. By the time he returned, they were gone. They'd probably died within an hour of his leaving, but he didn't like to think about that.

Lightning flashed next to the plane, jerking Finn back to the present. The mother screamed. The boy was probably terrified but too sick to make a sound. Next to Finn, the father clutched his seat.

No one asked if they were going to die, although he was sure they were thinking the question. Probably praying. Finn waited for a sense of regret, a voice that said nothing was worth this, that he should have waited.

And then he felt it. A sense of something other than himself. Even though he knew it was impossible, he would swear his parents were there with him, helping him. It was as if someone else took control of the plane, guiding his hands.

Not knowing what else to do, he listened to the silence, turning left, then right, dodging lightning and the wind shears, finding the calmest part of the storm. He flew lower when the invisible forces indicated he should, veered left, then up.

For the next hour he flew as he'd never flown before,

and gradually the power of the storm faded. Fifty miles outside of Anchorage, he saw the first hint of sunlight. A voice from the control tower crackled in his headset.

They landed less than thirty minutes later. An ambulance was waiting to race the boy and his family to the hospital. At the last second, the father turned back to him.

"I don't know how to thank you," the man said, shaking his hand. "I thought we were going to die. You saved us. You saved him."

Then he was running after his wife and climbing into the back of the ambulance.

Finn stood by his plane and watched the sun break through the clouds. Automatically, he checked the plane. Everything was fine. There wasn't a single mark to indicate what they'd been through. He climbed back inside, knowing whatever he was looking for wasn't there.

Maybe it had been his parents, maybe it had been something else. Flying was like boating. If a man did it long enough, he experienced things that couldn't be explained. For whatever reason, he'd been spared the night of the crash. He'd always thought it was to raise his brothers, but maybe there was another purpose. Maybe he'd been saved so that he could find his way to Dakota.

He loved her. Having to go through a near-death experience to figure that out made him an idiot, but he could live with that. As long as at the end of the day he got the chance to tell her.

He loved her. He wanted to marry her and have lots of babies with her. Hell, he needed to call Hamilton and tell the old coot he wanted to buy the business. Then he should let Bill know he was selling. Most important, he had to get back to Fool's Gold and tell Dakota how much he loved her and wanted to be with her.

He pulled out his cell phone and called Bill.

"I've been worried," his partner said. "I had to hear it from the tower that you arrived? You couldn't call?"

"I'm calling."

"You've been on the ground ten minutes. What have you been doing? Shopping?"

Finn chuckled. "Getting my passengers into the ambulance. Look, Bill, I'm out. You can buy me out of the business. I have to go back to Fool's Gold right away."

"This is about that woman, isn't it?"

Finn thought of Dakota and grinned. "Yeah. I'm going to figure out how to convince her to marry me."

There was a pause, then Bill said, "She's going to be really happy to hear that."

"How do you know?"

"Because she's standing right next to me. If her smile is anything to go by, I'm going to guess she'll say yes."

DAKOTA USED binoculars to scan the sky. Bill had told her in which direction to look, and when she saw the tiny speck of a plane appear, she began to jump up and down.

Finn landed and guided the plane off the runway. She was already running toward him.

They met on the grass by the tarmac. While there were a thousand things she had to say, right now she only wanted to be in his arms. Then she was, and he was holding her and kissing her and nothing had ever felt so right.

"I love you," he told her, then kissed her. "I love you, Dakota. You and Hannah and our unborn baby. I should have told you that before."

She was so happy, she wasn't sure she even needed to breathe. "You needed time."

"I got scared and then I took off." He cupped her face in his hands. "I want to marry you. I want us to be a family."

She searched his face. "Even though that means a lot of responsibility?"

He nodded, then kissed her again. "Who am I kidding? I was born to be responsible."

"You were a wild guy."

"For about fifteen minutes. I want to be with you."

Beautiful, amazing words, she thought happily. Perfect words, from the man who was exactly right for her.

"I love you, too," she whispered.

"You'll marry me?"

"Yes."

"We'll live in Fool's Gold?"

She wanted him to be happy. "Your life is here."

"No, it's not. I'm selling my half of the business to Bill. My brothers don't want it and I can use the money to buy Hamilton's company. I belong where you belong and that's Fool's Gold."

She flung herself against him. Being in his arms felt right.

"Hannah is going to be thrilled," she whispered. "She's really missed you."

"I've missed her, too." He touched her belly. "Soon she's going to have a baby brother or sister to boss around."

"One day you're going to have to show us all Alaska," she told him.

"I will, but right now, I'm ready to go home."

* * * * *

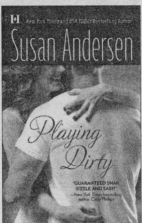

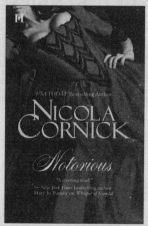

REQUEST YOUR FREE BOOKS!

2 FREE NOVELS
FROM THE ROMANCE COLLECTION
PLUS 2 FREE GIFTS!

YES! Please send me 2 FREE novels from the Romance Collection and my 2 FREE gifts (gifts are worth about $10). After receiving them, if I don't wish to receive any more books, I can return the shipping statement marked "cancel." If I don't cancel, I will receive 4 brand-new novels every month and be billed just $5.99 per book in the U.S. or $6.49 per book in Canada. That's a saving of at least 25% off the cover price. It's quite a bargain! Shipping and handling is just 50¢ per book in the U.S. and 75¢ per book in Canada.* I understand that accepting the 2 free books and gifts places me under no obligation to buy anything. I can always return a shipment and cancel at any time. Even if I never buy another book, the two free books and gifts are mine to keep forever.

194/394 MDN FELQ

Name	(PLEASE PRINT)	

Address		Apt. #

City	State/Prov.	Zip/Postal Code

Signature (if under 18, a parent or guardian must sign)

Mail to the **Reader Service:**
IN U.S.A.: P.O. Box 1867, Buffalo, NY 14240-1867
IN CANADA: P.O. Box 609, Fort Erie, Ontario L2A 5X3

Not valid for current subscribers to the Romance Collection
or the Romance/Suspense Collection.

Want to try two free books from another line?
Call 1-800-873-8635 or visit www.ReaderService.com.

* Terms and prices subject to change without notice. Prices do not include applicable taxes. Sales tax applicable in N.Y. Canadian residents will be charged applicable taxes. Offer not valid in Quebec. This offer is limited to one order per household. All orders subject to credit approval. Credit or debit balances in a customer's account(s) may be offset by any other outstanding balance owed by or to the customer. Please allow 4 to 6 weeks for delivery. Offer available while quantities last.

Your Privacy—The Reader Service is committed to protecting your privacy. Our Privacy Policy is available online at www.ReaderService.com or upon request from the Reader Service.

We make a portion of our mailing list available to reputable third parties that offer products we believe may interest you. If you prefer that we not exchange your name with third parties, or if you wish to clarify or modify your communication preferences, please visit us at www.ReaderService.com/consumerschoice or write to us at Reader Service Preference Service, P.O. Box 9062, Buffalo, NY 14269. Include your complete name and address.

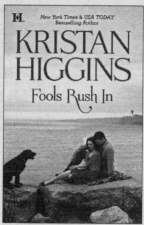

SUSAN MALLERY

77533	SWEET TROUBLE	___ $7.99 U.S.	___ $9.99 CAN.
77532	SWEET TALK	___ $7.99 U.S.	___ $9.99 CAN.
77531	SWEET SPOT	___ $7.99 U.S.	___ $9.99 CAN.
77529	FALLING FOR GRACIE	___ $7.99 U.S.	___ $9.99 CAN.
77527	ACCIDENTALLY YOURS	___ $7.99 U.S.	___ $9.99 CAN.
77520	DELICIOUS	___ $7.99 U.S.	___ $9.99 CAN.
77519	SIZZLING	___ $7.99 U.S.	___ $9.99 CAN.
77510	IRRESISTIBLE	___ $7.99 U.S.	___ $9.99 CAN.
77490	ALMOST PERFECT	___ $7.99 U.S.	___ $9.99 CAN.
77468	FINDING PERFECT	___ $7.99 U.S.	___ $9.99 CAN.
77465	SOMEONE LIKE YOU	___ $7.99 U.S.	___ $9.99 CAN.
77452	CHASING PERFECT	___ $7.99 U.S.	___ $9.99 CAN.
77384	HOT ON HER HEELS	___ $7.99 U.S.	___ $9.99 CAN.
77383	STRAIGHT FROM THE HIP	___ $7.99 U.S.	___ $8.99 CAN.
77372	LIP SERVICE	___ $7.99 U.S.	___ $8.99 CAN.

(limited quantities available)

TOTAL AMOUNT	$ _____
POSTAGE & HANDLING	$ _____
($1.00 FOR 1 BOOK, 50¢ for each additional)	
APPLICABLE TAXES*	$ _____
TOTAL PAYABLE	$ _____

(check or money order—please do not send cash)

To order, complete this form and send it, along with a check or money order for the total above, payable to HQN Books, to: **In the U.S.:** 3010 Walden Avenue, P.O. Box 9077, Buffalo, NY 14269-9077; **In Canada:** P.O. Box 636, Fort Erie, Ontario, L2A 5X3.

Name: _____
Address: _____ City: _____
State/Prov.: _____ Zip/Postal Code: _____
Account Number (if applicable): _____
075 CSAS

*New York residents remit applicable sales taxes.
*Canadian residents remit applicable GST and provincial taxes.

www.Harlequin.com